SOLDIER OF FORTUNE 1

VALIN'S RAIDERS

SOLDIER OF FORTUNE 1

VALIN'S RAIDERS

Tony Williams

22

For Alison and Mike

Arms consultants: Artemis, London

First published in Great Britain 1994
22 Books, Invicta House, Sir Thomas Longley Road,
Rochester, Kent

A CIP catalogue record for this book is available from the
British Library

ISBN 1 898125 24 4

10 9 8 7 6 5 4 3 2 1

Typeset by Hewer Text Composition Services, Edinburgh
Printed in Great Britain by Cox and Wyman Limited, Reading

1

The meeting took place in what once would have been called a bunker. Now it was simply known as basement 101. It was under a small, anonymous building in a small, anonymous town in Virginia. Outside, the streets were sizzling in a heatwave, but in the windowless conference room the temperature was a comfortable seventy degrees.

There were four men present: one FBI, one CIA, one DEA, and one from a government agency in Washington so secret that no one was even sure of its name.

All of the men sitting around the long, glass-topped table wore dark suits, white shirts, dark, striped ties and highly polished shoes. There were no ashtrays because no one smoked. The only refreshment available was bottled water and fruit. It could have been a convention of undertakers. In a way it was.

At precisely four-ten p.m. the man from the no-name government agency called the meeting to order. Not that it had been particularly rowdy before.

'Gentlemen,' he said. 'We all know why we're here today. We may speak freely as the room was swept for bugs less than half an hour ago. No notes will be taken, and as far as I'm concerned none of us are actually here this afternoon. I, for instance, am on the seventeenth green of the golf course at Camp David with our beloved president, as we speak.' He smiled, which was rare for him. 'And I'm sure the rest of you have similarly firm alibis.' The other men smiled too, but with little humour. 'So to the point of this little get-together. As I'm sure we are all aware, we are losing the drugs war. Have been losing it since the mid sixties. Things are going from bad to worse. Some parts of our country are in the grip of pure anarchy.' He paused as the other three men shifted in their seats. 'I know, I know. This is hardly news to any of us. But believe me, gentlemen, our intelligence from the war zones that we like to call the inner cities is that we haven't seen anything yet. New and powerful cocaine derivatives are appearing every day. Derivatives that make crack look as harmless as milk. We are facing a crisis, gentlemen, and I have asked you all to be present today to discuss a solution to at least part of the problem.' Then, turning to the man from the Drug Enforcement Agency, he said: 'Bob, you can take over from here.'

Bob 'Tank' Tankerton rose to his feet and looked at the other men. His nickname may have come from his surname, but it also fitted his build perfectly. He was a little under six feet tall, and in the dim lights that lit the room he appeared to be a little under six feet wide too. At least one of the other men thanked God they were on the same side. 'Gents,' said Tank. 'What our friend here said is perfectly true. We are in deep shit, and believe me, the shit is getting deeper every second. Cocaine is flooding into the country every day from south of the border. It comes in by boat, plane, automobile and truck, on foot, and probably ways we haven't even thought of yet. We manage to halt about ten per cent. We always have, always will. But as our success rate increases, we know that more is being smuggled in. Our only hope is to go to the source. And one of the biggest sources is a factory just outside Bogotá that processes the raw coca leaves into cocaine powder.' Tank saw the FBI man look at the man from the CIA. 'Yes, I'm aware that Bogotá is part of the sovereign state of Colombia. But this factory has been a thorn in my side for years. And that by definition is a thorn in all our sides. Agreed?'

There were nods all round.

'Very well. In that case, I know a man, an old friend of two of us here, and an old enemy of another. His name is Valin. Colonel James Valin. Ex-SAS, and right now a soldier of fortune, first class.'

The man from the CIA sprang to his feet.

'No,' he growled.

'Relax, Jack,' said Tank. 'I know you guys have got a history. But this is no time for old enmities. Valin is the best there is, bar none. We send him in with a squad of his mercs, and he'll blow that coke factory to kingdom come.'

'This is crazy,' said the man from the CIA. 'Do you really expect me to agree to send in a bunch of goddam psychopaths to sort out the business of the United States of America.'

'If we had a flag handy I'd salute it,' said Tank sarcastically. 'Listen, Jack, if you can come up with a better idea, one that doesn't compromise our position on the world stage, then I'll be ready to listen. If not, then with all due respect, shut the fuck up.'

The man from the CIA sat down, then said: 'Why not send in a platoon of Marines?'

'Jesus, Jack,' said Tank. 'We've still got a few ICBMs left under a field in Kansas. Maybe we should just lob a few of those in too.'

'In civilian clothes, I meant,' said the man from the CIA huffily.

'It's a nice idea, Jack,' said Tank. 'Don't think it's not been discussed. But if even one guy got killed or captured, then we'd be in the centre of a political shit-storm that would reach from here right to the UN building.'

The man from the FBI spoke for the first time since the meeting began. 'I agree with Tank,' he said. 'I don't know this character Valin, but I've heard some things about him. He seems like he knows what he's doing. Let's give him a whirl.'

The man from the CIA shook his head.

'At least listen to what he has to say,' said Tank.

'You mean he's here?' said the man from the CIA.

'Right outside,' replied Tank.

'Jesus Christ,' said the man from the CIA. 'You've had this well planned.'

'I had no option,' said Tank. 'A decision had to be made.'

'Shit,' said the man from the CIA.

'So shall I bring him in?' said Tank.

'Do what the hell you like,' said the man from the CIA.

Tank walked to the door of the room, opened it, and beckoned to whoever was waiting outside. The other three in the room looked towards the door as two men appeared, and Tank stepped back to allow them to enter.

The first to enter was a man of about forty-five, tall, with greying hair and a ramrod-straight posture that made him appear even taller than he was. He was casually dressed in civilian clothes, but his military bearing gave the impression that he was dressed in uniform, and probably always would. He shook Tank's hand warmly, then turned to face the room, and the men still sitting at the table saw that the right side of his face was marred with a bright-red scar that ran from his forehead to the lobe of his ear. The man who followed him into the room was younger and taller, but had such a languid air about him that he seemed smaller than his companion. He was blond, with a cowlick of hair that fell down over his forehead almost into one of his pale-blue eyes. He too was casually dressed, in a tartan shirt, jeans and high-heeled brown cowboy boots, and looked as if he would be more at home at a picnic in the park than in a crucial meeting in the war against drugs.

'Gentlemen,' said Tank as he closed the door, 'may I present Colonel James Valin and Lieutenant Mark O'Rourke, both late of the British Special Air Service. Colonel, you have already met Jack Bernard from the Central Intelligence Agency. Sitting next to him is Karl Landers, Federal Bureau of Investigation, and of course you also know General Avery.'

'General,' said Valin to the man from Washington. 'It's been too long, Mr Landers.' He nodded to the man from the FBI. 'Jack,' he said to the man from the CIA, who just shook his head in disgust and said nothing in reply.

'Please be seated, gentlemen,' said Tank to the newcomers. 'Would you care for some water?'

'I'd rather have a Scotch,' said Mark O'Rourke, 'but I suppose that's out of the question.'

'Sorry,' said Tank, 'we don't stock hard liquor here.'

'Never mind,' said O'Rourke. 'I think I can bear to wait until later.'

'Colonel,' said Tank. 'Any refreshment for you?'

'No, thank you,' said Valin. 'I share my young friend's distaste for water.'

'Colonel,' Tank went on. 'You know why I asked you and Lieutenant O'Rourke here this afternoon. I'd like to take this opportunity to show you, in more detail, the target that we wish you to destroy.'

He moved over to a console at the back of the room and pressed a button that hydraulically lowered the wall at the other end, revealing a screen. Another button lowered the dim lights still more, and a third projected a map of Colombia on to the screen, with Bogotá highlighted and a red cross marking a spot some twenty miles outside the city.

'The red cross marks the site of the factory,' explained Tank. 'It is on the outskirts of a small town called Santa Ana. We have informants in the town. Apparently a crack regiment of the Colombian army is based next to the factory to protect it.'

'Crack. Is that a joke?' asked O'Rourke, but no one laughed.

Tank pressed the button again and a picture of an industrial location appeared on the screen. It was surrounded by high fences topped with barbed wire. 'The factory itself,' he said. 'Only one gate in and out, guarded twenty-four hours a day. The fence is heavily electrified, and if you look closely you can clearly see the dead bodies of several small animals that have come too close.' A third click of the button and a larger map of the immediate area filled the screen. 'Should you accept the mission,' Tank said to Valin, 'you will of course be supplied with copies of all our intelligence reports. Now, as I say, we have men on the ground there – locals who know the area well. They tell us that the closest place for you to make landfall is an airstrip about four hours' drive away from Bogotá. Anywhere closer would prejudice the mission itself. Only they and I know exactly where the LZ is. And apart from Colonel Valin here, I think we'll keep it that way for now. Careless talk costs lives, as you all know.'

'How much?' asked Valin.

'Excuse me,' said Tank.

'How much are you prepared to pay for us to complete this exercise?'

'One million.'

'Dollars or sterling?'

'Sterling.'

'Cash?'

'Of course.'

'In what currency?'

'Half and half. Dollars and British pounds.'

Valin looked at O'Rourke. 'What do you think, Mark?'

'A piece of cake, boss.'

'So speaks the voice of the younger generation,' said Valin. 'And I tend to agree.'

'You'll take the job then?' asked Tank.

'I would hardly have bothered to travel to this God-forsaken spot in this unspeakable weather if I didn't intend to,' said Valin.

'How many men will you take with you?' asked Tank.

'We'll be a dozen, all told.'

'Against a regiment?' asked the man from the FBI.

'The odds will be on our side,' replied Valin.

'I really must object,' said the man from the CIA. 'I've never been involved in anything so shambolic in all my life.'

'You must have been,' said Valin. 'Weren't you at the Bay of Pigs?'

'I was *not*,' said the man from the CIA.

'You amaze me. Well, you were certainly in Vietnam. So was I. Briefly during the conflict – or was it a police action? And latterly for a longer time. I saw what you people left behind. If that wasn't shambolic, what was?'

The man from the CIA said nothing.

'Forget it, Jack,' said Tank. 'It's not your decision.'

'Then I'm leaving,' said Jack, who got up from the table and walked towards the door. 'And my report will be on the Secretary of Defence's desk by Monday.'

'So be it, Jack,' said Tank, as the man from the CIA stormed out of the room and slammed the door behind him.

Then they got down to serious business. The deal Tank offered was one-third of the fee down, the other two-thirds on completion.

Valin accepted.

'When will you go in?' asked Landers.

'As soon as we're ready,' replied Valin. 'The exact time and place will be on a need-to-know basis. And frankly only Tank needs to know. No offence.'

'None taken,' said the FBI man.

'So what's your next move?' asked Tank.

'You give us our money, and we go back to England to get the men together.'

'And then?'

'You'll be the first to know, Tank. I promise.'

Later that evening Valin and O'Rourke drove their hire car back to Washington DC and caught the first available flight back to Heathrow, with one-third of a million pounds in mixed currency in their luggage.

2

As dawn broke, four weeks to the day after the meeting in basement 101, an ancient, battered Douglas C47 Dakota, its fuselage patched and frayed, came out of the rising sun, flying under the Colombian radar with its engines throttled back to almost stalling speed, and touched down at the landing zone, four hours' drive outside Bogotá, sending up a puff of dust from the hard-packed earth.

The plane bounced along the makeshift runway and halted with its nose pointing into the dense foliage that surrounded the airfield, before turning to face the way it had come.

When the plane was stationary but with its engines still running, the passenger door in the side opened and a figure appeared. He was dressed in a tiger suit that had been pressed until every crease was like a razor-blade, with sergeant's chevrons on both sleeves, and black combat boots buffed to a mirror shine. He was carrying a Heckler and Koch G3 7.62mm assault rifle. Carefully he checked the terrain that was visible. When he was satisfied that nothing lurked in the undergrowth, he dropped to the ground and turned slowly in the back draught from the propellers, until he was again satisfied that there was no danger. Only then did he relax, and give the pilot the thumbs-up, at which sign he cut the engines. In the silence that followed, and as the dust created by the propellers drifted to the ground, the sergeant hung his rifle over his right shoulder by its sling and stretched. He was massive: fully six foot six, with a physique to match. He reached into one of his pockets and retrieved a purple beret. This he tugged over his blond hair, which was cropped into stubble, and then he banged on the side of the plane, shouting in a heavy German accent: ''*Raus*. Come on, you lazy bastards. Get deplaned, and into some semblance of order.'

One by one, another nine men left the plane and formed a ragged line. They were dressed in a mixture of military uniforms, the colours ranging from sand to deep khaki, to forest green, and civilian clothes, and all were heavily armed. The blond giant walked slowly along the column with a look of deep disdain on his face. 'Homos, all of you,' he said. 'Poofs.'

'You should know, Sarge,' said the man at the far right of the line in an American accent.

The sergeant paused, then walked back until he came to the man who had spoken, and looked him up and down. He was young – maybe twenty-five or six – and wore his dark hair long. He was dressed in a leather bomber jacket over a khaki shirt and mid-green army trousers. On his feet were a pair of dark-brown Doc Marten boots. Over his shoulder was slung an Uzi 9mm machine pistol, and around his waist a belt with a holster containing a Colt 1911 A1 automatic pistol. His GI steel helmet was adorned with a 'ban the bomb' symbol and the word 'PEACE' in black capital letters. He wore two different earrings: in the left ear a plain silver ring, while a red cross made of bone dangled from the other. A Walkman was tucked into a breast pocket of his jacket, and the earphones were around his neck. His eyes were shaded by mirrored aviator sunglasses. He badly needed a shave, and when he smiled his teeth were bright against the stubble that darkened his handsome face.

'What the hell did you say, Angel?' the sergeant demanded.

'Nothing, Sarge,' replied Angel. 'Just remarking what a beautiful morning it is.'

'Don't piss me about, boy,' said the sergeant. 'If you've got something on your mind, get it off now.'

'Not me, Sarge,' said Angel. 'Just waiting to get into some action, get home, and spend some of the dough I'll've earned today.'

'You haven't earned anything yet,' said the sergeant. 'Now straighten up and try and look at least a little like a soldier.'

'No problem, Sergeant Keller,' said Angel and came sloppily to attention. 'No problem at all.'

Keller walked back up the line of men. 'Right,' he said. 'I'm going to talk to the colonel. You men get busy unloading the plane. Angel, keep watch.' He checked his watch. 'Our transport should be here shortly.'

Without another word he turned and returned to the C47, jumped up through the passenger door and vanished. The other men also drifted back in the direction of the aircraft, piled together the weapons they were carrying and opened the door to the hold.

Angel stayed where he was, unslung his Uzi and watched the forest.

Inside the aircraft, Sergeant Keller went up to the flight deck where Valin and O'Rourke had made the latter part of the journey. He found them talking to the pilot. 'Sir,' he roared to Valin. 'All present and correct. The ground seems safe and the men are unloading the ordnance.'

'Well done, Sergeant,' said Valin. 'What time is the transport due?'

Keller looked at his watch again. 'In precisely fifteen minutes, sir,' he replied.

'This *is* South America, Sergeant,' said O'Rourke from his window seat. 'Don't be surprised if they're a trifle late.'

'No, sir,' said Keller. 'I'll be getting back outside to make sure those lumps don't break anything.'

'Carry on, Sergeant,' said Valin, and the German backed out into the main cabin.

'Now, you'll return tomorrow at the same time,' Valin said to the pilot in Spanish.

'*Sí*,' said the pilot, grinning through his moustache. He was himself formerly in the Bolivian air force, and enjoyed earning more in one night ferrying a crazy bunch of ragged soldiers than he did in a week of delivering parcels around the country.

'And if we are not here, you'll come back at the same time the next morning.'

'*Sí*,' said the pilot again. 'But if you are not here then, I am gone for good. To come again would be bad for my health.'

'We'll be here,' said Valin. 'Just make sure that you are. Because if you're not, there are people who know who you are. And for you to abandon us would be bad for *your* health. Do I make myself clear?'

'Perfectly. But believe me, sir, I am an honourable man. An ex-officer myself. I will be here as arranged. Just make sure that you are. It is a dangerous world out there. I would hate for anything to happen to you, so that we do not meet again. You owe me money, remember?'

'How could I forget?' said Valin, and clapped the pilot on the shoulder before leaving the flight deck, followed by O'Rourke, who winked at the Bolivian.

By the time the officers had exited the C47, the soldiers had unloaded the equipment and piled it up beside the runway. Sergeant Keller slammed the loading-bay door, then the passenger door, and whirled his finger to the pilot, who was looking through the window of the aircraft. The pilot replied with a thumbs-up, and taxied slowly away before gathering speed for the take-off. As the plane lifted off then banked away towards the sun, Keller said to Valin: 'I hope he doesn't abandon us. 'Cos if he does I'll have to find him and cut his throat.'

'If he does,' said Valin, 'I hope you're alive to do it.'

Keller grunted and walked over to inspect the boxes and bags that had been unloaded from the plane, while Valin and O'Rourke moved in the direction of the men who were taking a smoke break. Valin looked at them and smiled to himself. These were his troops, and he loved them all, as he had always done the men under his command.

'Everything copacetic?' he asked as he got closer.

'Mellow-D, Colonel,' replied a black man with a London accent, dressed in light-coloured fatigues and with a shoulder holster that held a huge Uzi Desert Eagle pistol under one armpit and spare magazines under the other. His hands clutched a Colt M16 Commando with a collapsed stock.

'Glad to hear it, Stoner,' said Valin. 'Are we treating you better than they did in the Foreign Legion?'

'Couldn't be worse,' replied Stoner, and smiled showing a set of broken front teeth. 'With the cash I'm getting here, I can get my Hampsteads fixed properly.'

'You don't have much luck with them, do you?' said Valin.

'Not a lot,' agreed Stoner, and laughed at the memories.

Johnny Stoner was born in the East End, when he had spent years colliding with the local law for every crime from hot-wiring high-powered cars, to running a string of prostitutes. Finally he skipped the country and after spending some time in jail in Marseilles, he joined the legendary French Foreign Legion, only to learn that the NCOs didn't take kindly to his sense of humour. His cockney wit earned him a severe beating which reduced his face to mush, after which he deserted and stowed away on a ship bound for England. Once back in his home country, he met up with some of his old mates and together they took part in a bank raid in south London where a security guard had been shot and badly wounded. All the members of the gang were caught, and Stoner received a ten-year jail sentence. Once inside, he at last got his teeth fixed by a prison dentist.

He was a model prisoner, but memories were long in the prison service. The security guard who had been shot had once been a screw at Wandsworth, and just before his sentence was complete, Stoner was paid a late-night visit by three warders, who reduced the good work the dentist had done to the rubble that was now visible whenever he opened his mouth.

Once released, and without friends or money, Stoner drifted through the twilight world of criminal London, until one day he found himself in a pub in Fulham where mercenaries were recruited.

As luck would have it, Valin and O'Rourke had been looking for men for the Colombian job, and although Stoner was a complete stranger to them, and even though he had had no experience as a mercenary, they liked the look of him and signed him up on the spot. It had been the same with eight of the twelve men who now waited on the airstrip for their transport to arrive. Even though Valin had been confident of his ability to carry out the mission, times had been hard for the colonel and his lieutenant. A mercenary job in southern Africa had gone disastrously wrong a short time before, so the offer from the Americans had been a godsend.

Valin shivered as he remembered how only he, O'Rourke, Keller and one other member of their squad had got out of Africa alive, and the dead bodies of their comrades that they had left unburied on the cruel veldt.

'Better luck this time,' he said to Stoner.

'I hope we *all* have better luck this time,' said a sardonic voice that Valin knew well.

'Me too, Chris,' Valin replied as a tall, rangy figure

rose from where he had been checking the fastenings of an ammunition box. 'Me too.'

Chris Spenser pushed back the brim of his Boston Bears baseball cap and looked hard at Valin. He was one of the oldest men present – forty-six, though he looked years younger. Born in Los Angeles in the late forties, at the height of the baby boom, as a teenager he had almost made it on the rock and roll scene of the mid sixties. But fate was against him. After seeing his best friend die from a drug overdose, he volunteered for the US army in late 1966, was chosen for the Marines, went through training with flying colours, and was immediately posted to Vietnam. In 1968, at the height of the conflict, he received a battlefield commission in the An Hoa basin, where he was wounded and posted back to Da Nang as a liaison officer. Later, promoted again, he went back into the fray. After his tour of duty was complete, he re-enlisted and stayed in Vietnam until the Americans pulled out in 1975, and it was there that he had first met Colonel Valin. Over countless drinks in the Hanoi Hilton they became firm friends as they bemoaned the state of the war and the calibre of the politicians back in Washington who could not see that it was unwinnable.

Once back in the USA, Spenser resigned his commission and tried to rebuild his life. He was not yet thirty, and again tried to make it in the music business. He grew his hair and joined a band. But bad luck struck once more. When the band broke up, Spenser was left high and dry in New York. One night in a bar on the Lower East Side he heard a young, successful-looking businessman decry all Vietnam veterans as baby-killers. Spenser had been drinking heavily, and an argument broke out that turned into a fist fight. Using the skills he had acquired in South-east Asia, he killed the businessman with a blow of the palm to the nose. Stunned, he sat on the floor by the body until the police arrived, and was arrested. He pleaded guilty to second-degree murder and was sentenced to life imprisonment. During his twelve years in jail he started a correspondence with Valin, and learned of his friend's head injury in a street fight in Belfast, his consequent early demobilization from the SAS on medical grounds and his new career as a mercenary. On his release in 1988, Spenser travelled to Europe, where he hooked up with Valin. Apart from the colonel, he was the only member of the squad to get away from the African débâcle alive, with just a flesh wound to show for it.

'This is the weirdest crew yet,' Spenser remarked. 'You reckon we gonna make it, Colonel?'

'Trust in me and the Lord, Chris,' said Valin.

'Sure will, Colonel,' replied the older man. 'But I tend to rely on my baby more.'

Spenser bent and tapped the gun case that held his 'baby'. A 7.62mm M134 GECAL electrically powered rotary Gatling gun, with six barrels and a cyclical firing rate of up to six thousand rounds per minute, it was powered by a battery pack and had been specially converted to be hand held. Normally a weapon of this kind is mounted on a helicopter gunship or land vehicle, and Spenser loved it all the more for that. Together, Chris and his 'sweet little rock 'n' roller' were like having a platoon of artillery at hand.

'My babies are better,' said a voice with a mid-European accent. It came from one of the men sitting on a nearby pile of boxes. He was smoking a strong-smelling cigar and wearing dark-green fatigues.

'Explosives,' sneered Spenser. 'Where's the subtlety in them?'

Maxim Resnick grinned at the American. 'And where is the subtlety in that oversized popgun you have there? With my equipment and my expertise, I could blow the head off a pimple on your face at a thousand yards and not leave a scar.'

Spenser grinned back. He had met the Russian only a few weeks before, when the group had got together for their first briefing and a short spell of training at the small farm in Norfolk that Valin had bought on his retirement from the SAS as a base for his private army. But already he felt a strong kinship with the leathery veteran of the Afghanistan campaign. Maybe it was the fact that Afghanistan had been as futile an exercise as Vietnam, or perhaps it was simply that he recognized and admired a truly professional warrior.

'We'll see, Max,' he said. 'We'll see.'

Resnick ground out his cigar with the toe of his boot and stood up. He was short. Maybe five foot six, but well built and fit-looking. From his hip hung a Czechoslovakian CZ 75 double-action 9mm handgun, and on his back was strapped a Kalashnikov AK47 with a banana-shaped magazine.

The Russian was a victim of the dramatic political changes in the East since the Wall had come down. When his regiment was disbanded, he drifted west into Germany and then across Europe until he ended up in London. His status as an illegal immigrant had prevented him finding work, but his grasp of English, which he had learned in a crash course as a boy soldier in the bad old days when an invasion of the West was the ultimate aim of his masters in Moscow, soon led him to the pub in Fulham where Valin and O'Rourke had been recruiting.

Resnick was an explosives expert. As he had boasted to Spenser, he could place a charge of Semtex and neatly blow a hole as large or as small as required in any target, or destroy it completely. On this occasion his ordnance was divided up into a dozen or so haversack-sized bags which had been neatly placed in the shade. Even though Semtex was stable, many of the men had seen the effects of heat on high explosive, and were not keen to see it again. They were taking no chances.

'And where the fuck's our transport?' said Spenser testily. 'We're like sitting ducks waiting here.'

'It'll be along,' said Valin, but when he checked his watch he saw that the vehicles were already ten minutes late.

'It's going to be a hell of a walk if they don't arrive,' said Spenser. 'Especially with all the junk we've brought with us.'

'Don't worry about a thing, Chris,' said Valin, and as if to back up his promise, the sound of heavy-duty engines reached them from some way off. The men all scrambled for their weapons and took up defensive positions as the sound of the engines grew louder, and an old British Ford three-tonner with a canvas tonneau over the cargo compartment, closely followed by a World War Two jeep, bounced into view through a gap in the jungle.

The noise of weapons being cocked was the next loudest sound as the two vehicles skidded to a halt about a hundred yards from the squad.

The driver of the jeep dismounted and walked towards the twelve mercenaries, his empty hands held far away from his body. He was wearing the white cotton suit of a peon, and leather sandals, and appeared to be unarmed, but half the squad trained their weapons on him, while the other half kept their guns on the three-tonner.

'Colonel Valin?' said the man as he drew closer, in English with a strong Spanish accent. He was about sixty, wrinkled and grey, but even under the barrels of the weapons that covered him, he had a youthful spring to his step.

'That's me,' said Valin.

A grin appeared on the man's face. 'My name is Jesús,' he said. 'I believe you were expecting me.' He pronounced his name in the Spanish way: '*Hey-zoos*'.

'That is correct,' replied Valin. 'You are very prompt. But as we have not met before, you must excuse me if I am cautious.'

'Of course, señor.'

'There is a question I have been told to ask you.'

'Please, señor.'

'Your army number, date of enlistment, and date of demobilization.'

The Colombian smiled. 'As if I could ever forget,' he said, and reeled off a number and two dates which Valin checked in a notebook that he had already taken from one of the pockets of his jacket.

'Correct,' said Valin. 'Are you armed?'

'No. I felt it safer. Please search me if you wish.'

'Thank you,' said Valin, and expertly frisked the man, until he was satisfied that he was clean.

'Who's in the truck?' asked Valin.

'Only Carlos, my son. He is alone and unarmed also.'

'Tell him to get out,' ordered Valin.

In a burst of rapid Spanish Jesús did as he was told, and a young man in his early twenties, dressed in jeans and a checked shirt, opened the driver's door of the truck and jumped to the ground.

'Angel, Stoner, check out the vehicle,' barked Valin.

The two men walked over to the truck, frisked the driver, searched the cab and opened the canvas cover at the back cautiously. When Stoner shouted: 'All clear, Colonel,' Valin relaxed and said: 'Once again, my apologies, but you realize we must be careful.'

The Colombian nodded. 'Of course, Colonel. I would have been disappointed if you were not.'

'Good. Bob Tankerton said that you knew your stuff.'

'Tank,' said Jesús with a broad smile. 'Have you seen him lately?'

'A few weeks ago.'

'If you see him soon, give him my regards. It must have been my old compadre who came up with the idea of asking me my army number, and those dates.'

Valin nodded.

'It was a good ploy. What other information does a man never forget? Tank, he is as cunning as a fox. But for now, Colonel, instruct your men to load up the truck. There are patrols in the area, and we don't want the army to know that you are here one moment earlier than necessary.'

'Agreed,' said Valin. 'Sergeant Keller, get the men to load the gear pronto.'

'Yes, sir,' replied Keller, then screamed at the men: 'You heard the colonel. Get this stuff loaded at the double.'

Within five minutes the ordnance was in the back of the truck, along with Keller and the rest of the squad, apart from Spenser, who, because he spoke reasonable Spanish, had been ordered to sit next to Carlos. Valin and O'Rourke were in the jeep, with Jesús driving, and as the two vehicles left the airstrip and nosed their way on to the narrow track that ran through the jungle, the jeep led the way.

'It's about four hours to Bogotá, according to Tankerton,' Valin shouted into Jesús's ear above the sound of the engine.

'That is correct, Colonel, but the army presence has become stronger on the roads over the last few weeks. It is almost as if they know that something is going to happen. We should wait until dusk before going the whole way.'

'That was not part of the original plan,' said Valin.

'Plans are made to be changed,' said Jesús. 'We do not want to be stopped for a check by a patrol. I have found a place where we can stay until darkness begins to fall. Believe me, sir, it is for the best.'

'What do you think, Mark?' Valin asked his aide.

'I think we should pay attention to the local intelligence, sir,' the younger man replied. 'We've got until the day after tomorrow to get back to the airstrip. Perhaps it would be better to carry out the operation under the cover of total darkness.'

'OK,' the colonel replied, and then said to the Colombian: 'Very well, Jesús, take us to your secure location. I'll let my top sergeant know what we're doing.'

Valin took a small, low-powered radio from his jacket pocket and spoke into it. 'Valin to Keller, over.'

In the back of the truck, Keller spoke into an identical radio, attached to the lapel of his tiger suit. 'Keller to Valin. Receiving you loud and clear. Over.'

Valin explained the change of plan to the German sergeant, who acknowledged it. 'You heard the boss,' he said to the eight men bouncing up and down on the bench seats along both sides of the truck. 'We go in tonight.'

3

About a quarter of an hour later, Jesús turned off the track and joined a wider road, paved with cracked and buckled concrete and stretching in both directions through the dense jungle. 'We go north here,' he explained to Valin and O'Rourke, 'then to an old ranch I know. We will be safe there until tonight. There is food and drink for you and your men. My wife and daughters are waiting, and they will take care of us.

'Just keep them away from the troops. I don't know everyone I've brought with me on this trip,' said Valin. 'Some of them are a little rough-and-ready, to say the least.'

'I have faith in your ability to keep order, Colonel,' said Jesús. 'Tank assured me of your trustworthiness and honour, in a message he got through to me last week.'

'I admire his faith in me, and yours too, Jesús,' replied the colonel. 'I only hope I can live up to it.'

Christ, I'd better, he thought, as he looked back over the past few hectic weeks. The day after the meeting in Virginia, the pair of them had got back to England, where Keller and Spenser were kicking their heels at the farm, and had started scouring the pubs on the mercenary circuit for fresh recruits. They had money, which was something. But even a third of a million wouldn't last long once they started paying for the men, their keep, arms and ammunition, transport, forged papers for some of them, and somewhere to hole up near their target. It had taken a week to hire eight new men, and Valin had detailed O'Rourke to take them up to Norfolk for basic training under the tender care of Sergeant Keller.

While Keller and O'Rourke were making the new recruits' lives a misery, Valin flew back to the USA to organize transport, weapons, and a hide-out as far south as possible. He found a ranch to rent in New Mexico, close to the Mexican border, where O'Rourke rejoined him. Together they purchased the state-of-the-art ordnance that the troops had recently unloaded from the C47, and made some forays into Mexico, making careful notes as to which roads were heavily guarded by the Border Patrol and which were not. The last thing they needed was to be stopped and searched by the US authorities before they even crossed the border. Valin had no compunction about killing any customs and immigration officers who got nosy, but it was a complication he could do without, and would certainly bring unwanted attention.

Valin and O'Rourke also flew to Mexico City and hired more cars under false papers that they had purchased from a charming gentleman who lived in the *barrio*, before flying on to Panama, where they organized the plane and pilot. When they arrived back at the farm, having been away for a fortnight, they were gratified to find that the men had been forged into some semblance of a fighting unit. Although how good they were going to be when it came to real action, only time would tell.

Under the canvas covering the back of the truck, the temperature was rising as the sun climbed ever higher in the sky. Keller mopped his brow with his sleeve and looked at the men as they lolled on the bench seats. Jesus, he thought, what a bunch. Why can't I find a regular job and not have to get involved with all this crap? Then he smiled to himself. What would I do? Get a milk round in Cologne, marry a fat hausfrau and settle down?

Once again he studied the men under his command, mourning the loss of the old friends that he had been forced to watch die in southern Africa. A pity some of them couldn't be here today, he thought. This is no time to be going into battle with untried troops. He looked up and down the length of the truck, trying to foresee what they would be like in combat.

Angel was OK, he thought. A bit cheeky and rebellious, but he had come through well in the short training period they had spent together. He was a hippie, that was true. But a hippie with a killer instinct if the stories about his basic training at Fort Bragg had been correct. Angel, aka Johnny Angelo, had been another young man who had volunteered for the US army. But in his case it was a peacetime army, and he had been earmarked as a communications operative because he had majored in electronics in college. This was the last thing that Angel wanted. He had craved action, and as if to prove it, he'd fought two military policemen in the last week of his basic. Angel was court-martialled, found guilty of assault and 'conduct unbecoming', slung into the brig and, after he had served his sentence, dishonourably discharged. But soon he went back, found one of the MPs and inflicted even more damage on him, before absconding to Italy, because of his fluency in the language of his father's home country. Hired by a radio station as a technician, he nevertheless soon tired of the job and, like most of the rest of the squad, drifted through Europe until he reached London, where the appeal of the mercenary life led him to the same recruiting pub as the others.

The Russian was OK too. Resnick was a real soldier, professionally trained by other professionals, and although Keller's father had fought on the eastern front during the war, and died soon after his return from the terrible effects of the campaign, the sergeant felt no animosity to the man. In fact he was glad to have him on his side. If Hitler had kept Russia as an ally, he reflected, we would never have lost the fucking war.

And then there was Stoner. Keller was not a great fan of blacks, but as they went he seemed like a reasonable guy. Sitting next to Stoner was the Frenchman. A bit of a mystery, that one. His name was Messelier, or so he said. A good-looking man of about thirty-five, he kept himself to himself, rarely mixing with the other troops. And by the look in his eye, there was something bad, very bad, in his past. But that was his business.

Messelier was wearing blue jeans and a combat jacket. His preferred side-arm was a Sig niner, and cradled across his lap was an Ingram MAC11 machine pistol with two clips welded together end to end, to give it a sixty-round capacity which the little gun could exhaust in about six seconds on full auto.

Messelier noticed the huge sergeant staring at him, and gave him a friendly nod. He could feel Keller's curiosity, but he had no intention of enlightening him. It was nothing personal. Just the way it had to be. Messelier had been a mercenary for some five years, since leaving the French diplomatic corps, where he had received an unusual training. An assassin, he thought. Me. A man with a fine-arts degree from the Sorbonne, and all it got me was a job as a paid killer. For when Messelier finished his studies at the age of twenty-three, not knowing how to use his education, his Uncle Claude suggested a safe, well-paid and permanent job in the civil service, where he himself had spent more than thirty comfortable years growing fat and lazy.

Messelier had applied, and been siphoned off from the other applicants and interviewed by the French secret service. His psychological profile had thrown up some useful insights into his character. He was a born killer, he was told. It came as some surprise, as he had never even been in a fist-fight. The man from the secret service made Messelier an interesting proposition. He would be fully trained in the art of murder, and in exchange for his services in that particular art he would take up the handsomely paid post of a chargé d'affaires in the Foreign Office in Paris.

Messelier jumped at the chance. He knew how popular diplomats were. They drove fast cars, made love to fast women, wore the best clothes and got the best seats at the opera. For a year he trained as a killer, taking to it like a duck to water. Then he took up his government position, and for another year he lived the high life, until one day he was contacted by the secret-service man who had interviewed him earlier. Messelier was given a gun, an address and a name. He was to go there and kill the named person. He did it without compunction. After all, it was what he had been trained for. Over the next five years he did it eight more times. He killed both men and women quite happily. Then one day, after he had knifed the mistress of a minister in the defence department who had been collecting indiscreet pillow talk and selling it to the highest bidder, her eight-year-old daughter had woken up and walked into the room and he had slit her throat too, almost without thinking. It was only afterwards that his conscience began to bother him. He started drinking heavily, and was warned that unless he stopped it would be his turn to be terminated by a fellow graduate of the academy for killers.

Messelier ignored the warning, and when his would-be assassin appeared some weeks later he dispatched him with ease. Then he himself disappeared, just like he had 'disappeared' so many others. He had planned this moment for months. Within the hour he was on a plane to Canada with a false passport. But he could not settle in the suburb of the Francophone city where he had been planning to begin a new life. Within a year he was travelling the world, looking for adventure, and fell in with mercenaries in Africa. He moved about the continent, picking up work where and when he could, under many different names, Messelier being just the latest. If Keller had known some of the other names under which he had operated, he would have realized why Valin jumped at the chance to take on the Frenchman for the current mission. But Messelier had sworn the officer to secrecy when he joined him, and Valin was a man of his word. In fact it was only chance that the Frenchman and the German had not run across each other before, although the likelihood was lessened by the fact that Messelier, knowing that the French government had a very long memory, had schooled himself in the art of keeping a low profile. So low in fact, that in some quarters of the mercenary world his nickname was 'The Invisible Man'.

The Frenchman mentally shrugged at the German sergeant's penetrating look. The German was a professional fighting man, and once hostilities began, all other personal likes and dislikes would be forgotten.

Next to Messelier on the flesh-numbing bench was another new recruit to Valin's private army. Messelier had had little opportunity to speak to him before, and offered him a cigarette, which he accepted. He was very young, nineteen or twenty at the most, and his name was Lenny Packard. He was Australian.

'How the hell did you get involved in all this shit?' Messelier asked him when both their cigarettes were lit.

'My old man,' said Packard. 'He was in Vietnam. He was killed there. I joined up as a boy soldier in the Ozzie infantry. It was boring. I got a three-month psychological discharge and headed for England. I heard there were people who signed up mercs, and I found this bunch in a pub in west London. What about you?'

'A long story,' said Messelier. 'I'll tell you sometime, my young friend. Is this your first time out?'

The Australian nodded.

'I hope you know what you're letting yourself in for.'

'A lot of money and a good time,' said Packard. But he was lying.

'I wish it were as simple as that,' said Messelier.

'Have you been in this game long?' asked Packard.

'Too long. Far too long.'

The Frenchman looked at Packard's fresh, new combat suit, the small holster on his left side holding what looked like a Beretta 1934 model, and the ancient 7.62mm FN FAL assault rifle with telescopic sight that he held between his knees. 'Where did you get your weapons?' he asked.

'They were my old man's. They were shipped back from 'Nam with his body. He was a sergeant. His Top came round and gave them to my mum. I've had them ever since.'

'I hope they bring you luck,' said Messelier.

'Me too,' said Packard.

Suddenly the truck lurched as it turned off the paved road on to what felt like a dirt track again, and Messelier peered through the gap in the canvas back of the truck. 'Looks like we're where we're going to,' he said to no one in particular.

Up front in the jeep, Valin looked ahead at the narrow track that Jesús was negotiating carefully. He picked up and cocked the M16 that was in the well of the vehicle, and O'Rourke took out the Browning 9mm semi-automatic handgun that he carried as a side-arm and worked the slide so that it was ready to fire. 'Just in case,' said Valin casually. 'This looks like a good place for an ambush.'

In the truck behind, Keller was of the same mind, and ordered his men to ready their rifles and machine-guns for action.

The two vehicles bounced along the track until it widened into a clearing that overlooked an abandoned farmhouse. In a dip about half a mile away was a tumbledown ranch house and behind it an equally dilapidated barn. '*Mi casa, su casa*,' said Jesús. 'Welcome to your temporary home.' He put his foot on the accelerator and the jeep, closely followed by the truck with his son at the wheel, headed towards the house. As they got closer, the front door opened and a woman emerged carrying a double-barrelled shotgun. 'My wife,' said Jesús proudly. 'The best cook and shot in Colombia.'

As they drew level with the front of the house, the woman raised her gun in greeting and called to someone inside. 'My daughters are in there, helping prepare your meal,' said Jesús reassuringly. 'We'd better hide these vehicles in the barn. Sometimes helicopter patrols take a look at these broken-down farms,' he said, as he swung the jeep around the house and through the huge double doors of the barn. He pulled up in one corner close to a dark-green VW Microbus, to allow room for the truck. With both vehicles safely inside, Jesús jumped out of the jeep with surprising agility, saying: 'Come along, my friends, let's eat.'

4

The soldiers leapt down from the truck one by one and joined Valin, O'Rourke and Jesús. Everyone then made their way back to the farmhouse. Two of the last three men to exit the truck were the McGuire brothers, Gerry and Daniel, who had come into the mercenary business by way of the IRA, to which they had belonged since their boyhood. The other was Pat Newman, an Englishman who had served in the parachute regiment for ten years before taking voluntary redundancy in the huge shake-up that had occurred in the British armed services in the early nineties. Gerry and Daniel were as alike as twins, even though Gerry was thirty and Daniel twenty-eight. They were large young men, with ruddy faces and bright-red hair that evinced their Irish ancestry.

The McGuires were good-natured and enjoyed a drink and a laugh with their mates, but they were also hardened killers who had demonstrated their loyalty to the Provisional cause with bombs and bullets and had quit their homeland only when they had appeared on the 'most wanted' lists of the British army, the Ulster Defence Force and the Royal Ulster Constabulary. They were dressed alike in British 'greens' and both carried at the waist Colt Combat Commander

.45 automatics, with eight-shot magazines, and, over their shoulders, Czechoslovakian V261 Scorpions in 7.65mm, fitted with suppressors. The weapons had all been supplied by NORAID, which displeased Newman, as he had done several tours of duty in Belfast, and had seen many of his friends brought down by similar weapons. But that, he thought, was then, and this is now. It was in the past and best forgotten, even though he still felt a frisson of anger at the memories. The ex-para favoured straight-legged army trousers, 'monkey boots', an MA1 jacket, a Smith & Wesson Model 59 in 9mm parabellum as a side-arm, and, as a carry weapon, an Ithaca Bear Stopper 12-gauge shotgun with an eighteen-and-a-half-inch barrel, a pistol grip and an eight-shot capacity.

Inside the house, the soldiers found Jesús's wife overseeing the preparation of a huge meal being cooked by her three daughters. 'Colonel,' said Jesús, 'allow me to introduce my wife Maria, and my three daughters, Sofía, Carlotta and Carmen.'

'Delighted,' said Valin, and introduced his men one by one to the four women. Maria was tall, well built and about fifty, her long, dark hair beginning to go grey. She wore a peasant-style black dress and boots, and leant her shotgun against the side of the fireplace as she greeted the men. But their attention was mainly on her daughters. They were beautiful and, as far as Valin and his troops could tell, ranged in age from about seventeen to twenty-two or three. All three were taller than their mother, slim but voluptuous, and had the same long, lustrous black hair. Sofía and Carlotta, who appeared to be the eldest of the trio, favoured simple white blouses with long, dark skirts and sandals, but Carmen wore tight blue jeans, knee boots and a plain, crimson cowboy shirt. The two older girls were unarmed as they went about their chores, although another pair of shotguns stood against the back door. On a cartridge belt around her waist, Carmen wore an open gunfighter's holster which contained an old-fashioned single-action Colt Peacemaker.

All four women spoke English to some extent, and all seemed delighted to greet the arrival of the mercenaries. And so, on a day that was to change the lives of everyone present, the twelve soldiers who made up Valin's Raiders met the six men and women who comprised the Delgado family.

The ground floor of the ranch house was one huge room that combined living, dining and cooking areas. At the back, a wood stove was covered with bubbling pots and pans that exuded a mouth-watering aroma. Next to it was a sink with an old hand-operated water pump. The living area had been swept neatly, and two long trestle tables had been set up, with plain benches as seats. In the opposite corner to the cooking area, a wide staircase led up to the first floor and disappeared into the shadows.

'A drink, gentlemen, to celebrate your safe arrival,' said Jesús, who produced a bottle of tequila, salt, lime, glasses and half-a-dozen six packs of warm Budweiser from under the sink.

'All the comforts of home,' said O'Rourke, who helped himself to a beer, sat at the table, lit a cigarette and watched the daughters as they went about their business.

'There'll be plenty of time for that later, Lieutenant,' said Valin. 'First of all I want guards placed at the perimeters. We'll take it in turns to eat, and replace the guards on a two-hourly basis.'

'Sir,' said O'Rourke, rising smartly to his feet. 'Sergeant,' he said to Keller. 'You heard the colonel.'

'Sir,' echoed Keller, and then turned to the two Irishmen. 'You McGuires take the first duty. We'll get you a snack sent out as soon as we've eaten ourselves. Then you can come back and eat at your leisure in two hours' time.'

'Be sure to save us plenty,' said Daniel. 'We'll have a hell of an appetite by then. Come on, Gerry, we'd better find a comfortable pair of hidey-holes to watch the front and back.'

'Carlos will show you a couple of places we've discovered that give you a good view of the road in and out,' said Jesús. He poured out another torrent of Spanish to his son, who smiled and opened the door to allow the brothers to leave.

'Use your radios if you spot anything suspicious,' ordered Valin as they went through the doorway. 'Otherwise maintain strict radio silence. Understood?'

'Yes, sir,' replied Daniel briskly, as if he had never fought several bitter small-arms battles with Valin's previous regiment, possibly even when Valin was serving with them. 'Leave it to us.'

'And save us a couple of them beers, boys,' was Gerry's parting shot as he left the house.

When the McGuires had gone to take up their guard duty outside, the rest of the men piled their carry weapons against one wall and sat down to eat. The Delgado women had done them proud. On top of the stove were two huge pots of meat stew with chillies that brought tears to the men's eyes, plus a ratatouille of local vegetables and a huge saucepan of rice. In the oven was hot bread, and for dessert a fruit pie. As the men ate, Carlotta boiled up a pot of the strong, bitter local coffee, which Jesús laced with tequila.

Carlos returned, only to be dispatched almost immediately to take the McGuires plates of food, which he did before eating himself, and although the men ate huge portions of everything, there was still plenty for the women, and even some left when the guards came in after their stint.

During the meal, Spenser found it almost impossible to keep his eyes off Carmen, and she could hardly keep her eyes off him. He was amazed. It seemed like years since he had been with a woman. The last one he could remember had been a hard-bitten prostitute in some French port or other before leaving on a mission. He had not enjoyed it much, and had decided there and then that he would not bother again. But the sight of the slim young woman in her tight jeans and shirt, with a handgun slung around her waist, had rekindled something inside him, and it had not gone unnoticed.

'Sweet thang, ain't she?' said Angel as he dug into his stew. 'Trouble is, she could be your daughter, man.'

'I don't have a daughter,' said Spenser, refusing to rise to the bait.

'I'm only kidding, man,' said Angel. 'Hell, I'm jealous. I haven't had a woman look at me like that since I don't know when. Just don't let her momma see, or she might use that shotgun on your ass.'

Spenser smiled. 'I'll take your advice, Angel,' he said. 'I'll be very careful about how I behave.'

'Good idea, man,' said Angel. 'I'd hate to see you get hurt before we even get to the coke factory. Seems like you and me might enjoy sharing a line before we blow the shit out of the place.'

'We just might do that,' agreed Spenser, and went back to trying to look at Carmen without letting the others notice.

When the meal was finished and the plates were stacked in the sink, Valin lit a rare cigarette and said to Jesús: 'Is this your place?'

'No, sir,' came the reply. 'The original owners vanished about a year and a half ago. That often happens in this part of the world. It happened to my own brother too, many years ago. Up until then I was a friend of the regime. But now I would do anything to see them destroyed. Why else would a man who served long and loyally in the army be helping a foreign country to fight a battle on his own soil?'

Valin nodded. 'So you just moved in?'

'That is correct.'

'And do you and your family live far away?'

'No. Eighty kilometres or so, on the road to Bogotá.'

'And what exactly happens tonight as far as you're concerned?'

'Carlos and I will take you in, leave you and the transport, and then vanish.'

'And the women?'

'They will take the VW you saw in the barn,

load it up with all their utensils and leave us before noon.'

'And we just leave the truck and the jeep at the airstrip?'

'Correct, Colonel. Maria, Carlos and I will take a little drive through the jungle in a day or two to see if they have been discovered. If not, we drive them home. If they have . . . well, there are plenty more vehicles around.'

'You have a good attitude, Jesús,' said O'Rourke. 'You should have joined up with our mob. Scrounging is a way of life in the British army.'

Jesús smiled, and was just about to answer when Valin's radio squealed and Gerry McGuire's unmistakable accent came through. 'McGuire to home. There's a vehicle coming down the track. Four bodies on board. They look like army.'

Valin looked hard at Jesús and said: 'This had better not have anything to do with you.'

5

'No, Colonel, I swear,' said Jesús.

'Did you hear me, Colonel? Over,' said Gerry McGuire on the radio.

'I hear you, Gerry,' said Valin. 'What's the story? Over.'

'Definitely army, Colonel. Four in a jeep, all with side-arms, carry weapons and an LMG mounted in the back. An M60. They're coming real slow. I can take them out. What do you say?'

'No. We don't know if they're alone. Just let them come. Give me an ETA.'

'Two or three minutes to you.'

'Stay where you are then. Keep an eye out for reinforcements. We'll take care of them this end. No more radio contact now unless you see any more troops. Over and out.'

Valin put his radio back in his pocket and rapped out a stream of orders. 'Mark. You, Newman and Angel get over to the barn and secure the transport. Keller, take Stoner and Messelier and find cover that gives you a clear view of the front. Now double.' The six men grabbed their carry weapons and ran out of the house. Valin took out his radio again and pressed the send button. 'Daniel, are you listening?'

The younger McGuire came on immediately. 'That's a roger, boss.'

'Where are you?'

'Behind the house.'

'Stay there, and keep down. Over and out.'

'The rest of you come upstairs with me,' Valin said. 'And Jesús, just act as naturally as possible. Tell the army you're squatting here or something. Lose your weapons too.' Then, to the youngest of the four women: 'Carmen, take off that belt.'

'But . . . '

'No arguments, girl.'

Reluctantly the youngest daughter loosened the buckle on her gun belt. Then Valin turned to the remainder of his men. 'Come on, you lot, upstairs,' he barked, and led Spenser, Resnick and Packard up to the top of the house.

The four men ran past three open doors that looked into rooms long neglected and littered with broken furniture, over the bare floorboards to a room overlooking the clearing in front of the house. Valin, Resnick and Packard cocked their carry weapons as they went, and Spenser, who relied on his Gatling, unholstered the Star Model MD.45 ACP selective fire that he had carried since Vietnam and put a round in the chamber. They reached a window covered with torn and dusty brocade curtains just in time to spot a new, long-wheelbase Wrangler jeep painted dull grey and with an open top and a machine-gun mounted on a swivel in the back. Inside were four men in grey army uniforms. 'Militia men,' said Valin. 'Now I wonder what they're looking for.'

'Us?' said Spenser.

'I don't think so,' replied Valin. 'Otherwise there'd be more than just four of them. Unless of course we're losing our fearsome reputation.'

The jeep drove slowly to the front of the house and the four men got out. One, with a captain's chevrons on his shoulders, carried a Walther PPK semi-automatic handgun, while the other three all held Colt AR-15 semi-automatic rifles. They appeared to be ready for combat, though not particularly suspicious of the ranch house.

Then, as Jesús appeared from the veranda and walked towards the soldiers, they cocked their weapons and the officer called out to him in Spanish: 'Who are you?'

'My name is Delgado. Jesús Delgado.'

'What are you doing here?'

'My family and I . . . We have lost everything. We were looking for a place to stay.'

'This house has been put under the control of the Militia. You have no right to be here.'

'My apologies, señor. We will leave immediately.'

'Who else is here?'

'My wife and four children.'

'Let me see them.'

Jesús turned and beckoned, and Maria, Carlos and the three daughters came out on to the veranda and joined him by the jeep, as the soldiers covered them.

The officer stepped forward and said: 'You have very beautiful daughters, señor. Perhaps I can see my way to letting you stay here for a while after all.'

'Thank you,' Jesús replied. 'But we are happy to move on.'

'If I say you stay, you stay,' said the officer, reaching

forward and touching Carmen's hair. Valin heard Spenser catch his breath.

'What is your name, girl?' asked the officer.

'Carmen, señor.'

'Then, with your father's permission, Carmen, you and I will become better acquainted inside.'

'Señor, no,' Jesús protested. 'We will just get our truck and leave.'

'Not at all, Señor Delgado. My sergeant, the corporal and I will go inside, where they will look after you and your family. And Carmen and I will go upstairs for a little while.'

'No, señor, please,' said Maria. 'She is my baby.'

'Be quiet, woman,' snapped the officer. 'Sergeant, Corporal, see these people inside. You,' he said to the private who had been driving the jeep, 'stay here and keep guard.'

'Captain,' said the private, coming to attention, as the sergeant and corporal herded the rest of the family inside, leaving the officer to bring Carmen with him.

'Son of a bitch,' hissed Spenser.

'Cool down, Chris,' Valin whispered. 'Let him bring her upstairs, and you can deal with him.'

The waiting mercenaries heard voices from below, then footsteps on the stairs. They flattened themselves against the wall behind the door of their room, in case he chose it for his tryst, but as they had hoped, he took Carmen into the first room at the top of the stairs. 'Not too many home comforts here,' they heard the officer say. 'But never mind, I'm sure our passion will outweigh the lack of comfort.'

'Please, señor,' said Carmen. 'You are hurting me.'

'Go, Chris,' said Valin. 'But keep it quiet.'

Spenser reholstered his pistol, from under one arm drew the needle-pointed, razor-sharp Marine Ka-Ba knife that he had also owned since his days in the service, and crept out of the room, silent in his rubber-soled combat boots.

He slid down the hall, keeping close to the wall to minimize any creaks from the loose boards, until he reached the room at the top of the stairs, and peered through the open doorway. Carmen was lying on an old, stained mattress, her blouse ripped open to expose bare breasts, with the captain over her, his back to the door, opening his fly.

Carmen saw Spenser in the doorway, knife in hand, but with extreme presence of mind, showed no emotion. The officer started to drop his trousers. Perfect, thought Spenser, as he moved forward, put his left arm around the captain's neck, covered his mouth with his hand, jerked back his head and put the knife into his right kidney, twisting the blade viciously. The officer kicked once and died without a sound. Spenser lowered his body gently to the floor.

'Thank you,' the girl said. 'You saved my life.'

'Thank me later,' said Spenser. 'We're not out of this yet. Now cover yourself up, girl.'

Carmen looked down at her nakedness, blushed, and pulled her shirt across herself. Spenser gave her his hand and pulled her upright, then turned as he heard a sound behind him. Valin was standing in the doorway screwing a silencer on to the barrel of the Smith & Wesson 459 that he carried as a side-arm.

'Good work, Chris,' he said. 'Cover me on the stairs.'

Spenser wiped the blade of his knife on the captain's tunic and returned it to its sheath, then drew his automatic and followed Valin to the head of the stairs, closely followed by Carmen, Resnick and Packard.

The colonel crept down the first couple of treads, keeping in the shadows, and squinted down into the room below. The rest of the Delgado family were sitting on one of the benches under the watchful eye of the corporal, as the sergeant slumped against the door frame smoking a *cigarillo*, his rifle leaning against the wall beside him.

Valin's first shot hit the corporal in the chest, sending up a puff of dust from his jacket, the second punched home an inch or so away from the first, and the man went down like a felled tree. The sergeant barely had time to register what was happening before Valin's third slug ripped through his throat and he died clutching at his neck.

Valin crept down to the ground floor with his finger on his lips, as Jesús, his wife and children rose as one from the bench.

'Quiet,' hissed Valin. 'There's still one outside.'

'Is Carmen all right?' asked Maria, then, seeing her youngest daughter at the top of the stairs next to Spenser, relaxed.

Valin checked the bodies of the two soldiers for signs of life, then pulled the sergeant's body away from the door and looked through the filthy window at the private outside.

The young enlisted man was lounging against the front mudguard of the jeep, his rifle at port arms, unaware of what had just happened inside the house. Valin rapped on the glass to draw his attention, and showing only his hand and the sleeve of his jacket, beckoned imperiously for the private to come to the door. The boy slung his weapon over his shoulder and mounted the steps to the veranda. As he approached the doorway, Valin kicked open the door and shot him straight between the eyes, blowing off the back of his skull and sending a spray of blood, bone and brain across the boardwalk.

Valin stood in the silence that followed the violent death of the young soldier, feeling the heat of the sun as it rose to its zenith and seemed to fill the cloudless sky above the house. The jungle that surrounded the clearing looked dry and dusty in the bright sunlight, and already flies were buzzing around the bodies. He pulled out his radio, pressed the send button to all stations and called in his men. One by one they arrived, and stood in the clearing in front of the house and looked at the body at his feet.

6

'Don't just stand there,' barked Valin. 'There's another three bodies inside. Newman, Stoner. Get them shifted. You McGuires help them. Mesellier, get up to the track and keep an eye out. We still don't know if they were on their own.'

As Messelier doubled away, Angel, who was looking into the Wrangler, said: 'They weren't wearing their body armour or tin hats. And they're still in the vehicle. I reckon they were just looking for a nice, comfortable place to have a drink and while their duty away.' He reached into the back of the jeep and came up with a bottle of tequila. 'See. There's another bottle in here too. I guess our boys were just searching for a place to chill out. They sure found it.' He chuckled. 'Anyway, Colonel, it's a damn nice truck we've inherited. It's even got a si-reen.'

'We might put it to some good use later,' replied Valin. 'You seem pretty keen, Angel. Why don't you try the late private's uniform for size. It looks like it'll fit you nicely, and there's hardly a speck of blood on it. Then you can lead the way into town with the si-reen, as you call it, on, all the way.'

'Jeez, Colonel,' protested the American.

'That's an order, Angel.'

Angel shook his head, put down his carry weapon, climbed up on to the veranda and looked at the body of the private. Meanwhile, Stoner, Newman and the McGuires went inside to remove the other three bodies, and Jesús joined Valin on the corner of the veranda to catch the slight breeze from the north.

'You saved our lives, Colonel,' said the Colombian. 'Not to mention my youngest daughter's virtue.'

Valin smiled at the older man, and his choice of words. 'It was my duty. If we had not been here, you would not have been here. Any of you.'

'That is not the point. We *were* here. And you and your men's actions prevented our women being raped one by one, and all of us killed afterwards. That is the army's way. And for that I thank you.'

'I can only repeat that it was our duty. But it was also a pleasure.'

'If you can call killing four men a pleasure.'

'*Touché.*'

'So what now, Colonel?'

'I think we'd better leave. Sooner or later someone will come looking for these four. I think we'd better make ourselves extremely scarce before they do. We'll hide the bodies behind the barn, then get the transport and leave.'

'Where to?'

'I don't think *we* should go anywhere. You've done enough, Jesús. It'll be safer if we split up. Give us a map and point us in the right direction and we'll find the factory. We've been studying intelligence on it for the past three weeks. If we can't find it by ourselves by now, we deserve to blow the mission.'

'No, señor.'

'What?' Valin growled.

'You have saved our lives. Now we owe them to you. So we will come with you on the mission. There are four hundred men in the barracks next to the factory, and there are just a dozen of you. I think another six soldiers would be most welcome.'

'No, Jesús,' said Valin. 'Four of you are women. And you . . . '

'You think I am an old fool, and my womenfolk are weak?' Jesús interjected.

'I didn't say that.'

'But you thought it.'

Valin made no reply.

'Well, let me tell you, señor. I may be old. But I served my time in the army as you know. When the army was the friend of the people. And when it changed, I took to the jungle and the mountains. And my family came with me. My daughters have been sharpshooters since they were no taller than the rifles they were firing.'

'OK, OK, Jesús,' said Valin, putting up his hands in a gesture of surrender. 'You win. But you and your family will be under my command. And you will take orders from me and my lieutenant, just like the rest of the grunts.'

'Understood,' said Jesús.

'Right. We'd better get back to them then. Tell my men of your new status, and let's work out what we do next.'

Meanwhile Spenser had gone to the other side of the house, away from the stench of death, and lit up a cigarette. He heard footsteps on the veranda and turned as Carmen came round the corner behind him.

'I wanted to thank you, señor,' she said.

Spenser kept his face grim. 'You have already. Anyway, it was nothing.'

'It was.'

He shook his head.

'May I call you Chris?' she said, then paused.

'If you must.'

Spenser could have kicked himself. For the first time in years he was feeling something for a woman. So why was he behaving like this?

He realized he was coming close to blowing it, by the look on Carmen's face. 'Whoa, time out,' he said. 'Listen, I'm sorry. I'm a bit shaky. It's been a while since I've killed a man like that.'

'I understand,' Carmen said quietly. 'I too have killed men.'

'*You* have?'

'Don't be so surprised, Chris. This is a strange country.'

'I'm beginning to see that.'

'So, once again I thank you.'

'I'd do it for you anytime.'

'I know.'

He smiled. 'You're pretty sure of yourself.'

'I am. Do you want to kiss me?'

'How did you know that?'

He realized it was a pretty naïve question, even as he said it. It had been obvious since the moment he first saw her, and he knew it.

She smiled. 'I am a woman, and I saw you look at me when . . . ' She touched her breasts. 'When I was naked.'

'Any man would have.'

'Not the way you did. Not in a dirty way. I could feel you were ashamed for me. That I had been treated that way.'

Spenser nodded, and she came into his arms and they kissed. Then they heard someone running towards them, and before they could part, Angel, dressed in the private's grey uniform, which had hardly been touched by the detritus from his head wound, came round the corner and skidded to a halt. He looked at Spenser and Carmen and grinned broadly. 'Sorry, guys,' he said. 'Didn't mean to break anything up. But the boss wants to talk to all of us.'

7

Valin addressed the troops from the veranda, as they stood in the clearing in front of the house. 'Ladies and gentlemen,' he began. 'It seems that we have acquired reinforcements. Against my better judgement I have agreed that the Delgado family will join us in our mission.'

He heard a rumble of discontent from his men and raised his hands. 'Listen. We can use all the help we can get. Don't knock it. These people are willing to put their lives on the line for us, so I don't want to hear a word against it. They will take orders like the rest of you, and will be treated as such. Understood?'

The men mumbled what could just about be construed as a positive response, and Valin went on. 'Our immediate plan is to move out of here as quickly as possible. Sergeant, contact Messelier and tell him we'll collect him ASAP. The rest of you, saddle up, and let's get gone. From now on we are on full battle alert.'

Valin dismissed them and the troops went to the vehicles. After collecting their weapons from inside the house, Maria and the women took the Microbus. Carlos got into the driving seat of the Ford truck, with Spenser riding shotgun again. Jesús drove the old jeep as before, with Valin and O'Rourke as passengers, and

Angel took the wheel of the Wrangler, with Stoner in the back, looking after the light machine-gun.

As the hands of Valin's old service watch approached eleven hundred hours, the convoy of four vehicles, Angel leading the way, drove along the track through the jungle, picking up Messelier as they went, and headed back to the main road to Bogotá, where they turned north once again.

'There is another jungle track about three kilometres down the road,' Jesús informed Valin. 'We could drive in and bivouac until dusk.'

'Good idea. We don't want to be on the road for a moment longer than necessary. We could meet another patrol at any time, and I don't want to start a fire-fight unless it's absolutely unavoidable.'

Valin called up Angel on the radio and told him to drop back and let Jesús take the lead. Angel complied, and shortly afterwards Jesús aimed the jeep at what looked like a wall of impenetrable jungle. Miraculously, the vegetation opened up to reveal an overgrown track and all four vehicles left the main road.

They drove on for fifteen minutes or so until Jesús brought the jeep to a halt. 'This will do, Colonel,' he said. 'I don't think anyone will follow us in.'

'I'll mount a guard just in case,' replied Valin. 'And this is as good a place as any to check our ordnance.'

Within fifteen minutes, Stoner was on guard duty, the McGuires were tucking into the remains of the meal that the women had brought with them, and the weapons experts were checking their armaments.

Resnick was fiddling with his explosives, well away

from the main party, while Spenser unpacked his Gatling, wiped off the excess oil, and tested the action, before checking the pile of cartridge belts that held his ammunition.

As he was working, Carmen joined him, once again wearing the Colt .45 on her hip. 'That's a hell of a gun,' she said.

Spenser smiled proudly. 'The latest model, and the best. I liberated it from a British depot in Somalia. Don't tell the colonel. But then they shouldn't even have been there. Nor should I.'

'How do you feed the shells?'

'I need a loader. I guess I'll use Packard on this trip.'

'I should be proud to do it for you.'

'You would?'

Carmen nodded. 'Please show me how it's done,' she said.

On the other side of the clearing, Newman sat and covertly looked at the McGuires. They had finished eating and were busy checking their weapons. Bastards, he thought, as he listened to them chatting to each other. Fucking bastards. And in his mind's eye he was no longer sitting in the Colombian jungle smearing insect repellent on every exposed inch of skin to combat the clouds of insects that zeroed in ceaselessly. Instead he was on the streets of Derry on a cold, dark February morning two years before. His squad fanned out behind a heavily armoured Land Rover as it inched its way between the parked cars, and a dismal mixture of rain, sleet and snow drizzled on to the pavement. Next to the paratrooper were his best mates: Corporal Jimmy Reid and Private Lenny Malin. They were on a routine patrol looking for whatever turned up, when Reid took a sniper shot that cut through his body armour as if it were butter and killed him instantly. Newman saw the round hit, and his friend die, and the two steps he took after he was dead, before he tumbled to the hard, wet tarmac, with a rind of ice on the kerbstones, and lay still.

The paras never caught the sniper. They couldn't even locate where the shot had come from, although they suspected it was from the roof of a block of Republican flats that overlooked the street they had been patrolling.

Newman stayed with Reid until the ambulance arrived. The young officer in charge had ordered him to take cover, but for one of the few times in his army career, Newman disobeyed a direct order, and sheltered his dead friend's body with his own. Afterwards he didn't know why. But something told him not to let the cold, hard rain fall on to the corporal's face, and he didn't.

The next day he was up on a charge, and was confined to barracks for a month. He didn't care. He hated going out into town with his mates anyway, especially now there was one less of them. Hated the way that the population treated the British soldiers, spitting on them, deliberately ignoring them in shops and pubs, and shouting obscenities after them in the street.

Lenny Malin did not survive the tour of duty either. He took a shotgun blast in the leg, fired by a fourteen-year-old boy, and was invalided out. In many ways Newman was happy to take voluntary redundancy when it was offered. He had not lost his bottle, but he was close.

And now, thousands of miles away from home, he was being forced to listen to the Ulster brogue again. He touched the Military Medal that he had won in the Falklands, which he kept hidden in the breast pocket of his army blouse, and fingered the trigger of the shotgun he carried, dreaming of using it on the two Irishmen. Trigger, pump, he thought. Trigger, pump. And then maybe some of the pain would go away.

Messelier and Packard were sitting together with their backs to the bole of a huge fern, slapping the bugs that were targeting their hands and necks. 'This is the life, eh?' said the Frenchman sardonically. 'A soldier's life for me.'

'It could be worse,' replied Packard, lighting a cigarette. 'We might both be sitting in an office, earning peanuts and pretending to be scared of the boss.'

'Too true, my young friend. Too true.'

'So what exactly *were* you doing before this?' asked Packard.

'Ah,' said Messelier. 'I told you, it's a long story.'

'I'm sorry,' said the younger man. 'If you don't want to talk about it. I know we're not supposed to ask questions like that. But I thought we could be mates.'

'We will be, I'm sure, if we live that long. And don't apologize. Sometimes a man needs to talk.' Messelier paused and looked up through the thick fronds of the fern. 'I was a killer,' he said. 'A legalized killer for my government. I was like James Bond in those stupid films. Licensed to kill. But I killed once too often. An innocent child. It was not my finest hour.

Afterwards, I went . . . How do you say? Off the rails . . . I was an embarrassment. So my government decided to eliminate me. But I killed the man they sent to kill me, and then I ran away. But I could not stay away from killing. It is like a drug. You may find that too, Packard. But I hope not. So here I am. Back in the killing fields. But at least today, the people we are up against will fight back. No more children, I hope. I couldn't do that again.'

'You may have to.'

'If I do, I do. I just hope it won't come to it.'

'Did you kill many people?'

'Enough. And this is enough talk, my friend. I wonder if there is a drink around.'

'Tequila, I think.'

'Ah, warm tequila. But it will do. Let's go and find Angel. I believe he knows where it is hidden.'

Messelier and Packard found Angel sitting in the driving seat of the Wrangler. 'Angel,' said Messelier. 'What the hell did you do with the booze?'

'A man after my own heart,' said Angel as he produced a bottle from under the seat. 'But don't let the boss see. I don't think he approves.'

'So, how are you doing, Angel?' asked Packard, after all three of them had taken a surreptitious swig.

'Not bad. But I don't think the geek who was wearing this goddam suit before me had taken a bath for a month.'

'You are not exactly the flowers in May,' said Messelier. 'But I thought it would have been impolite to mention it.'

Angel grinned. 'But that's the life in this man's

army,' he said. 'It's a dirty job, but someone's got to do it.'

All three laughed out loud, and the bottle went round one more time.

Valin saw the three of them drinking, but said nothing. Both Packard and Angel had never seen real action before, and he trusted Messelier to take care of them. A drink or two would bond the three together, and in a way Valin envied the two youngsters their innocence. They have a lot to learn, he thought. Please God that they learn it before it's too late.

And so the day went. The sun reached its peak, then started to drop towards the west, and the squad prepared themselves for the night – and the killing to come.

8

As the afternoon lengthened, Colonel Valin called his troops together for a briefing. He spread maps and diagrams over the bonnet of the Wrangler, and the rest of the squad gathered round him. Carlos had replaced Stoner on guard duty, and Jesús would brief his son later in his native language.

'Very well, ladies and gentlemen,' said Valin. 'I believe we are all aware of our objective tonight.' He held up a grainy photograph of the factory complex. 'This is the place. A small factory that quite legally converts raw coca leaves into cocaine, on the outskirts of the town of Santa Ana, about twenty miles from the capital and with a population of some seven thousand. As you can see, the complex is surrounded by an electric fence. There is just one way in and out: a gate guarded by half-a-dozen soldiers from the barracks next door.' He held up another photograph of a grim, block-built structure. 'There are approximately four hundred soldiers billeted here, so our first job is to get as many of them away from the vicinity as possible. That is Resnick's job. Maxim, the floor is yours.'

Resnick rose from the running board of the truck where he was sitting, and walked over to stand next to his commanding officer. 'I have with me, as you are all well aware, a quantity of high explosives,' he began. 'I intend to take some of it and cause a diversion in Santa Ana. I shall be looking for a gas station near the centre, and when I find it, I intend to destroy it in the most spectacular way possible. It that doesn't bring the soldiers out, nothing will. I'll be needing a volunteer to accompany me, and cover my back. Any offers?'

Sofía raised her hand slowly. 'I will come with you, señor.'

'Can you drive?' asked Resnick.

Maria smiled at his question. 'She is the finest driver in Colombia,' she volunteered proudly.

'Can you steal a car?' asked Resnick.

'Any car you can show me,' replied Sofía brazenly. 'I am the queen of the car thieves.'

'We didn't realize that we had such talent available,' said Valin. 'And that's very good. It'll look better if you go into town as a couple. Less suspicious. Can you use a machine-gun, Sofía?'

The young woman nodded.

'Excellent. We have several new Heckler and Koch MP5K personal defence weapons with us. Do you think you could handle one?'

'Show me, and I'll tell you,' said Sofía.

'Lieutenant,' said Valin, and O'Rourke climbed into the back of the three-tonner and came back out holding a stubby, vicious-looking weapon with a folding stock and sound suppressor, complete with a holster and belt. 'Welcome to the future,' he said, as he pulled the MP5K from its holster and punched home a short magazine. 'Thirty rounds,' he explained. 'Nine mill, and it goes some.' He tossed the weapon to

Sofía. 'You'd better get some practice in. Don't worry about anyone hearing. The silencer is very effective.'

'Thank you, señor,' she said, almost curtseying, and O'Rourke winked at her.

'So much for the big diversion,' said Valin. 'At the same time, Stoner and one other will be destroying an electricity substation that feeds the town, plus the telephone exchange that is conveniently located next door. We need to cut communications as much as possible, and keep these bastards in the dark in more ways than one.' He held up another photograph, showing the generator building, with a dark, brick-built edifice next to it. 'They'll take this vehicle.' He slapped the bonnet of the Wrangler. 'And rejoin us as soon as possible back at the factory. Mr Stoner, in a previous life, has had some experience with HE, and Maxim has been giving him a crash course since we got together. Are you happy with that, Max?'

'He is a good student,' said the Russian. 'I'd rather do the job myself, but sadly I can't be in two places at once. Just remember, Johnny,' he said to Stoner, 'to wait for my diversion to stir up the hornet's nest before you blow up anything.'

'You're the boss,' said Stoner.

'I'm going to team you up with Angel,' said Valin. 'Driving an army vehicle, and dressed as he is, you shouldn't have much trouble getting in close. The communications and power complexes are subject to routine patrols according to our intelligence sources.' He nodded at Jesús, who nodded back. 'But I'm going to need you back at the factory pronto. This jeep is the best cover we've got. We're going to have to get through those gates somehow, and we might have to use it as a Trojan horse. So, Angel, try not to lose it.'

'Trust me, boss,' said Angel.

'Meanwhile,' Valin went on, 'Sergeant Keller, with his sniper rifle, will have taken up a position on the hilltop that overlooks both the factory and the barracks.' Keller was lovingly cleaning a .50-calibre Browning Barratt Model 82 A-1 semi-automatic sniper rifle with a ten-round magazine holding shells that could punch their way through the skin of an armoured car, and fitted with a 10x40 Trijicon optical gunsight with tritium-powered red and black dots for night and day shooting. 'The rifle he is caressing is accurate up to two and a half thousand metres, but tonight he'll be less than half that distance away, and he is a good shot, believe me. There are a few of us here who owe our lives to his talent.'

Keller smiled darkly, and carried on cleaning his weapon.

'Gerry,' Valin said to the elder of the McGuire brothers. 'I want you to take a pair of night glasses and act as his spotter. Daniel, you'll be with the rest of us in the main assault team. We'll go in and take the charges with us, which Resnick will set off as soon as he catches up.'

'And if he doesn't?' asked O'Rourke, then looked at the Russian and put his hands up. 'No offence, Maxim,' he said.

'Then I will set the charges,' said Valin sharply. 'Or you, or whoever's around. It's not a difficult job. The preparation's the hard part, isn't it, Max?' Resnick nodded. 'But he *will* return,' said Valin confidently. 'He wouldn't have lasted three years in Afghanistan if he couldn't get across a hick town guarded by an army made up of conscripted old men and boys. And I didn't take on this job to fail, is that understood?'

O'Rourke nodded. 'Just checking, sir,' he said.

'Fair enough, Mark,' said Valin. 'Any other questions so far?' There was silence, so he continued. 'Our main man covering the barracks itself will be Chris Spenser and his Gatling. I believe he has a new ammunition feeder that he's been showing the ropes to this afternoon. Your job, Chris, is to keep the remaining soldiers bottled up in that building. It's not going to be an easy job, so I'm going to put Messelier, Packard, Maria and Carlotta with you. Three of them armed with H and Ks, and the other with the grenade-launcher.' His eyes found the two women. 'It's going to be dangerous – one of the most dangerous jobs of them all. But I need your manpower, or should I say womanpower. I need a lid kept on that place, so if you have a problem with it, speak now.'

The older woman looked at her daughter, and they both smiled. 'Today is as good as any other to die, señor, said Maria. 'We have seen death once already today. Another glimpse will not kill us.' And she giggled like a schoolgirl at her own joke.

'Fine. Good attitude. Newman, Lieutenant O'Rourke and myself, plus Jesús, Carlos and you, Daniel, will go into the complex. We secure it and destroy it. Simple.'

He looked round the clearing at their still faces and paused. 'Afterwards we get out of town fast and get back to the airstrip. We will meet up at this spot here.' Bending over one of the maps on the bonnet of the jeep, he found the location he was seeking. 'There is a crossroads on the south side of the town. That will be our RV. We make our way there as best we can. It's a four-hour drive back to the airstrip. The plane flies in at dawn. That means we need to leave Santa Ana at two hundred hours at the latest. I don't intend to leave anyone behind. The pilot has told me he will make one more trip at the same time next day. But that may be impossible. If the army discovers the location of the airstrip, it *will* be impossible. So I need everyone at that rendezvous on time. I don't care how you get there. Just be there, and we'll all be drinking champagne by noon tomorrow. But we've got to be flexible. The odds are against us, even with the help of Jesús and his family. But we have surprise on our side, and the latest weapons that the American taxpayers' money can buy. We have to get in and out before they even know what's hit them. Just remember that and we'll be OK. There are K-rations in the truck. I suggest we eat now. We don't know when we'll get another chance.' He paused again. 'That's it, ladies and gentlemen. It only leaves me to say good luck, and good hunting.' He began to fold up his maps.

Resnick took Sofía to one side. 'Do you want to try out that gun?' he asked. 'I want to make sure you can cover me properly.'

'I'd love to,' said the girl with a smile. 'Where shall we go?'

'A little way into the jungle,' he said. 'I'll get some spare magazines from the truck. Wait here. Do you want anything to eat?'

'A picnic,' said Sofía. 'How lovely. Yes, please. Whatever you're having.'

Resnick went over to the truck and collected four

spare full clips for the Heckler and Koch, a box of one hundred 9mm bullets, a pocket full of K-ration tins, and a bottle of water. The time for drinking anything stronger was over. He went back and joined Sofía, who by now had strapped the weapon to her hip, and after she had told her mother where she was going and why, they struck off into the jungle.

'This is far enough,' said the Russian after they had gone a few yards. 'Do you want to eat first? Or shoot first?'

'Shoot.'

Resnick took the gun from her and showed her its simple workings. 'Single shot or full auto,' he said. 'Use the auto. If nothing else, you'll scare the shit out of anyone you shoot at . . . Sorry.'

'For what?'

'For my language.'

'I have heard worse.'

'That's no excuse. I apologize.'

'I accept.'

Resnick felt himself redden. 'Right,' he said, to cover his embarrassment. 'Safety off.' He handed her the weapon. 'It's ready to go. Try aiming for that yellow tree over there.' He pointed to a tree some thirty yards away.

Sofía unfolded the stock, wedged it against her hip, flexed her knees, lowered the weapon slightly and pulled the trigger. The 9mm Teflon-coated shells silently stitched a neat line up the bole of the tree, and she moved the gun slightly from left to right and chopped the trunk off neatly about five feet up. By then the gun was empty, and she pulled out the used magazine and stuck it into the waistband of her skirt. 'Next,' she said.

'That's good,' said Resnick. 'You weren't kidding. If you're as good at stealing cars, it's money in the bank.'

'I am,' said Sofía. 'Better. Can we eat now?'

Back in the clearing, the men were talking among themselves. 'What do you reckon?' said Daniel to his brother.

'What the hell do I know?' replied Gerry. 'But I've got to be honest with you, little brother, something in my water tells me we're up shit creek.'

'So what do we do?'

'What the hell *can* we do? We came into this with our eyes open. We've got nowhere else *to* go. We follow Valin or we die where we stand. I reckon there's a couple of guys in the squad would be glad to nail our Republican hides to a tree.'

'Bloody Brits.'

'You never spoke a truer word.'

Messelier and Packard were sharing a can of cold pork and beans, sitting on the tailgate of the truck. 'Glad you came?' asked the Frenchman.

'I wouldn't have missed it for the world.'

'You're a strange guy, Packard. I would like to have met your father.'

'He was a strange sort too, so I'm told.'

'So we're going to be keeping the barracks pinned down. That's good,' said Messelier. 'We can watch each other's backs. I want to come out of this episode alive.'

'Me too,' agreed Packard.

But he was lying again. He didn't want to live. Indeed that was his main reason for signing up with

Valin's Raiders. The same reason he had joined the Australian army, and then worked himself a discharge on psychological grounds when he found out that he would probably never come within a mile of combat. Lenny Packard wanted to die because he was a killer himself, and he hated it.

The first man he ever killed was the driver of an overland truck transporter with three wagons hitched up to its Volvo tractor. The man had been speeding in a cloud of dust along the highway fifty miles from the lonely sheep station that Packard's mother had inherited from his late father. For years, ever since he was a kid, Lenny had practised with his father's rifle, using ammunition illegally bought from a friend of a friend, so that his mother wouldn't find out, and he was a crack shot. He had slaughtered every animal that came into his sights, large or small. But animals were not enough. Now he was hunting for bigger game. And finally, one morning after he had borrowed the family pick-up truck, he had driven alone to the main road, hidden his vehicle behind a clump of scrub, and taken up his position on a ridge overlooking the highway.

Not much traffic used the route, and Lenny had to wait for hours under the burning sun until a target presented itself. But he was patient, and he knew someone would come along eventually.

First of all he saw a dust cloud, far away, which gradually materialized into the mighty roadliner. He smiled and squinted through the telescopic sights at the dirty windscreen through which he could see the head and shoulders of the driver. He exhaled and squeezed the trigger gently. The rifle kicked into his shoulder, and for a second he thought he had missed. Then the big, turbo-driven tractor swerved slightly to the right, then more violently to the left, and the cab and the three containers jackknifed slowly, the front wheels of the Volvo dug into the sand at the side of the road, and the tractor and its trailers began to roll over and break up, until the cab exploded into flames.

Lenny put the FN FAL back into its case and returned to his pick-up. He was not interested in the driver of the juggernaut. He was dead. Strike one.

Messelier had said that he was a strange guy, and Lenny Packard had told him that his father was too. And he'd spoken the truth. But what he didn't know was that his old man often took the rifle out on hunting expeditions, and buried the humans that he had sniped in shallow graves all over the outback. But he wouldn't have been surprised. Not in the least. And the police didn't draw any conclusions from the fact that the mysterious disappearances of tourists and transients in the area ceased when Joe Packard went to Vietnam, only to return in a pine box. They were just grateful. And of course they didn't suspect young Lenny when the disappearances started again some fourteen years later.

But Lenny hated himself for the compulsion that had driven him to kill half-a-dozen people over the next five years. Hated himself, but didn't do much about it. He lacked the nerve to either turn himself in to the authorities or kill himself. But he knew that the only way to stop himself killing more innocent people was for him to die, and as he sat next to Messelier he prayed that it would happen soon.

On the other side of the clearing Spenser and Carmen were going through the procedure to keep the Gatling shooting smoothly once again. 'I've loaded the belts with a mixture of shells,' explained the American. 'High-explosive. . . armour-piercing. . . tracers. You name it. But where we are, it's going to get hot in more ways than one. I hope you can handle it.'

'Trust me,' said Carmen. 'Where are you going after the mission is over?'

'Christ knows. Back to England, I suppose. Until we get another job. What about you?'

She shrugged eloquently. 'Who knows?'

'Have you ever been to England?'

'No, I have never been outside Colombia.'

'Maybe you'd like to.'

'I hear it is very cold and damp there.'

'Only sometimes.'

She nodded. 'Maybe . . . ' she said.

Angel lounged in the front seat of the liberated jeep smoking a joint, while Stoner checked the M60 mounted in the back. 'You reckon we'll have to use that?' asked Angel.

'Chances are,' replied Stoner. 'I was trained on one similar in the Legion.'

'That's good news. I'd hate to go on the mission with someone who didn't know what he was doing.'

'You scared, kid?'

'Shitting my pants. This calm exterior is just a pose.'

'Give us a hit on that joint, then, because I ain't exactly looking forward to tonight myself.'

Newman collared Keller as the sergeant carefully put his Barratt back in its case. 'I need some grenades, Sarge,' he said.

'Help yourself,' said the German.

'I hope that Irish bastard is a good spotter,' Newman muttered.

'He should be. I had a talk with him last night. Seems he spent some time on the south side of the Irish border spotting a Yank who was picking off British troops.' Keller smiled grimly. 'Some of your mates maybe.'

'Don't remind me.'

'Forget it. We're all on the same side now.'

'Sure,' said the ex-para as he went off to fill a sack with grenades and collect another box of cartridges for his shotgun. 'Sure thing.'

Away from the main group, Colonel Valin was giving his lieutenant his final briefing.

'This is it then, Mark,' he said.

'It certainly is, sir.'

'You don't seem too happy.'

'I just don't know if this lot are ready.'

'As ready as they'll ever be.'

'It's not going to be easy.'

'It never was. Just keep them together and we'll be all right.'

'If you say so, sir.'

'I do. I'm going to speak to Jesús. I'm still not crazy about taking the Delgados with us.'

'I think they can take care of themselves, sir.'

'It's not them I'm worried about. It's us.'

Valin left O'Rourke and went over to where the Delgado family, minus Sofía and Carmen, were sitting together, talking in low tones. 'Everything OK?' he asked.

Jesús nodded at him.

'Still determined to come with us?'

'Of course.'

'Then we move out in a couple of hours.'

9

In the jungles of Colombia, the dusk comes early and quickly. By six in the evening, beneath the dense foliage of the tropical forest, it was almost dark, and Valin ordered his men to pack up and move out. There was only one difference in the travel arrangements: Carmen was now in the cab of the Ford truck with her brother and Spenser.

Before they left the clearing, Jesús approached Valin. 'Spenser,' he said. 'What kind of man is he?'

'One of the best,' replied Valin. 'I've known him for years.'

'I think he is interested in Carmen.'

'With all due respect to you, Jesús, who wouldn't be?' said Valin. 'She is a beautiful young woman. And he did kill the man who was going to rape her earlier today. That kind of thing forges bonds.'

'She is beautiful, yes. But crazy in the head, I think. Is he married?'

'No.'

'How old is he?'

'Does it matter?'

'These days, I suppose not. The whole world is going mad.'

'So does it matter if a few more join in?'

'I suppose not,' the old man sighed. 'And what about the Russian?'

'Resnick?'

'Yes.'

'What about him?'

'Sofía is going into town with him to blow up the gas station.'

'Someone had to.'

'I just don't know, Colonel. Here I am with three daughters all of marriageable age, and none of them has shown any interest in men, except now, two of them seem to have fallen for men who may not live through the night.'

'It could be worse.'

'I suppose so. At least neither of them fell for the president,' said Jesús, and he burst out laughing.

Valin laughed too, then said: 'So are you OK about it?'

Jesús shrugged. 'I suppose so,' he said again. 'At least we know they can take care of them.'

'Like I said,' observed Valin, 'it could be worse.'

One by one the vehicles pulled out of the clearing and took the track back to the main road. Only Jesús in the lead jeep showed any lights, and the pace of the convoy was torturously slow. But eventually they made it on to the blistered main road and with a roar of his engine Angel took the lead. While they had been hanging around, Jesús had gone through the maps with the young American and his British passenger. The road to Bogotá was as straight as any in the region, with no turn-offs to negotiate, and the fact that an army vehicle was leading the convoy was bound to ensure a safe passage.

The two jeeps, the Microbus and the old Ford truck, now all with headlights on, clocked up an average speed of just over thirty miles per hour. The surface of the road began to improve as they got closer to Bogotá, and other traffic started to appear, but they saw no sign of any military presence until they had been travelling for just under three hours, when they suddenly came up behind an army convoy.

Angel slowed down to almost a walking pace, and looked over his shoulder at Valin in the jeep behind him, who gave him a hand signal to stop. The young American allowed the jeep to coast to a halt at the side of the road, and his commanding officer exited his vehicle and jogged up to join him.

'What do we do, boss?' asked Angel.

'You overtake that convoy and get into town. Check out the substation and the telephone exchange. Use your siren if you have to. Jesús tells me this is a regular army convoy, not Militia, so they shouldn't be interested in you. Militia and army don't exactly get on in this country. We'll follow behind. You recce the area, and check back with me. Meet us at the crossroads RV just this side of town that we looked at on the map. And another thing . . . '

'Boss?'

'Jesús tells me there's a midnight curfew on the town. It's just come into force. I don't like it a bit. More military activity in the area, and now a curfew. It stinks. I've got a gut feeling we may be expected.'

'Shit, boss,' said Stoner from where he was sitting behind the trigger of the LMG. 'I knew something like this was going to happen. Why didn't the old geezer tell you before? Is he playing both sides against the middle? Because if he is . . . ' He made as if to get out of the jeep.

'He told me this morning,' said Valin. 'I just chose not to share the happy news until now. So relax. Move out, Angel, and take it easy.'

'That's my middle name, Colonel,' said Angel as he jammed the Wrangler into gear, and set off after the convoy, headlights on full beam and the siren already screaming.

I'm too old for all this, thought Valin as he headed back to the other jeep. Far too old.

10

Angel sped past the convoy with the pedal to the metal, and screeched off ahead at about seventy miles per hour.

'Slow down a bit, for Chrissake,' shouted Stoner from the back, above the roar of the slipstream and the scream of the engine. 'Or you'll have us off the fucking road.'

Angel looked over his shoulder with a grin. 'Relax. I used to drive superstocks at the San Marino stadium, back in the good ol' US of A.'

'This ain't the good old US of A,' screamed Stoner. 'And I ain't wearing a seat belt.'

'If you're that worried about your health you shouldn't be here,' Angel yelled back, but slowed down slightly. Even so, they arrived at the outskirts of Santa Ana within half an hour, no longer constrained by the speed of the slower vehicles in the convoy. So the first members of Valin's team made contact with their target at slightly before twenty-two hundred hours on day one of the mission.

As the Wrangler passed the first few scattered dwellings, Angel dropped speed even further, to less than thirty, and kept an eye out for roadblocks.

Stoner moved forward, knelt behind the driver's seat and said: 'Looks pretty quiet.'

'So far,' said Angel. 'Hey, Stoner.'

'What?'

'You speak any Spanish?'

'No. You?'

'No. So what happens if anyone tries to speak to us?'

'We shoot the fucker, that's what happens.'

Both men laughed.

They cruised towards the town centre, and the closer they got, the more military presence they felt. At one point a three-ton personnel carrier, with a full complement of soldiers in combat gear, crossed in front of them, and there were foot patrols every quarter of a mile or so, but non paid them much attention.

'I wonder if this is usual, or for our benefit,' said Angel. 'And where are all the civilians? There's hardly any about, and it's still two hours to curfew time.'

'Christ knows,' replied Stoner. 'Just take it easy, and we'll be cool.'

Angel found the town centre and turned the jeep in the direction of the telephone exchange and electricity substation.

'It should be just down here,' he said to Stoner, as he steered into a side street.

'Keep driving,' hissed Stoner. 'We've got company.'

Parked between the two buildings they were looking for was another personnel carrier, and Stoner had spotted the glow of a cigarette in the back as someone took a drag.

Angel drove by slowly and turned off at the next

corner. 'Shit,' said Stoner. 'It ain't gonna be as easy as we thought to take them out.'

'We'll manage,' said Angel. 'Do you want to take a look at the factory and barracks?'

'Might as well,' replied Stoner, and Angel headed back towards the town centre, then headed west in the direction of the complex. On the way, two jeeps full of soldiers passed them going in the opposite direction, and they spotted three more foot patrols.

The factory was not difficult to find, as it was brightly lit and the glow of the lights could be seen for a mile or so. Angel stopped the jeep at the brow of a hill less than half that distance from the factory, and he and Stoner scoped the view.

The factory and adjoining barracks lay in a depression between two hills. One was the hill where the two mercenaries were parked; the other, behind the complex, had once been cleared of vegetation but now seemed to be partially reclaimed by the jungle.

'Can we get off this road?' said Stoner. 'And up on the other side? Looks like the ideal place for a sniper to cover the whole area.'

Angel nodded, put the jeep into gear and let it drift down towards the factory. About a quarter of a mile before the slip road that led to the complex, he spotted a track off to the right, killed his lights and drove on to it. It was a slow and difficult climb, even with the Wrangler in four-wheel drive, but eventually they found the top of the second hill, and from the cover of the new growth of trees and ferns had an uninterrupted view of both the factory and the barracks beyond it.

Stoner took out his binoculars and swept them across the two brightly lit buildings, which lay close together. The slip road back to the main road sloped gently upwards towards the entrance to the factory, and a side road led off it that, two or three hundred yards down the hill, went up to the barracks. Trucks, jeeps, personnel carriers and a few regular cars painted in army colours were parked on the U-shaped drive in front of the building. There was a fair amount of activity – soldiers moving about on various tasks, vehicles coming and going – but nothing to suggest that they were on any particular state of alert. The factory was busy too, with civilians moving from one building to another, and at the gatehouse that covered the entrance Stoner spotted at least six heavily armed soldiers on guard, and a couple of jeeps parked with their drivers at the wheel.

'This is the ideal place,' he said to Angel. 'Get Keller up here with that rifle of his and he'll have complete control of both the factory and the barracks.'

'Yeah,' agreed the American. 'And once we knock the lights out, it'll be chaos down there.'

'They're bound to have an emergency generator,' said Stoner. 'Now where the hell could that be?'

'Who knows?' said Angel. 'In the basement, probably. Maybe we'll get lucky, and Spenser will knock it out with that Gatling of his.'

'Maybe,' agreed Stoner. 'We'd better get back to the colonel, and tell him what's happening. We've seen all we can here.'

'OK,' said Angel, and he turned the jeep round on the track, drove back down to the road and headed back into town, where he picked up the main road again. He found the rendezvous without difficulty, and swung off the road into the shadows of the jungle, where Messelier appeared out of nowhere like a wraith and led them to where the other three vehicles were waiting, parked out of sight.

'What's the good word?' asked Valin when Angel and Stoner joined him at the command post he had set up in the back of Jesús's jeep.

'Lots of activity,' said Stoner. 'Patrols everywhere. Motorized and on foot. Not much civilian presence, though. I get the distinct feeling that the authorities know something's up, but not exactly when it's going to happen. We found the telephone exchange with no bother. There's a truck full of army watching it and the substation next door. Then we took a shufti at the factory. We found an ace spot for Keller to snipe from. Up on a hill overlooking it. It's ideal.'

'Right,' said Valin. 'Good work.' He called Jesús, Keller and O'Rourke over, who listened as Stoner repeated his story. 'What do you say, Jesús?' asked Valin.

'It's exactly as I thought, Colonel,' replied the Colombian. 'As I told you this morning, I suspected as much.'

'But you don't think we're particularly expected tonight of all nights?' Valin asked Stoner.

'That's not the impression I get. It feels like they're on a yellow alert. Waiting for something or someone, but that's all.'

'It's just as well that only Tank and Jesús knew what day we were due to make our strike, then, isn't it,' said Valin.

'You think someone's tipped them off that you were coming?' asked Jesús.

'That we were coming, yes. But not exactly when,'

replied Valin. 'Otherwise they'd have been waiting at the airstrip this morning to blow the plane out of the sky. But it certainly doesn't make our job any easier.'

'I've got a suggestion, Colonel,' said Stoner.

'Let's hear it then.'

'We're never gonna get four vehicles through the centre of town. It's twenty-three hundred now, and already all the civilians are off the street, and we didn't see one civvy car moving around. I suggest we go in the back way, get Sergeant Keller and his spotter up on the hill overlooking the compound in Jesús's jeep. It's the ideal place. We leave the Microbus here, and put the rest of the Delgados in the truck. That way, at least there'll be one vehicle here to get us back to the airstrip if anything happens to the rest. Not that I think it'll come to that. Then Angel and I take Resnick and Sofía into town in our jeep to set up the diversion. He blows the petrol station, then they steal a motor and get back to you. We wait five minutes or so to give whoever leaves the barracks to see what's occurring time to get away, then we blow the substation and the telephone exchange, and get back over to you. By then you should have the factory and barracks pretty well sewn up, and in we go and blow the place to kingdom come.'

Valin looked at O'Rourke. 'Mark?' he said.

'Sounds good to me, Colonel,' replied the lieutenant. 'Let me check the maps to see what road we need to take to get round to the other side of town.'

O'Rourke picked up a map case, opened it and scanned the contents by the light of his torch. 'Yeah,' he said. 'That works.'

'Good,' said Valin. 'Mark, get everyone together for a final short briefing, and we'll be off.'

A minute or two later the squad gathered together in front of Valin. The Delgado women wore the dead soldier's body armour, which had been in the captured jeep, and had all been issued with Heckler and Koch MP5Ks. Messelier carried a South African-manufactured ARMSCOR 40mm multi-shot grenade-launcher, a semi-automatic six-shot drum revolver – a single-barrelled weapon with a folding stock. It looked like a sub-machine-gun and apart from the cylinder was about the same size. It had a forward and back pistol grip. Its muzzle velocity was 80 metres per second and it had a combat range of 425 metres. It swung open like a revolver for loading and could fire any combination of high-explosive, smoke, gas, illumination and anti-riot rounds. Loaded with a full cylinder, it weighed only 7kg; and the weight was between the hands, where it should be. It was fitted with an occluded sight that was used with both eyes and was self-graduated to 375 metres, where the user picked out a red dot. It was one hell of a weapon and it felt good in Messelier's hands as he slotted in the HE grenades that he would use on the first strike. In his pockets he carried a dozen smoke grenades and more HE for later use. Spenser had his Gatling on his shoulder and Sergeant Keller was nursing his Barratt.

'Revised plan,' said Valin. 'But only slightly. What happens now is that Stoner and Angel lead us in. They've scouted the area, and have an overview. Then they take Resnick and Sofía into town. Sergeant Keller, you take up your position with Gerry on the hill looking down on the factory. Chris, you find a field of fire at the bottom of the hill. We all wait for the diversion explosion, then the electricity to go, and we put a blanket on the barracks, then blow the factory. Rendezvous here, and head back to the airstrip. Any questions?'

There were none.

'OK,' he said. 'Saddle up, people. We're in business.'

11

Everyone piled into their designated vehicle and all three set off, with the captured jeep at the front, leaving the VW safely parked with its keys in the exhaust pipe. They took the road that dissected the highway they had come in on, and headed round the edge of Santa Ana. For this final part of their journey, O'Rourke joined Angel and Stoner in the Wrangler to check the route.

After about twenty minutes the lieutenant tapped Angel on the shoulder and told him to slow down. A quarter of a mile or so further down the road there was a turn-off towards the town, and O'Rourke told him to take it. The two jeeps and the truck turned off into the blackness of the jungle, and with their headlights cutting through the darkness they headed towards the factory.

The road came out the other side of the factory, about two miles from the centre of Santa Ana. Valin got Jesús to flash the lead jeep, and then jumped out and ran forward. 'You go on,' he said to Angel. 'We'll follow in about three minutes, and the truck can come about three minutes after us.'

'The turn-off is about a quarter of a mile past the slip road to the factory,' said Stoner. 'Don't miss it, for fuck's sake.'

'We won't,' said Valin. 'Now go, go, go.'

The lead jeep peeled off down the road, past the factory, and at the last moment Angel killed the lights and spun the wheel so that the vehicle shot off on to the track leading up the hill.

'Perfect,' said Stoner, looking back through the fern fronds. 'No one saw a thing.'

Within six minutes they were joined by the other jeep and the truck, and the squad dismounted. 'Jesús,' said Valin. 'Let Gerry take over and drive your jeep up the hill.'

Jesús tossed the Irishman the keys, and slid in behind the wheel, while Keller, with sniper rifle and twenty spare magazines, climbed into the passenger seat. They took off.

Meanwhile, Resnick had carefully stashed four knapsacks of high explosive into the rear of the Wrangler. Then he turned, and from one of the cavernous pockets of his jacket took three radio transmitters. He handed one to Valin, tossed the second to Stoner, and held up the remaining one in the air. 'Lieutenant,' he said. 'Give me a little light, will you?'

O'Rourke shone his torch on the transmitter in Resnick's hand. 'Stoner, Angel. This is how you blow the packages I will leave with you,' said the Russian. 'Colonel. This is how you blow the rest of the charges in case I do not return. It is simplicity itself.' He paused for effect, then went on. 'In the right-hand corner' – he pointed with his finger – 'is the on/off switch.' He touched the button, and a tiny green light glowed on the face of the remote control. 'It is now armed. Stoner, do not turn yours on until I have blown up the garage, and you have placed your charges where they will do the most damage. Colonel, I hope I will be back here to do the job, but just in case, do not turn *yours* on until you hear the two separate blasts, and you have put the explosives where they will destroy the factory. When they *are* switched on, you simply touch this red button at the bottom and the charges blow.'

Resnick indicated the button in question, but was careful not to touch it. Then he switched off the transmitter and the green light died. 'But be careful,' he warned. 'All three are live, and one could trigger the rest.' He saw the looks on their faces and grinned. 'But don't worry. They won't. They only work up to a distance of a mile or so, and they're all tuned to different frequencies. But just to be on the safe side, keep them turned off until you need to use them. Everyone clear?' Stoner and Valin grunted their assent. 'I want *all* of you to understand,' the Russian said to the rest. 'Who knows what will happen in the next hour or so?'

The others mumbled at his words, and Resnick nodded. 'Now I've also added a hand detonator to each package in case anyone fancies committing suicide in a very spectacular way. Open the knapsacks and you'll see a short length of knotted cord. It works rather like the pin on a hand-grenade. Pull it and the charge blows. But there is no time-delay. When the cord is pulled, the charges blow there and then. So don't pull them. That's my advice. Unless you are in a position where you're going to die anyway.' He looked round at the serious faces, lit by the dim reflection from O'Rourke's torchlight. 'Cheer up,' he said. 'It may never happen. Right. I think we will leave now.'

Then he helped Sofía into the back of the Wrangler, and joined her.

'Just keep the charges out of the line of fire until I get back, Colonel,' the Russian said. 'We don't want any accidents, do we?'

Valin smiled. 'Course we don't,' he said. 'And good luck.'

'Thank you,' replied Resnick. 'See you back here shortly.'

Angel got behind the wheel of the Wrangler and started the engine.

'Drive carefully, Angel,' said O'Rourke, as the American put the vehicle into gear.

'Will do, Ell-Tee,' replied Angel. 'Watch yourselves now.'

He spun the wheel and slowly nosed the jeep through the undergrowth back on to the main road, and was away.

'Right, the rest of you,' said Valin when the sound of the engine had receded into the distance. 'Get yourselves ready.'

12

Angel expertly sent the jeep rocketing towards the town centre. He wanted to get the charges laid and blown as quickly as possible, and make it back to where the real fighting was going to be, as soon as he could.

'You want us to pick you up after?' he shouted to Resnick in the back.

The Russian looked at Sofía. 'What do you say?'

'No,' she replied. 'I'll get us a car. Trust me.'

'Don't bother, Angel,' Resnick shouted back. 'We'll make it on our own.'

Then he pulled Sofía close and said: 'You know of a gas station?'

'Of course. I've been here a thousand times. I know just the place,' she said, grinning. 'It's right opposite the police headquarters. I hate those bastard pigs.'

Resnick grinned back. 'Perfect. We'll give them something to think about too. A little bonus,' he said quietly.

'I hoped you'd say that,' said Sofía, leaning forward and tapping Angel on the shoulder. 'Take the next turn on the left,' she said. 'There's a gas station down on the right.'

The jeep bounced over the cobbles that formed the

side street, and skidded to a halt outside a deserted petrol station. Opposite it was a brick-and-wood building with an illuminated sign that read 'POLICIA'. Resnick and Sofía baled out, taking two of the knapsacks of explosives with them.

'Good luck, guys,' said Angel as he gunned the engine. 'Don't take any wooden nickels.' With a screech of tyres, he was gone.

'Couldn't wait to say goodbye,' said Resnick.

'Who could blame him?' replied Sofía. 'With that lot over the road.'

Resnick cocked his Kalashnikov and smiled at her. 'Don't worry about cops,' he said. 'They're easy meat. Now we need a car.'

'I'll check round the back,' Sofía replied. 'There should be something.' Then she was gone.

Resnick kept a careful eye on the police building as he looked for the cover of the underground petrol tanks. It wasn't hard to find. Between the twin banks of pumps, he found a manhole, sealed with a cast-iron lid. With difficulty he hoisted the cover off, and saw the four line feeds that took the various grades of petrol and diesel into the tanks. He smiled and dropped one of the knapsacks down into the hole, then replaced the lid.

The Russian stood up as he heard the snarl of a powerful engine. An ancient, dusty-pink Chevrolet sedan, with Sofía at the wheel, turned the corner from behind the workshops at the back of the garage and purred to a halt beside him. Sofía wound down the window and leaned out. 'Like it?' she said.

'Very interesting,' Resnick replied. 'But will it get us where we want to go?'

'Count on it,' Sofía replied. 'Are you ready?'

'Won't be long,' Resnick said. 'I just want to give the local police a nice surprise.'

He threw his carry gun into the car and loped off across the road, carrying the second knapsack over his shoulder. The police station was very quiet and he hesitated for a moment before lobbing the sack down into the area in front of it, and then hopped over the metal railing that separated the building from the street. There were no signs of guards. Very lax, he noted. He dropped down about six feet, found the sack and shoved it into a grille that he reckoned was the exhaust for the air-conditioning system. He turned, pulled himself up and over the railings again, and ran back across the street to join Sofía in the Chevrolet, which smelt of damp and cat's piss. 'Drive,' he said. And she took off.

At the end of the street he told her to stop. 'Let me out here,' he said. 'Go at least two streets down before you stop. Then park around a corner, close to a building. Otherwise the concussion will blow out the windows.'

As soon as Resnick was out of the car, Sofía accelerated away again, and the Chevy spun round a corner just as he was taking cover behind the nearest house. There he took out the remote control he carried in his pocket, laid it carefully on the pavement, reached into his pocket again and removed a pair of plugs and carefully inserted them in his ears. He had laid enough charges to know how quickly a demolition expert could go deaf. Then he picked up the remote again, turned on the green light, and touched the red button.

The petrol station and the police headquarters erupted simultaneously. From his position behind the corner of the house, Resnick watched as the package he had placed under the manhole cover in the garage blew it straight up through the roof canopy above, on the crest of a pillar of fire, with an enormous bang. In the same split second, the front of the police station seemed to lift a dozen feet in the air, then blew out, burying the two police cars parked in front in a pile of rubble and broken bodies. There was a frozen silence for an instant, then Resnick heard a deep rumble from the bowels of the earth, and with an explosion that made the previous one sound like a pin dropping, the buried petrol tanks blew out in a sea of boiling fuel, and every window close by imploded as one.

Back at the factory the waiting soldiers heard the explosions echo across the silent town, and watched in awe as the mushroom cloud from the petrol tanks began to rise.

'Shit,' said Packard. 'Was that nuclear?'

'Good job!' said Valin. 'That should stir things up.'

It was not long before he was proved correct. Within half a minute the barracks was like an ant's nest. Troops came out of every exit, hastily buckling on equipment, and dived into the cars, jeeps and trucks that were parked outside, before racing in the direction of the fireball.

'Excellent,' whispered O'Rourke. 'We've just got rid of a hundred and fifty of the opposition.'

'They'll be back,' observed Valin drily. 'Now come on, all of you. Move back to the factory. And keep in the shelter of the trees. We don't want to be spotted yet.'

After Angel had dropped off Resnick and Sofía, he had sped back in the direction of the telephone exchange, and skidded the jeep to a halt on the corner of the main street and the side turning that led to it, just as the Russian slid the manhole cover back into place after laying the first charge.

'You wanna do the thing?' Angel said to Stoner.

'What about the guards?'

'Leave them to me,' Angel growled, and leaving the engine running, he pulled himself out of the driver's seat, hopped into the back and got behind the trigger of the LMG. 'I've used one of these before too. Get up there and lay the charges. If you're spotted I'll give you cover. You can drive when you get back. Quick. I feel a big bang coming on.'

As the words left his lips, the petrol station and police headquarters blew.

Angel and Stoner turned towards the source of the explosions as one, and had an excellent view of the carnage over the tops of the houses in between.

'Jesus Christ,' said Stoner. 'What the fuck's he got in these bags?'

'Plant 'em and let's find out,' urged Angel. 'Look out, here come the sightseers.'

The guards on the telephone exchange and electricity substation had rushed out at the sound of the bombs, and together they ran around the side of the exchange and stood, open-mouthed, in a group gawping at Resnick's handiwork.

Angel squinted through the sights of the light

machine-gun, squeezed the trigger and let go a burst of high-explosive shells that cut the guards down where they stood, hacking lumps of flesh from their bodies as they hammered home. Then he raked the body of the personnel carrier that was still parked where he and Stoner had seen it earlier. One of the bullets hit the petrol tank and the back of the truck bounced up as the fuel exploded and spewed forth a pair of soldiers, their uniforms ablaze. Angel cut them down with another burst.

'Lay the charges,' the American shouted to Stoner, who could hardly hear him for post-explosive concussion, which had set bells ringing in his ears. 'Before any more of the mothers get here! Slash and burn. Slash and burn.'

Stoner didn't have to be told twice. He shot down the street like a greyhound, kicked open the door to the substation and threw a knapsack inside. Then he slammed the door shut, vaulted over the fence that divided the generator from the telephone exchange and did the same there. He turned and sprinted back to where Angel was waiting, leaping over the bodies of the fallen soldiers as he did so. As he ran along the street, Angel was firing at the front of the buildings, where faces had appeared at the windows. He laughed out loud as they vanished, and shouted out to Stoner: 'Come on, you fucker! Get a move on.'

Stoner dived into the driver's seat, crashed into gear and slammed his foot down. As the Wrangler roared off, Angel fired one last, long burst down the street as they went. Stoner almost immediately slammed on the brakes, slewing the jeep to a halt in the middle of the road, and took the radio transmitter from his pocket.

He thumbed the on switch, hit the red button and behind him the street erupted as every electric light in town, and for miles around, went off.

'Fucking A,' yelled Angel. 'Let's get the fuck back to the boss.'

Stoner trod down again as the dust pall settled behind them, and at long last, the citizens of Santa Ana began to show themselves on the streets.

Valin's group heard the second explosion too, a second after the lights went out in the barracks and the factory.

That was Keller's signal to start firing, and his first bullet ripped through the tunic of a young subaltern on his first day of guard duty at the factory gates, which was also to prove to be his last, for he was dead before he hit the ground.

The German's second bullet smashed through the windscreen of one of the jeeps parked by the gatehouse, killing the driver, while the third slammed into the gatehouse itself, sending the inhabitants to the floor in panic.

Good man, thought Valin as he watched the mayhem that Keller's bullets were wreaking on the guards outside the complex. With the rest of his group he was under light cover at the top of the slip road, equidistant between the factory and the barracks next door. Turning to Spenser, he said: 'Chris, let them have it.'

The American smiled, and squeezed the trigger of his Gatling, sending a stream of bullets spewing towards the barracks, where they tore holes in the brickwork and shattered the windows. As he did so, Carmen fed the ammunition belt to the gun as if she had been doing it for years.

Packard, Maria and Carlotta took up their positions, two on either side of Spenser, and added to his barrage of fire a hail of bullets from their Heckler and Kochs. Messelier pulled the trigger of the ARMSCOR grenade-launcher, and the first projectile smashed through a window on the second floor of the barracks, blowing out a chunk of wall as it exploded. The others meanwhile collected the knapsacks of explosive and advanced towards the factory. Resnick knew where they would be when he got back, and if he didn't, well, *c'est la guerre*. Keller kept firing as they went, and when they were close to the gate they dropped to the ground and destroyed the gatehouse with automatic fire and one perfectly placed grenade from Newman.

13

The second, and bigger, explosion at the petrol station knocked Resnick on to his back, and he sprawled into the gutter before he jumped to his feet and ran in the same direction that Sofía had driven the Chevrolet, so that he could escape the intense heat from the blazing motor fuel. He tore round the corner that he had seen her take, and there she was, waiting for him beside the car, the driver's door open and the engine running. He saw a look of relief cross her face in the flickering reflection of the fierce fire that burned behind him, lighting up the street like neon. 'Thank God,' Sofía said. 'I thought you might have been caught in the explosion.'

'An expert like me?' the Russian replied as he dived across the front bench seat on to the passenger side. 'No chance. Now, can you get us back to the factory without getting caught up in all the excitement we've caused?'

'Sure I can.' And she dropped the Chevy into gear and set off. 'You did a good job there. If that doesn't bring out the soldiers, nothing will,' Sofía said as she accelerated.

She took a circuitous route through the narrow streets of Santa Ana, and rejoined the main road to the factory complex. As they were negotiating a particularly narrow street, they saw, heard and felt the explosion that Stoner had detonated, to their left, and the solitary street lamp that illuminated the street winked out. Sofía flicked her lights to full beam and glanced at Resnick. 'You taught them well,' she said.

Resnick grinned back at her. 'Thank you.'

Once on the main road, they passed a stream of army vehicles going in the opposite direction, towards town, and Resnick gave Sofía the thumbs-up. 'Worked like a charm,' he said. 'And our crew seem to be working up ahead,' he added, as he heard the rattle of gunfire from the direction of the barracks and the factory.

Sofía slammed the Chevy through the leaves that hid the side road from the main drag, and skidded to a halt beside the empty Ford three-tonner.

'They've taken the charges and gone to the factory,' said Resnick after taking a quick look inside the truck. 'They didn't have much faith that we'd make it back. Come on, let's find them before someone blows himself up.'

Carry guns at the ready, they set off in the direction of the shooting. As he went, Resnick glanced at his standard-issue Red Army watch. A quarter past midnight.

Stoner and Angel did not have such good luck getting across Santa Ana.

After the explosion had wrecked the utility buildings, Stoner hit the Wrangler's accelerator again and it fishtailed up the street, leaving behind it twin trails of burnt rubber. He sent the vehicle into a four-wheel skid as he joined the main road, almost losing control, but he straightened up and roared off towards Valin and the rest of the squad.

'Whoa,' yelled Angel. 'Easy, man. Hang loose a little.'

'I thought you liked hot-rodding,' Stoner said. 'What's the problem? Scared?'

'Bastard,' shouted Angel, grinning manically.

Stoner glanced behind him and the pair exchanged looks of exultation. 'Did you see them go?' he shouted. 'Amazing.'

'Awesome,' agreed Angel. 'She-it. One to the visiting team.'

Then, as they reached another crossroads, from the right a jeep appeared containing four soldiers of the regular army. The one sitting in the passenger seat hit the siren and motioned for Stoner to stop. Instead Angel opened fire with the LMG, exhausting one belted magazine of ammunition, and rapidly reloading a second. Two members of the patrol were hit, but a third loosed off a burst from the M16 he was carrying. Half-a-dozen bullets rattled off the Wrangler, and two caught Stoner. One hit his left shoulder, just above the edge of his flak jacket, sending a spurt of blood across the dashboard; the other penetrated his left side. Three more of the heavy lead slugs punched through the windscreen.

At the moment he was hit, Stoner lost control of the jeep, which hit the low kerb, careered across the pavement, slammed into a house front, bounced back across the street again, and scraped along the body of a parked Nissan saloon in a shower of sparks. All the while, Angel poured bullets into the grille of the army jeep, which suddenly lost its radiator in a cloud of steam and pulled over, disgorging the two uninjured soldiers, who stood and poured a hail of lead at the back of the retreating Wrangler.

'You OK, man?' asked Angel after they had taken the next corner on two wheels, sped down the road and into the shadows behind a small block of flats, where Stoner halted the jeep and slumped forward over the steering wheel.

'I'm hit, man. I need a medic,' he said through gritted teeth.

'Is it bad?'

'Bad enough. Is there a medical kit on board?'

'Sure,' said Angel. There was a padlocked box with the Red Cross symbol on it, attached to the inside of the vehicle. He broke off the padlock with the butt of his Colt .45 and looked rapidly at the contents, then lifted out several items to examine them more closely by the flame from his Zippo lighter. 'Good,' he said. 'This stuff is written in American, at least. Now let's see.' He picked up a handful of disposable hypodermics, full of liquid. 'She-it,' he said in amazement. 'Morphine. Want some?'

'No. Any bandages?' asked Stoner.

'Some.'

'Then take a look at my fucking shoulder and side, I'm losing blood here.'

Angel did as he was asked, ripping open the material of Stoner's jacket and shirt to inspect the wound. The first bullet had passed straight through Stoner's shoulder. The entry wound was blue and puckered in the light of the Zippo, but the exit was the size of his fist and weeping blood. And he could see the white of bone splinters inside the wound.

'I'll do what I can,' said Angel, 'but you need a doctor.'

'And there's never one about when you need one. I've been hit in the side too.'

Angel investigated the second wound. The bullet was still inside Stoner's body. There was not much blood visible, and Angel feared serious internal injury and bleeding.

'Man, I'm not up to this,' he said.

'Do what you can, man, and let's get the fuck out of here before another patrol shows up.'

'You in pain?' said Angel.

'Not yet. Just numb. Like when I got hit with a baseball bat a couple of times.'

'You will be.'

'Thanks.'

Angel helped Stoner across to the passenger seat, then collected what he needed from the medical kit and got to work. Speedily he treated both wounds in Stoner's shoulder with antiseptic powder, then put a dressing in the front and back and hastily wrapped a bandage round his upper arm and under his armpit. As for the wound in his side, he simply attached a dressing with tape. 'That'll have to do for now, bro,' he said. 'We'll get someone to look at you later. How you feeling?'

'Like shit.'

'That's the shock. Here, swallow a painkiller.'

'Morphine? I don't want to be knocked out.'

'No. I'm saving that for me. This is just regular drugstore stuff. Come on, quick, man. We need to get out of here.'

'I told you, I'm not in pain.'

'And I told you, you will be. Just take these and shut up.'

Stoner swallowed the pills, washing them down with a mouthful of water from the canteen slung around his waist, and Angel got behind the wheel. The Wrangler was running smoothly enough, but as soon as he moved off he knew something was wrong. He got out and walked to the back of the jeep. 'Shit,' he said. 'We got us a flat.'

'What do we do?' asked Stoner weakly. The pain was beginning.

'Well, I ain't no grease monkey. I ain't about to change the fucker. And I don't think we belong to the local branch of the Automobile Club, so I reckon we just drive it as it is. It'll be bumpy, and mess you up, but it can't be helped. Sorry, man.'

'Just drive, Angel. Don't worry about me,' said Stoner. 'I'll survive.'

'You got it, Stoner.'

Angel put his foot down and the jeep bumped across the pavement, slowly gathering speed, but he felt the drag of the flat tyre and knew that pretty soon he would be driving on bare metal.

He managed to get up to about twenty miles per hour before the bumping got too bad, and he kept at that speed to save Stoner from too much pain.

Shit, he thought to himself as the jeep limped along in the direction of the fire-fight at the factory, this could take for ever. He glanced up at the face of a church clock lit by the moon. A quarter past twelve.

By midnight the soldiers left in the barracks had got themselves organized and were returning fire. They were sending up flares which bathed the area in a dull red glow, and tinged the smoke from Messelier's grenades pink, as it drifted down the hill towards them. Spenser and his team had dropped back slightly to gain cover from the trees at the edge of the jungle. 'Keep firing,' he yelled. 'Keep them interested in us and let the boss get inside the complex.'

The Gatling ate up another belt of ammunition, and in the comparative silence as Spenser threaded in a new one, the three mercenaries and the three women with them heard a clanking sound from the road beside the barracks. Spenser, Messelier and the women had heard the sound before and knew what it was. Packard just looked at them in the darkness. 'What the hell . . . ?' he said.

The noise got louder, and gun barrel first, a late-model American M1A1 tank rumbled round the corner. It was armed with a 120mm main gun, the M256 smooth-bore cannon using either kinetic-energy, armour-piercing, fin-stabilized tracer, or high-explosive anti-tank multipurpose chemical. It was perfect for the climate, as it was fitted with a cooling system that allowed the crew to wear normal combat suits rather than chemical suits, for it was fully equipped for chemical and/or nuclear warfare. The tank was painted in camouflage green, and as its treads clattered across the tarmac, the gun turret swung in the direction of Spenser and the rest. The American recognized it for what it was: a sixty-seven-ton monster with a 1500hp motor, driven through a four-speed automatic transmission. Known as 'Whispering Death', the tank could reach a top speed of forty miles per hour on tarmac. It had a thermal sight, laser rangefinder, and also carried a coaxial 7.62mm machine-gun. It was not to be messed with, as Saddam Hussein and his cronies had discovered to their cost in the Gulf War.

'Fall back,' Spenser screamed. 'Fall back and take cover.'

The group split and dived back into the jungle as the tank fired its big gun, and earth, trees, and bushes were thrown twenty feet in the air.

The squad fell back even further as the tank fired again, and Packard grabbed a grenade from the half a dozen hanging on the front of his body armour and raced towards the tank and the barracks. This was the moment he had been waiting for, and he felt a crazy elation as he ran.

'Packard,' yelled Messelier. 'Don't.' But it was too late: he was gone.

The Australian ran out from the shelter of the trees, across the cleared area in front, across the slip road, over the low wall that separated it from the front of the barracks, across the parking area towards the tank, whose machine-gun chattered and ripped up earth and tarmac all around his feet. He pulled the pin from the grenade, kept running, jumped up on to the side of the vehicle above the tracks, and popped it deftly into the machine-gun slot. When the grenade exploded, and the tank lifted an inch off the ground, smoke and flame roaring out of every orifice in its armour plating, he was already running back towards his mates.

He never made it. A sharpshooter inside the barracks, using the lull in the shooting coming from the foliage, took careful aim and fired. The bullet hit Packard square in the back, and went through his flak jacket like a knife through butter. He leapt into the air, fell, rolled and was still.

Spenser stepped out from the edge of the jungle and poured half the contents of an ammunition belt into the window from which the sniper had fired.

'Bastard,' he screamed as he sprayed the window. 'Fucking bastard.'

At the factory gates, Valin and his squad had been pinned down by fire from the complex itself. Either there was a squad of Colombian army inside, or the management and workers had been issued with weapons, and knew how to use them. Valin broke radio silence and called up Keller as the tank opened fire on Spenser's group, and Packard made his suicidal run.

'Keller. Come in. Over,' he said.

'Colonel, Keller. They've got a fucking tank over there. Over.'

'Forget that. Spenser will sort it. Who the hell's inside the factory? Can't you see? Over.'

'I'll try, Colonel. Over and out,' said Keller, then, to Gerry McGuire: 'You heard the colonel, McGuire. What can you see?'

'A whole lot of nothing, Sarge . . . Wait. Third window along, second floor. Gun flash.'

Keller let the red dot of the sight creep along the wall of the factory until it found the window. He saw a shadow move in the light from the flares and the burning tank, and fired.

'Hit,' hissed McGuire. 'I saw him go down.'

14

As Resnick and Sofía were racing towards the rest of their party, they heard the reports from the tank's big gun as it fired on Spenser and his crew, and the deeper thud as Packard dropped the grenade through the machine-gun port and killed it.

'What's that?' said Sofía, sliding to a halt.

'Artillery of some kind,' replied the Russian. 'Christ knows what kind of ordnance they've got up there. Keep going, but be careful.'

They snaked through the jungle, until Sofía almost ran over her mother, who was standing by the bole of a tree, gun at the ready.

'Mama, what's happening?' she demanded.

'My darling, you're back. Thank God. Get down, there's a tank firing on us.'

Resnick peered through the foliage and saw the M1A1 burning, and Packard's body lying where he had fallen. 'Relax,' he said. 'One of ours dealt with it.'

'Is he all right?' asked Maria.

'No. It looks like he paid the ultimate price.'

'The poor young man. He had no life.'

'But he gave it to save the rest of us,' said Resnick, not for a moment suspecting Packard's deeper motive. 'For that we must be grateful. Where are the others?'

'Hiding from the tank's guns. Has it really been destroyed?'

'Yes. Have no fear, Señora Delgado. Now come on, let's find Spenser, and hope there are not other casualties.'

Angel was worried about Stoner. The Brit seemed to have gone into deep shock, and the way the jeep was handling was not helping.

'Hey, Stoner, you all right, man?' he asked.

Stoner didn't respond, so Angel pulled to the side of the road. Up ahead, he could see the light from the flares and hear the popping of rifles and light machine-guns, plus the heavier booming from the tank. It wasn't sounding good. And from behind he heard more explosions, as the havoc that Stoner and Resnick had wreaked spread. But one thing was sure. Before long, the soldiers who had left the barracks to check out the diversion in town would be alerted to what was going on back at the factory and barracks, and come looking for them.

'Stoner,' said Angel again, more alarmed than he pretended. 'Come on, man. Talk to me.'

Stoner opened his eyes and groaned. 'Jesus,' he said. 'I feel terrible.'

'Listen, man,' said Angel. 'We're caught between a rock and a hard fucking place. Sounds like our buddies have got troubles of their own up ahead. There's bigger guns than ours being used. And those fucking army guys are going to be hot on our tails, PDQ. And this fucking jalopy is going nowhere fast.'

'How far's the factory?' asked Stoner.

'Ten klicks, maybe less.'

'How much ammo is left for the LMG?'

'Coupla belts. A few thousand rounds.'

'Then get me into the back and I can hold the army off for a while. You go ahead on foot. I'll be useless in a fire-fight. I can do more good here as a diversion.'

'Are you sure, man?'

'Sure I'm sure. Just give me some more of those pills, and I'll hold off the bad guys until hell freezes over. You go on ahead. They need more troops up there by the sound of it.'

'OK, man, if you're really sure.'

'Got any cigarettes?'

'Cigarettes, joints. You name it.'

'Leave me what you've got.'

'I'll just keep a coupla Js for myself. I might need them later, the way things are going. I can scrounge some smokes when I get up ahead.'

'Whatever. Just give me what you can spare and go.'

Angel took a pack of Marlboro from his pocket and gave it to Stoner, plus half-a-dozen ready-rolled joints that he had in his shirt pocket.

'Jesus, man, that uniform you're wearing stinks,' said Stoner.

'I know. But orders is orders. I hope someone's takin' care of my leather jacket. It cost me five hundred bucks.'

Angel steered the Wrangler towards the ditch at the side of the road, slewed it round side-on, so that it half-blocked the road, and helped Stoner out of the front passenger seat and behind the machine-gun. He checked that there was a fresh belt of ammo ready to fire, that Stoner's M16 was loaded and cocked, and finally he took the Desert Eagle from its holster under the Londoner's arm without disturbing the bandage, worked a cartridge into the breech and put it into his lap. Then he hopped out of the vehicle and stood beside it. 'You gonna be cool, babe?' he asked.

'Cool as ice. Thanks for the medical treatment, Angel. You did fine.'

'Any time, man. Any time at all.'

'I hope it's a long time before I need it.'

'Me too.'

'Gotta light?'

Angel hesitated. 'Only my Zippo. My old man gave it to me . . . Oh, what the fuck. Here.' He thrust the lighter into Stoner's hand, then helped himself to a cigarette from one of the packs, and Stoner lit it for him.

'Thanks, pal,' said Angel. 'See you later.'

'Hope so,' said Stoner.

'I'd better,' retorted Angel. 'I want my fucking lighter back.'

Then, with his Uzi slung over his shoulder, he set off at a trot towards the factory.

Spenser's squad had regrouped at the edge of the jungle, joined by Resnick and Sofía. They were all safe, apart from the unfortunate Packard.

'And I promised to watch his back,' said Messelier. 'Damn good job I did of it.'

'It wasn't your fault,' said Spenser, with one eye on the barracks, which had fallen silent since he had shot the sniper.

'What do you think is happening?' asked Resnick.

'I reckon they're deciding whether to come out and try and overrun us,' replied the American.

'You'd better give Sofía and me some covering fire, and we'll join the boss. Sounds like he's having trouble over there,' said the Russian.

'No problem,' said Spenser. 'Come on, guys. You heard what the man said. Let's shape up here.' As he moved towards the open space, his Gatling at the ready, he shouted: 'Carmen, come and feed me.'

The girl showed a mouthful of white teeth as she did what he said. 'Come on, mama,' she chided. 'We're needed.'

Valin and his squad were indeed in trouble. It was proving more difficult than he had thought to get inside. Cutting the electrical power to the complex had not killed the current to the perimeter fence. There had to be an auxiliary generator inside the factory, but he had no idea where, and being pinned down outside by withering fire from the factory buildings, despite Keller's sharpshooting from up on the hill, was not going to help him find it. He had suffered no casualties so far, but it was just a matter of time.

It had been quiet at the barracks for a few minutes, but suddenly Spenser and his troops opened fire again, and within a minute Resnick and Sofía came zigzagging across the open space behind them as bullets tore up the tarmac about their feet.

'What's the hold-up, Colonel?' said Resnick as he dropped down next to Valin.

'The sodding fence is still live, and we're pinned down here.'

'Give me one of my charges,' said the Russian. 'I'll soon sort this out.'

He grabbed a knapsack, took out the remote control

he still had in his pocket, made some deft changes, jumped up and ran towards the perimeter of the factory, where he slid the bag next to one of the fence supports, wormed his way back, and switched on the control. 'Heads down,' he said, and pressed the red button.

The support was torn from the ground by the explosion and the fence itself split open in a shower of sparks.

'Come on,' said Resnick. Let's get inside and find some cover.'

Valin, O'Rourke, Daniel McGuire, Newman and Sofía didn't need to be told twice. They sprang to their feet and hared through the gap in the fence, firing their carry weapons as they went, with Resnick in the lead.

From their position up on the brow of the hill, Keller and Gerry McGuire had a good view of what was happening down below, and so far no one on the other side seemed very interested in returning their fire.

'They're in,' said McGuire. 'Resnick must've got back and planted a charge.'

'Thank Christ for that,' said the German. 'I thought we were going to be here all night. If we're going to catch that plane, we'll have to get out of here before long. He looked at the luminous dial on his watch. A quarter to one. Time was passing quickly, and he too was aware that soon the troops who had gone into town would be back to reinforce the men in the barracks. 'Come on, Colonel,' he said almost to himself. 'Get a move on.'

He was not wrong. At the same time as Keller was

whispering to himself, Stoner saw the lights of the first troop carrier as it made its way back to the barracks.

He flicked away his fifth cigarette on the trot and checked the action of the LMG as the truck turned the corner, a quarter of a mile or so away, and started to lumber towards him.

By luck or by judgement, Angel had picked the perfect place to leave the disabled jeep. The road narrowed as it reached the top of an incline, and both sides were flanked by dense vegetation and strung with barbed wire. Unless troops were prepared to make a full-frontal assault up the metalled road, take to the jungle or try to use the ditch on the right-hand side as cover, they would just have to shoot it out.

Stoner pulled back the bolt and fired the LMG. Bullets ripped into the front of the big truck, killing the driver and passenger instantly, and the vehicle slid to the side of the road and nosed into the barbed wire. Stoner kept on firing, strafing the canvas-covered cargo area where the soldiers were sitting, and sending those he didn't hit looking for safer cover.

'Number two for the visiting team,' he said to himself as he lit another of Angel's cigarettes with the Zippo.

Angel heard the bark of the LMG as he arrived back at the track leading off the main road and found the three-tonner, parked and empty, next to the ancient pink Chevrolet. His leather jacket was in the cab of the Ford where he had left it. He looked back and wished Stoner good luck as he ripped off the stinking army tunic he was wearing and slid the jacket on, checking the pockets to see if the Walkman was still there.

He stopped for a moment to admire the lines of the Chevy, and check out the paint job. Pure rock and roll, he thought, as he picked up his Uzi and headed off towards the fire-fight.

He found Spenser, Messelier and the three women where they were still pinning the barracks down. 'Yo, man,' he said to the other American as he joined them. 'Nice work.'

'Where's Stoner?' asked Spenser, giving the red-hot Gatling time to cool down.

'He's been hit. He's keeping an eye on the road between here and the town.'

'Hit bad?'

'Twice. One bullet broke his shoulder up, and he took another round in his left side. It isn't looking good. He's in a lot of pain.'

'And you just left him?'

'Had to make a judgement call, Chris. You know how it is. He told me to leave him. He's a brave guy. So how's it going here?'

'Fine. You going to join the boss?'

'Seems like that's where I'm needed. You guys seem to be managing here all right.'

'Well, get going then.'

Taking advantage of the fresh hail of bullets that Spenser pumped at the barracks, Angel tore across the slip road in the direction of the factory. He saw the hole in the electrified fence and charged through, his machine pistol ready to cut down anyone who got in his way. He slid to a halt at the corner of one of the buildings and peered round just in time to see Valin's distinctive form entering a door into the next.

15

Stoner lit another Marlboro, and looked down the hill. There was a lot of activity going on there, as the army vehicles piled up behind the wreck of the first personnel carrier, which was blocking the road.

He grinned to himself. His shoulder and side hurt like hell and he swallowed more painkillers, then listened to the sound of the battle for control of the factory that was going on behind him.

Shit, he thought, I wonder if I'll get out of this one alive, as his fevered brain replayed events from his life over and over again.

He remembered his first brushes with the law when he was just a teenager, stealing from Woolworth's, then his move into more serious crimes as he climbed the underworld ladder. He recalled his time as a runner for a drug-dealing syndicate – ironic, considering the mission he found himself on now. Cocaine had been the drug of the early eighties, and Stoner had dealt his fair share round the West End and City, and sampled enough of his own product too, with the yuppies who made up his clientele at the time.

Then he had graduated to running a string of high-class whores to service the very same wheeler-dealers with too much money to spend, whom he had met when he had sold them drugs. It had been an easy life. Money, sex, fast cars, and as much dope as he could use. But he'd been too flashy, made a lot of enemies, and eventually one had grassed him up to the police.

While on the run, he'd made his aborted attempt to join the French Foreign Legion. What a dummy! A black cockney who didn't speak a word of the language, and who'd been used to getting up at noon, spending all day and night in relentless hedonism, trying to join the toughest army in the world. But at least they'd taught him how to use a variety of weapons, and some basic martial arts. If only he'd been able to keep his mouth shut, he might still have all his own teeth.

You've got to laugh, thought Stoner, as he lit the first of the joints that Angel had left, made himself more comfortable on the metal seat behind the LMG, and wished that the troops down the hill would do something before he died of boredom. Or my wounds, he said to himself. I wonder just how bad they are.

Not that learning to shoot and stab, garrotte and gouge in the Legion had done him much good. If he hadn't been willing and able to use a gun, perhaps he wouldn't have taken up armed robbery when he came back to England, which culminated in the shooting of the security guard, and his spell in prison.

Stoner's gloomy thoughts were rudely interrupted when the troops below opened fire, sending bullets ricocheting off the jeep. At last, he thought, a bit of action, and he pulled two grenades off the clips that secured them to the front of his flak jacket, released the pins and lobbed them down the hill. One exploded between the front wheels of the abandoned personnel carrier, which began to burn as the fuel caught, and the second bounced into the ditch where three soldiers were taking cover and burst in a shower of shrapnel that tore their bodies apart.

Slash and burn, he thought, as the grenades went off. Slash and burn.

Back at the barracks, what Spenser thought was going to happen, happened. The soldiers inside had got over their surprise at the attack and the efficiency with which the lights had been cut off. Someone had managed to get an emergency generator working, and now that they had light to see by once more, they regrouped at the back of the building. By sheer force of will the commanding officer, a major, calmed the conscripts who had seen their friends cut down before their eyes, and their armour destroyed, and split them into two groups, which advanced up the roads on either side of the building.

Spenser and his group slaughtered them as they came. It was almost too easy to cut them down in droves as they tried to get across the open area between the barracks and the edge of the jungle.

The women retched at the sight of the blood and guts that their bullets were producing, and almost stopped firing.

'Keep going,' screamed Spenser. 'Keep firing. Don't let them get close.'

Reluctantly they opened fire again and the sound of their weapons joined with the hammering of the Gatling and the explosions from the grenades that Messelier kept lobbing from the ARMSCOR in their direction, while the slugs and shrapnel tore through the advancing men again until they fell back. 'Well done,' said Spenser as he ordered his troops to cease fire. 'That's evened the odds a bit.'

Angel raced after Valin, through the open door that the boss had used, and into the factory proper. It was illuminated with dim emergency lights from the same source that had kept the outside fence live. He could hear the sporadic rattle of gunfire as the defenders put up a last bid to fight off the invaders. As Angel looked round the room, he saw one civilian and a couple of soldiers sprawled across the floor where they had fallen, their clothes bloodstained and their weapons still clasped in their hands. He ignored them, well aware that Valin and his men would not have passed without checking that they were dead. He was more interested in the equipment that filled the room. It was packed with all sorts of vats and tubes that he didn't have a clue about. But one thing he knew he would recognize: pure cocaine. And if he had anything to do with it, before the factory was destroyed he would make sure that he took some with him.

Suddenly he heard a sound from behind a bench that had been dragged to one side of the room. He walked towards it, finger on the trigger of the Uzi, and kicked the bench aside. Cowering on the floor was a man; he was small and dark, and wore a lab coat.

What have we here? thought Angel. Someone the others missed; that was rather careless. With the toe of one combat boot, he pushed the man, who looked up fearfully. 'Don't worry,' said the American. 'I won't shoot you unless you try and shoot me first. Are you armed?'

The man let go with a stream of breathless Spanish.

'English? *Inglés*?'

The man shook his head, and rattled on again in Spanish.

Shit, thought Angel. Sure wish I'd paid more attention to my Spanish lessons in high school. He held up his hand to silence the man. 'Come on,' he said, pulling him up by the arm. He marched the trembling man ahead of him with the tip of the barrel of his machine pistol close to his back. Up ahead he caught sight of Newman covering the backs of his comrades. The former para spun round when he heard the footsteps of the American and his prisoner, and brought up his shotgun ready to fire. 'Steady, man,' said Angel. 'Friend.'

'Angel!' said Newman, and gave one of his rare smiles. What little he had seen of the American hippie, he'd liked, even if they were as different in outlook as was humanly possible. 'You made it. You and Stoner did a good one on the electrics. Where is he?'

Angel frowned. 'I don't know, man,' he said. 'He took a couple of hits, and the jeep's U/S, and I left him up on the road taking care of business. I sure wish I could get back with some transport. Listen, check this guy, will you? See if he's carrying.'

Newman did as Angel asked, and frisked the man in the lab coat expertly. 'Clean as a whistle,' he said. 'Not even a nail file.'

'Good. Let's find the boss. He might be able to get something out of him.'

They moved forward past smashed equipment and more bodies, until they caught up with the main party.

'Hey, Angel,' said O'Rourke. 'Good to see you.'

'Likewise, Ell-Tee.'

'Who's this?' asked the lieutenant, nodding at Angel's prisoner.

'Fuck knows, he doesn't speak English. Or won't.'

'Colonel, Jesús,' O'Rourke called. 'Over here. We need a translator.'

Valin and the Colombian joined them.

'Angel. Good job,' said Valin. 'Where's Stoner?'

Angel explained about the jeep and Stoner's wounds, and Valin said: 'We're nearly finished here. As soon as we are, you and Newman get the transport and go and pull him out. Meanwhile, let's have a word with our friend here. Jesús, will you do the honours?'

Jesús questioned the prisoner in Spanish, and listened intently to his answers. After a minute or two he held up his hands and the prisoner fell silent.

'He is a scientist, Colonel,' said Jesús. 'A chemist, and he is here under duress. Also, he is a pacifist. That is why he did not join in the fighting. He hates the government. They have murdered his family. You were correct: the authorities knew that someone was coming to try and destroy the factory.'

'Yes, I got most of that,' said Valin. 'How did they know?'

'A moment,' said Jesús, and started talking in Spanish again.

The chemist spat out an answer.

'An American came here.'

Valin smiled grimly. 'I thought as much,' he said. 'Ask him if he knows who.'

Once more there was a stream of Spanish from both men.

'He saw him. You heard the description. Does it ring a bell?' said Jesús.

'Yes,' said Valin. 'It does.'

He then spoke to the chemist in his native tongue, and everyone understood his affirmative reply.

'He's coming with us when we leave,' said Valin. 'Back to the States. Lieutenant, I'm putting you in charge of his safety for now. We need him to positively identify the man who informed on us. Take good care of him. Right, let's finish up here. We'll clean up the last of the resistance. Resnick, start placing the charges. And all of you, be careful.'

16

O'Rourke stayed with the chemist, who said his name was Ramón García, while the rest of the group moved through the factory, Resnick laying charges as they went. They met more sporadic resistance, but soon dealt with it. Angel and Newman worked together, the American keeping a sharp eye out not only for armed men, but also for the drugs he was seeking. He finally found what he was looking for in a small store-room. It was a junkie's dream. Plastic bags of cocaine were piled floor to ceiling, and even the air seemed imbued with the drug.

'Shit,' said Angel. 'Christmas Day, and the snow is on the ground.'

He picked up a bag and weighed it in his hand – a kilo, he guessed – and put it inside his leather jacket, which he zipped up tightly.

Newman gave him a questioning look. 'Purely for personal consumption,' said Angel as he ran his finger along a shelf, picked up the residue of coke on his finger and rubbed it on his gums. 'She-it. Ninety-eight per cent pure, or I'm a monkey's uncle.'

'You will be if you take too much of that stuff.'

'Want some?' asked Angel.

'Not for me, thanks.'

'Suit yourself . . . Hey, and don't tell the boss. I don't think he's into dope.'

'I'm sure he's not,' said the Englishman. 'How much is that little lot worth?'

'On the streets back home? Cut? Shit. A quarter of a million bucks maybe. Maybe more.'

'Is that what you came here for?'

'No. I came for the foreign travel, adventure and to make new friends. What about you? This is just a bonus. Take one for yourself.'

'No thanks, Angel.'

'Your loss. Come on, let's go. I want to finish up here, and pick up my man Stoner.'

By the time they had found the rest of the team, the battle for the factory was almost over. The last few defenders had surrendered to Valin's men and stood sheepishly under the guard of Carlos and Daniel McGuire, and Resnick was busily setting the charges where they could do the most damage.

Angel looked at his watch as he joined them. Twenty past one. Time was running out fast.

'Angel, Newman,' barked Valin. 'Get a vehicle from somewhere and go and fetch Stoner.'

'Right away, Colonel,' said Angel.

'And be quick,' underlined Valin. 'We've got to get out of here fast.'

Stoner had exhausted the ammunition in the LMG, and used up the half-a-dozen grenades he had with him. The soldiers below had fanned out into the jungle by the light of the burning vehicles on the road, and were advancing up the hill.

His wounds were giving him a lot of pain, and he took his M16 and the Uzi automatic and left the jeep. Although he didn't know it, single-handedly he had managed to kill or wound thirty men, and destroy or disable six vehicles.

He scrambled into the ditch that ran parallel to the road and took stock. His movement had drawn fire from even closer, confirming that the opposition was moving up on him. Behind him he could still hear the battle of the barracks and factory, and wondered if any help would be forthcoming from the team. He guessed that it would, but had no way of telling how soon.

Better move my black arse, he thought to himself. Keeping himself low, he started wriggling back towards the crest of the hill, which was a few hundred yards behind him, in order to put it between himself and the Colombians below.

Even more bullets thudded into the ground around him as the enemy realized that they were no longer threatened by the LMG, and Stoner fired a warning blast from his M16, using the lull it caused to scuttle back further.

Come on, Angel, he thought, as he checked his watch. Let's see some action.

Angel and Newman ran back through the factory and across the slip road to where Spenser and his group were still keeping the lid on the barracks.

'How's it going over there?' said the Vietnam veteran.

'Pretty good,' replied Newman. 'No casualties, and the place is ours. What about here?'

'We've been lucky. We only lost Packard when he took out the tank.'

'Any sign of anything from the direction of the town?' asked Angel.

'Nothing,' replied Spenser. 'Stoner must be still blocking the road. But it can't last.'

'We're off to get him,' said Newman. 'We need transport.'

'The truck's still where we left it, and there's an old jalopy like something out of *American Graffiti* there, too,' said Angel. 'Resnick and his partner must've requisitioned it. We'll use that.'

'Come on then, Angel,' said Newman. 'We're wasting time. If we don't get out of here quick, we'll miss our airlift out of this God-forsaken dump.'

'Keep up the good work,' Angel said to Spenser, and the two men vanished into the darkness, equipment jangling as they went.

They ploughed through the undergrowth towards where the vehicles were parked until suddenly they came under automatic fire from their left.

'Shit,' they groaned in unison as they hit the ground, and brought their carry weapons up into firing position.

'Who the fuck is it?' hissed Angel.

'Christ knows,' whispered Newman, as he tried to get a fix on whoever was shooting at them. 'Either Stoner's copped it, or it's a pincer movement from the barracks.'

'I hope it's the barracks,' said Angel. 'Otherwise there'll be soldiers all over us like a rash. Come on, let's move.'

As they did so, the firing started up again. Newman

spotted a muzzle flash and returned fire, then heard a hoarse scream as his shotgun load hit home.

'Gotcha,' he said triumphantly.

There was more firing immediately, bullets whistling through the leaves around them, thudding into the trunks of trees and kicking up dirt. Both men returned fire as they tried to outflank the ambush in order to reach the vehicles. They might never have made it, except that from behind they were joined by Messelier and Maria Delgado, who gave them the advantage of the extra firepower of his Ingram and her Heckler and Koch. A brief but heavy gun battle followed before the ambushers finally dropped back.

'Thanks,' said Newman when the four made contact. 'Who the hell was that?'

'God alone knows,' said Messelier, as he heard gunfire from further down the road in the direction of the centre of Santa Ana. 'But it sounds like Stoner's still keeping someone pinned down. Go and help him. We'll cover you.'

Newman and Angel didn't waste another moment. They pushed through the undergrowth, keeping their ears and eyes open for any further opposition, but none was forthcoming, and within a few minutes they found the two vehicles parked where they had been left, seemingly undisturbed.

Angel made straight for the Chevrolet. The wires under the dash, which Sofía had stripped and used to start the engine, were still hanging free. He touched one to the other and the motor turned over, missed, caught, and then, as he jammed his foot on the accelerator, roared into life.

'GM,' said Angel proudly. 'Made with union labour

on American soil, and still starts first time, old as she is.'

'Can we discuss the pros and cons of car manufacturing at another time?' suggested Newman as he got into the passenger seat. 'We've got work to do. Drive the fucker, will you?'

Without another word, Angel shoved the Chevy into gear, put his foot down, wrestled the wheel round, and joined the main road, heading towards where he had left Stoner. The wounded man was by then putting up a desperate rearguard defence against the soldiers who were swarming up the road to where he had left the jeep. They looked as if they were in danger of overrunning him where he lay in the ditch at the brow of the hill, using his remaining ammunition in a frantic attempt to stay alive.

Suddenly he heard the sound of the motor from behind him, turned and saw the Chevrolet, lights blazing, heading his way at top speed. He didn't recognize the car, but considered any alternative to where he was an improvement.

As he got closer to where he had left Stoner, Angel banged his fist on the horn. The Londoner emptied the last of the M16 magazines down the hill at the advancing troops, then dropped the rifle, dragged himself to his feet, ignoring the pain from his wounds. Desert Eagle in hand, and blasting a few shots downhill, he turned and staggered in the direction of the speeding Chevrolet.

Angel recognized him as he stood upright. 'He's there,' he screamed at Newman. 'My buddy made it.' He put his foot down harder, and the old car almost seemed to leap up the incline in Stoner's direction.

As Angel and Newman looked through the windscreen at Stoner's halting advance, troops appeared at the top of the hill and started firing down at them. Angel slammed on the brakes, spun the wheel, jerked on the handbrake and felt the back wheels break away as he slammed the heavy car into a perfect one-hundred-and-eighty-degree turn almost in its own length.

'Open the back door,' the American shouted to Newman as he held the car still on the foot brake, waiting for Stoner to get to it.

The wounded Englishman was hobbling down the road as fast as he could, firing his Uzi automatic over his shoulder as he came, and Newman added shotgun fire from his Ithaca.

'Come on, Stoner,' Angel screamed out of the open window on his side. 'Come on, man. You can make it.'

Bullets were tearing at the ground near Stoner's feet as he made for the Chevy, and others were slamming into the back of the car, until Angel feared that the petrol tank would be hit.

'Come on, man,' he screamed once more, and saw Stoner make the final effort to reach the open rear door, when a slug hit him in the thigh and he stumbled.

Angel feathered the accelerator as, almost in slow motion, Stoner put out his hand to pull himself into the car. Just then, a burst of bullets stitched up his back, neck and head, and finally blew his face away as he dropped to the ground, slid along on his front and lay perfectly still, the Zippo lighter he held in one hand slipping from between his lifeless fingers and bouncing in front of him.

'Beat it, Angel,' said Newman between shotgun blasts. 'He's copped it.'

'No, man, he'll be OK. Just let me get him inside.'

'No, you bloody fool. His head's gone. He's dead.'

'I want to see.'

Newman turned the shotgun round and stuck it into Angel's face.

'It was your fault we were too late,' he growled. 'If you hadn't stopped to pick up those drugs, we could've got him out. Now drive, before we get killed as well.'

Angel stared at him for a few seconds in the light from the dashboard, a terrible look of guilt on his face, then stamped on the accelerator again. The bonnet of the big old Chevrolet lifted and the car took off back in the direction of the factory with a scream of protest from its rear tyres.

17

Inside the factory everything was set. The prisoners that Valin's men had taken had been disarmed and sent off into the night. The last thing he wanted was any more spare baggage. He realized that he could not leave any of the Delgados behind. With a traitor operating back in the States, the family's cover could be blown at any moment, so they had to be taken out if at all possible. And then there was Ramón García. He alone could positively identify the turncoat, even though Valin had a fair idea of who it was from his description. The only witness. As such the chemist was indispensable.

'Right, Colonel,' said Resnick as he checked the last of the charges. 'Time to go.'

'Everyone,' roared Valin. 'Get back across the road. But be careful. There'll still be some resistance. And I haven't lost any of you . . . Yet.'

The troops bailed out, taking García with them under the watchful eye of O'Rourke. They sped across the road, bent double and zigzagging as they went, attracting only sporadic fire from the barracks – where for the present at least, the defenders seemed to have lost interest in the battle – until they were all back in the safety of the jungle, where they met up with Spenser's crew.

'OK, Resnick,' said Valin when they were all accounted for. 'Let her go.'

'A pleasure, Colonel,' said the Russian. He switched on his transmitter for the third time that night and calmly touched the red button.

The entire factory complex shuddered, as the charges that Resnick had so carefully placed exploded simultaneously. A brilliant flash, almost bright enough to blind them after the dim light that was all the attack force had seen for hours, burst through the windows as a thunderclap rang around the valley where they stood. Slates, bricks, wood and glass shot upwards, as the full force of the blasts was felt by the building, then rained down in a cacophony, as if a giant orchestra of tone-deaf musicians was tuning up.

Everyone ducked at the explosion, except Resnick, who watched proudly as the roof of the factory dropped between the walls as they were blown apart.

Excellent, he thought.

Up on the hillside, Keller and Gerry McGuire watched the explosion too, and felt the blast of hot air pull at their clothes.

'Time to go,' said the German, starting to pack away his sniper rifle. 'Money for old rope, wasn't it?'

'We're not home yet,' replied the Irishman.

'Too true. But at least we've done what we came for.'

Angel and Newman were about halfway between where they had left the dead Stoner and where the truck was parked, when the explosion occurred. They watched the pillar of fire, smoke and debris rise up in front of them, and Newman, in triumph, simply said: 'Yes.'

For once Angel had nothing to say. He knew he was at least partly to blame for Stoner's death, and the knowledge filled him with anger. Anger at himself, anger at the Colombians, and anger at the people who had sent both of them to risk their lives for money. He put his foot down violently, and the Chevy rocketed back towards the others.

'Let's go,' said Valin as the factory crumpled. 'Everyone back to the truck, and watch out for soldiers in the jungle.'

The thirteen of them, Valin, O'Rourke, Spenser, Daniel McGuire, Messelier, Resnick, Jesús Delgado, his wife, son, and three daughters, and Ramón García, who had thrown away his lab coat and was now less conspicuous in blue jeans and a dark-green shirt, set off back through the jungle in the direction of the track that led off the main road.

But their troubles were just about to start. They were met by a murderous hail of bullets, and Carlotta Delgado's white blouse blossomed red as a round hit her above her left breast and knocked her to the ground. The brief lull in resistance was over, as soldiers from the barracks joined the men who had ambushed Newman and Angel earlier, and who had been scattered when Maria and Messelier came to their comrades' assistance.

'My daughter,' screamed Maria, dropping her Heckler and Koch and rushing to Carlotta's aid.

'Daniel,' shouted Valin. 'First aid.'

Valin had always prided himself in having a medic

with the squad when they went into a fight. But the last soldier with real battlefield first-aid experience who had been part of the group still lay somewhere in southern Africa, felled by a bullet from a tribesman's muzzle-loading rifle at the end of their last, ill-fated excursion into enemy territory. And for this mission, there had just not been time enough to recruit another, so Daniel McGuire, who had picked up his knowledge by patching up the wounds of his IRA brethren on the streets of Belfast, had been appointed official medic.

The Irishman dodged bullets to get to Carlotta, flinging off his backpack and digging out the medical kit that he had been given. Valin, Maria and Daniel dragged Carlotta behind the shelter of a tree, trying hard to ignore the gasps of pain she made as they did so. Only there, out of the direct line of fire from whoever was preventing them reaching their transport, did Daniel dare to show a glimmer of light from the torch that he carried.

What he saw filled him with trepidation. He knew that it was beyond his meagre skills. A bullet had ripped through the young woman's body armour and torn open an artery in her chest, from where rich, red blood pumped in sync with the beating of her heart. And with every second that passed, the rhythm was becoming weaker.

He pulled her flak jacket open, and tore the flimsy material of the blouse below, to expose bare breasts streaked with gore, and examined the wound. But he knew, even as he looked at it, that there was nothing he could do. She was too far gone. What she needed was a hospital, blood transfusions, treatment for shock, and an expert surgeon to patch her up. Out here in the field, in half darkness, with his mud-caked hands, no proper equipment, and under fire, he knew that she had only minutes to live.

'Colonel,' Daniel said. 'I can't . . . '

Maria Delgado looked at him. 'Save her,' she cried, as the bullets from the ambushers drove them to take further cover. 'Please, señor. In the name of God.'

'I can't,' Daniel repeated, holding a pad of gauze over the wound in an attempt to staunch the flow of blood. 'She's too badly hurt. It's impossible.'

And as if to underline his words, the young girl stiffened, rattled deep in her throat, and was still.

'Christ Jesus,' screamed Maria, made the sign of the cross, and threw herself across her daughter's body.

'I'm sorry, Colonel,' said the Irishman. 'It was no good.'

'I understand,' said Valin. 'There was nothing you could do. Now come on, both of you. We've got to get out of here.'

As he spoke, Jesús scrambled to join them, and when he saw his wife covering his daughter's lifeless body with her own, tears sprang to his eyes.

'Jesús,' said Valin, touching the man's shoulder. 'I'm so sorry.'

'Lord,' said Jesús. 'Have mercy on her eternal soul.'

'Amen to that,' said Valin. And ours too, he thought. The situation seemed desperate. His men, and the civilians he had promised to care for, were pinned down by the ambushers, who had had time to dig themselves in. Valin looked at his watch. It was almost two o'clock, their deadline to get away, and they were in big trouble.

* * *

Angel and Newman and Keller and Gerry McGuire arrived back at the truck at almost exactly the same time. They got out, stood beside their three vehicles and listened to the sound of gunfire coming from the jungle.

'Goddam,' said Keller, 'that's not from the barracks. It's too close. They must've met some resistance on the way back here.'

'Angel and I were ambushed in the jungle before,' said Newman. 'We chased them off, but they must have regrouped. And it sounds like there's more of them now. We'd better go and give the rest a hand.' He took a hand-grenade from one of his pockets. 'A little reinforcement from the rear. That'll shake the bastards up.'

Keller nodded his agreement, and the four men readied their carry weapons, the German once again trusting to his Heckler and Koch G3, and in single file they snaked into the thick foliage to seek out the enemy.

Although the ambushers had made themselves as secure as possible, they were not seasoned campaigners, and were not expecting to be attacked from behind. So when the four mercenaries came up from the rear, guns blazing, and Newman dropped his grenade into their midst, panic swept through them. The soldiers were caught in the crossfire from in front and behind, and within a matter of seconds their line broke and they retreated towards the barracks, inflicting no more losses on Valin's people.

The soldiers, the Delgados and García stood together looking down at Carlotta's corpse, and O'Rourke switched on his torch. The light was very faint in the enormity of the jungle, and she looked very small. Maria bent and pulled the torn edges of her blouse over her naked breasts and the dreadful wound that had killed her. Jesús, Carlos, Carmen and Sofía had tears running down their cheeks, but Maria remained dry-eyed.

'We should bury her here,' said Valin.

'No,' said Maria firmly.

'No,' agreed her husband. 'We shall take her with us, and bury her somewhere better.'

'None of us may get out of here alive,' said Valin. 'You may not be able to bury her at all.'

'Then at least we'll all be together in death,' said the dead girl's mother.

'Carlos will carry her,' said Jesús, and spoke in Spanish to his son, who nodded back. 'And if he falls, I will carry her. If I fall, Maria, and so on. This place is bad. We will find a good place for her to lie.'

'Very well,' said Valin, knowing it was useless to argue. 'But let's go . . . Now.'

Maria and Jesús helped Carlos hoist Carlotta's body on to his back, where her blood stained his shirt. Valin found Maria's Heckler and Koch and handed it back to her, while Daniel replaced the useless first-aid kit in his backpack. Once ready, the sixteen survivors of the battle for the factory, plus one of the three casualties, made their way back to their transport.

18

The Delgados walked together, Carlos leading, carrying Carlotta's lifeless form, followed by Carmen and Sofía, supporting their mother, with Jesús bringing up the rear, head bowed.

'What happened?' Gerry McGuire said to his brother, who looked shaken and ill.

'What do you think happened? She copped one, and I couldn't do a thing for her.'

'Poor wee bitch.'

'She bled like a stuck pig, Gerry. I tried to help, but she died on me. Just like our sainted sister all those years ago on the Falls Road.'

'No, Dan, don't.'

'We were there, Gerry. Both of us. You tried to help, but could do nothing. You know what it's like to lose someone. To feel their life trickle through your fingers.'

Gerry McGuire did. Very well indeed. He hardly needed reminding, and he knew that his little brother had to be feeling deep pain to bring up the subject at all. When the elder of the McGuire brothers had been a lad of thirteen at the height of the Troubles, he had been sent on an errand by his mother to fetch some bacon for his father's tea.

'Take your wee sister with you for a walk, Gerry,' his mother said.

'Oh, Mam, she's a baby. I don't want the boys to see me with her.'

'The devil take the boys of yours, and you take your sister. You've got to look after her. You're getting to be a man now, Gerry, and you should take on some responsibility for others. And I've put twenty pence in the envelope with the list for you. On the way back buy some sweeties. And share them. But don't give Bridie enough to make her sick.'

Gerry McGuire had very little intention of giving his sister any sweeties at all. If he was going to be forced to run the gauntlet of his mates' jeers as he went down the street hand in hand with someone who was little more than a toddler, and a girl to boot, sister or no sister, then at least he'd get his just reward.

'OK, Mam,' he said. 'I'll take her,' he said, picking up the envelope into which, for safety, his mother insisted on putting the shopping list and the money for his father's supper.

Bridie was playing in the tiny front garden of their council house. When Gerry took her hand, she came willingly. She worshipped both her older brothers, even though they teased her mercilessly and always hid their sweets from her prying eyes. So when Gerry wanted to take her for a walk, she was as pleased as Punch. *He* wasn't, however, and hardly made any reply to her constant prattle as they headed towards the grocer's. Then he saw them. Half-a-dozen poorly dressed boys astride bicycles that for the most part had been cobbled together from stolen parts. And all waiting at the corner as if they just knew that he was on his way, ripe to be teased.

Oh no, he thought, as he saw them. Not now. As he drew level with them, the gang started to whistle, shout and laugh at their unfortunate friend's predicament.

'Got your wee girlfriend with ya, eh, Gerry?' said one.

'He loves his little sister, right enough,' said another. 'Look, he can't bear to be parted from her for a minute.'

'Stop it, will ya?' said Gerry. 'I'm doing an errand for me mam. Now what's wrong with that?'

'So you are, Gerry,' said yet another of his pals. 'But who's taking who for a walk?'

And the boys dissolved into laughter.

'Jeez, but you're impossible,' said Gerry, and hurried his sister past the gang, his ears burning and continuing to do so all the way to the shops, where, kicking his heels outside a newsagent's on the other side of the street, was his eleven-year-old brother.

'Hey, Dan,' Gerry shouted. 'Get yourself over here and look to Bridie. Our mam's made me bring her, and I've got to go for our dadda's tea.'

'Look to her yourself,' replied Daniel, not looking up.

'Dan, I'm warning you.'

'Don't make me laugh.'

Gerry let go of Bridie's hand and left her standing on the pavement as he made to get hold of his brother. But she didn't realize what was happening. She thought that it was a trick to lose her, and she ran after her brother as fast as her little legs would carry her. Across the pavement, down the kerb and into the road, where a motorcyclist, doing a very legal twenty-eight miles an hour, tried to swerve to avoid her, but skidded on the slick surface, wet from recent rain, lost control, his back wheel swinging round to scoop up Bridie and fling her against a lamppost, head first. Her skull split open with a sound like a paper bag full of water being dropped on to a hard surface, and Gerry, hearing the screams of the women in the street, looked round to see his sister lying in the gutter, blood and brains sliding out of the hole in her head. He couldn't believe what he was seeing, and ran back to her, his little brother just a few steps behind. Gerry threw himself down next to Bridie, and tried to scoop the warm mess back inside her skull, spitting and kicking at the passers-by who tried to stop him, as Daniel looked on in horror.

There were a dozen witnesses who said that he'd abandoned the little girl on the pavement, and she in her innocence had chased him into the street, and a dozen more to say that the motorcyclist had been obeying the speed limit. So, hard as he had tried in the years since, he could never forgive himself for what he had done to the child that he had been charged to take care of. The little sister that deep down inside he'd loved, and would never watch grow up.

No, he didn't need reminding what it was like to lose someone. And though he'd seen sudden death dozens of times since, nothing could ever blot out the horror of that day. And he knew that it was the same for his brother.

'It wasn't your fault, Dan,' he said, touching him on the shoulder. 'You did what you could, didn't you?'

'Course I did. But it was precious little.'

* * *

The soldiers got back to the transport and climbed in. Carlos put his sister's body into the back of the truck, before going back to the driving seat, and the rest of the family climbed into the back too, with García, Keller, Resnick and Spenser joining them. The McGuires got into the Chevy with Angel driving again, and Valin climbed in beside Carlos. Messelier and Newman got into Jesus's old jeep with O'Rourke at the wheel, leading the convoy, and they set off.

As the three vehicles reached the main road, O'Rourke, up at the front, saw the glare of headlights from the direction of the town. The vehicles that Stoner had wrecked had finally been cleared off the highway, and the cars, jeeps and personnel carriers that had been bottled up there started the remainder of their journey back to the burning factory, their occupants bent on destroying the perpetrators of the outrage against the Colombian economy.

'Jesus, they're after us,' O'Rourke said to his passengers, 'and we've still got to get past the bloody barracks.'

The three vehicles sped back towards the track that led to the ring road round Santa Ana, and comparative freedom.

But as O'Rourke had so truthfully pointed out, the barracks was between them and it.

A roadblock had been set up across the main road, manned by the last of the troops Valin's men had left alive, and they were more than ready to avenge their fallen comrades and their lost honour.

O'Rourke spotted the roadblock at about the same time as the troops guarding it saw the convoy and opened fire. He slewed the open-topped jeep to the side of the road before it was properly in range, and the truck and the Chevy pulled in sharply beside him.

'Looks like we've got a little problem,' said Valin laconically from his perch on the passenger side of the three-tonner.

'Don't worry, boss, I'll get through,' said Angel through the open window of the Chevrolet. 'You guys,' he said, turning to Gerry and Daniel, 'you wanna get out? I'm going straight through, and it'll be a bumpy ride.'

The two brothers looked at each other, and each for his different reasons, some recent, and some long in the past, grinned strained grins, and said: 'Let's do it,' in chorus.

'We probably won't make it,' said Angel, picking up his steel helmet from the seat next to him and putting it on.

'What the hell?' said Gerry. 'No one's going to live for ever.'

19

The Chevrolet leapt forward, and the McGuires poked their silenced Scorpions out of the rear windows into the slipstream, as the defenders of the roadblock raked the highway with fire.

Back at the truck, Valin buttonholed Resnick, saying, 'Haven't you got anything to slow down that lot?' as he pointed at the headlights of the vehicles coming up behind them and getting dangerously close.

'Just the thing, Colonel,' said the Russian. 'I brought along a few land-mines, just in case. I was going to leave them as a goodbye present when we turned off the main road.'

'I think you'd better leave them as a goodbye present now, don't you?'

'Anything you say,' said Resnick, who grabbed a knapsack out of the truck and ran to the jeep, dived into the back and shouted to O'Rourke: 'Get me back a bit.'

The lieutenant hauled on the wheel of the jeep and headed back the way they had come, his passengers hanging on to the sides for balance.

Bullets were tearing at the Chevy as it got closer to the roadblock, which consisted of a five-ton truck and a Ford staff car. Angel ducked down over the steering wheel, and the McGuires let go twin volleys of bullets from their silenced machine-guns.

Half a mile or so back down the road, Resnick shouted for O'Rourke to stop the jeep, and he leapt out carrying the knapsack, pulling out its contents – three flat, disc-shaped, NATO-standard M-19 anti-tank mines – as he went. These he placed on the road in a Z-shaped pattern. Then, as O'Rourke turned the jeep round again, he threw the knapsack to the side of the road and ran back to the jeep, leapt in, and yelled: 'Go, go, go!'

Meanwhile the Chevy was just a couple of hundred yards from the roadblock, and a hail of bullets was ripping through its bodywork. The windscreen imploded in a shower of glass, the radiator blew up in a cloud of steam, the bonnet flew upwards and both front tyres exploded, but still it kept going. By a miracle, no one in the car had been hit, but it couldn't last. A 9mm bullet slammed into Gerry McGuire's left elbow, but he kept firing his Scorpion, changing magazines every few seconds. Then his brother felt a terrible blow to his chest. He looked down and saw blood, but assumed that his body armour had prevented serious injury, and laughed out loud as he carried on pumping bullets out of the window.

A second bullet hit Daniel in the groin, but his adrenalin was flowing, and he felt nothing. When a third ripped into his neck he fell back against the seat behind him.

Another bullet hit Angel's tin helmet and his head rang, but the thick bulkhead of the Chevy was protecting him from fire as he aimed the dying vehicle at the side of the staff car. The heavy old saloon slammed into it, knocking it off the road, and then itself spun in a full circle, sending soldiers flying, hit the edge of a ditch, bounced back on to the road, and then rolled over half-a-dozen times in a shower of sparks, before coming to rest back on its wheels.

Angel sat at the wheel, almost mesmerized, before he made a move. The driver's door was jammed, but the passenger door sagged open, and, grabbing his Uzi from the floor where it had finished up, he kicked it open. 'You guys in the back OK?' he shouted to Gerry and Daniel.

'I've been hit in the arm,' said Gerry in a dazed voice.

'What about your brother?'

'He's been hit too.'

'Bad?'

Before Gerry had time to answer, the first vehicle in the convoy of Colombian soldiers coming from the town, an armoured personnel carrier, hit one of the land-mines that Resnick had laid, and was tossed up into the air before landing broadside and bursting into flames. Behind it was a jeep. The driver of the jeep swerved as the first land-mine exploded, and hit another. The vehicle was flipped right over, spilling men and guns, and landed on its top next to the personnel carrier, and the two of them completely blocked the road.

'What the fuck was that?' said Angel.

'Christ knows,' said Gerry.

'We'd better get out of here, Irish. Come on, and bring your brother,' Angel said urgently.

'The door's stuck.'

'Use the window.'

Gerry leant over and touched Daniel on the shoulder, but his head slumped down, and when the elder of the two brothers felt for a pulse on the younger's neck, there was nothing.

'Daniel,' he shouted. 'Daniel, are you all right?' But there was no answer.

'He's dead,' Gerry moaned. 'Oh Christ, my poor little brother's dead.'

The troops back at the jeep and truck saw and heard the first vehicle in the pursuing convoy hit the landmine too. 'Nice work, Resnick,' said Valin, as he watched the truck burning.

'Your confidence in me is most gratifying, Colonel,' replied the Russian. 'But shouldn't we press on and see what has happened to Angel and his comrades?'

Valin looked towards the roadblock. 'Of course. Mount up, people,' he said. 'We have more work to do.'

At first Gerry refused to leave his brother, and Angel had to lean into the car and almost drag him away from the body. 'It's no good, man,' the American insisted, after he too had felt for a pulse. 'He's gone.'

'I can't leave him here.'

'We can't take him with us.'

Christ, thought Angel. At this rate we'll have more dead bodies with us than live ones. 'Come on, Gerry, let's find some cover and wait for the rest,' he said firmly.

As more bullets thudded into the body of the Chevrolet, at last Gerry forced his way through the window and joined Angel on the road.

'This way,' said the American, and dragged Gerry across to a slight knoll, where they threw themselves down and started to return fire at the remnants of the defenders of the roadblock, as the Ford three-tonner and the jeep headed in their direction.

'I'm going back for him,' declared Gerry, when the firing died down as some of the enemy guns were turned on the approaching vehicles. He stood up, only to be cut down by a bullet in the leg.

'You fucking crazy bastard,' screamed Angel as he loosed the remains of a magazine on to the road. 'Why couldn't you wait a minute until they got here?'

That was all it would have taken, as the truck and the jeep screeched to a halt at the other side of the roadblock, and Valin's troops threw themselves into battle, Maria's Heckler and Koch automatic spitting lead up at the front, for she was determined to avenge the death of her eldest daughter.

The last of the defenders who stayed to fight were cut down within seconds, while the rest fled. For a moment silence reigned.

'I'll be back,' said Angel to Gerry. 'Hold on.' He quit the knoll and ran towards his comrades.

'Angel, you made it,' said O'Rourke. 'Where are the McGuires?'

'Daniel's still in the car. He's dead. Gerry's up there,' Angel said, gesturing back the way he had come. 'He's been hit. Don't know how bad.'

'Are you OK?'

'Can't seem to be anything else.'

'You're lucky,' said Newman, who had been standing next to the lieutenant. 'I'll go and see how he is.' He melted away towards the knoll that Angel had indicated.

So one of them's dead, the ex-para thought as he went. Good job. I wish it had been me who'd done it. Let's see if the other survived. From his pocket he drew a knife, a Randall No. 1, as sharp as a razor from constant honing. He found Gerry McGuire lying where he had fallen, his Scorpion still clasped in one hand. Gently he knelt beside the Irishman, took his gun from him, and said: 'Are you all right?'

McGuire looked up at Newman through eyes glazed with pain. 'Thank God you're here,' he said. 'Help me. I've got to get back to my brother.'

'Too late for him, old son,' said Newman. 'He's dead.' He lifted the knife and kissed the blade. 'And so are you.' The last words he whispered almost lovingly as he slit McGuire's throat. 'That's for my mates,' he cooed as he cleaned the knife on the dead man's tunic. 'The ones you and your like murdered for that shithouse called Northern Ireland, you Republican scum.'

He looked down at the dim form of McGuire's body, put his knife away, then removed several playing cards from another of his many pockets. There were a dozen or more of them, all from different decks. But they all had the same motif: the Ace of Spades. He removed one, tucked it into the collar of the Irishman's jacket and stood up. Then he walked down to the Chevrolet, wrested open the back door and checked Daniel's body to make sure he was dead. He was. Newman took another of the cards, slid it into the pocket of the dead man's blouse and slammed the door shut on him.

20

Newman returned slowly to the others, a feeling of well-being suffusing his whole body after what he had just seen and done. Even if he didn't make it back himself, he thought, at least he'd done something to avenge all those friends who'd been brought home from Ulster in wooden boxes, or invalided out to spend the rest of their lives becoming increasingly bitter, and trying to live on army pensions.

'How is he?' asked Angel.

'Dead.'

'He can't be.'

'He is. How many more bodies do you want to see tonight? He was hit at least three times. There's nothing you can do – any of us can do.'

'I want to see him.'

'I told you, there's nothing you can do. He's dead, Angel. Get it through your head.'

'What's going on here?' It was Valin.

'The McGuires. Newman says they're both dead,' said Angel. 'But Gerry was alive when I left him.'

'Why would he lie?' said Valin harshly, sensing the panic in Angel's manner. 'Now mount up, soldier. We're late.'

It was almost two-thirty and they still hadn't left

Santa Ana for the long drive back to the airstrip. They were late, and Valin knew the pilot would not hang around.

'But, Colonel,' protested Angel, 'Gerry might still be alive.'

'They're *both* dead,' said Newman. 'Take my word – I've seen enough dead bodies in my time.'

'I just want to be certain,' said Angel.

'OK,' said Valin, beginning to lose his patience. 'Check.'

Newman said nothing as Angel went up to the ridge, where he found McGuire's body and the card. He knew what it meant, and that it was too late to do anything about it. He went back to where Newman and Valin were waiting. 'So?' said Valin.

'Dead,' said Angel. 'Just like he said.' He looked at Newman, who looked straight back.

'Satisfied?' asked Valin.

'Sure.'

Newman's eyes narrowed, but he said not a word, and all three got back into their vehicles, and the convoy, now reduced to just the truck and the jeep, moved off.

They sped down the road nose to tail, O'Rourke in the lead again, until they came to the jungle track that led to the ring road. For the next few miles it was slow going, and Valin, sitting next to Carlos in the truck, could hardly contain his impatience. They would need to be very lucky to reach the airstrip on time. It meant a straight run with no more delays, and the way their luck was running, that seemed more and more unlikely.

They returned to the rendezvous point they had

chosen, but which they had not had to use, and picked up the Microbus.

Jesús carried his dead daughter to it, and the rest of the family, apart from Carlos, joined him inside.

Valin went over for a word, and the Colombian joined him outside the bus.

'What are you going to do with Carlotta's body?' Valin asked.

'We have decided to take her home.'

'But I thought you were coming out with us and García.'

'It is impossible, Colonel. We have to bury our daughter.'

'But you may all be in danger. You know there is an informer back in the States.'

'So be it.'

'Jesús, I beg you to reconsider. Bury your daughter by all means. But do it out by the airstrip, then come on the plane with us.'

'Without the benefit of a priest?'

'If necessary. She's dead now, and words mean nothing to her.'

'They mean much to Maria and me.'

Valin realized once again that it was pointless to argue with the Colombian, and changed the subject. 'We're going to need petrol and diesel soon,' he said.

'We have laid stashes all along the highway,' said Jesús. 'The first is about forty kilometres away. We can be there in a little while and fill up the tanks.'

'Bless you.'

'It is nothing.'

Valin looked through the window of the bus and saw the body of the Delgados' daughter laid out on the back seat, and knew what a gigantic lie her being there made of the old man's words.

'Your other children maybe. Let them come then. They could make a fresh start in America,' he said.

'Carlos? He speaks no English.' Jesús then saw Valin's face, and said: 'All right, I will ask them. But for now, we had better leave. Time is passing, and there are many soldiers between us and our destination. And all of them will be looking for us.'

Don't remind me, thought Valin tiredly. 'Of course,' he said, and returned to the truck.

The convoy reached the fuel dump without any problems. Once there, Jesús and Carlos busied themselves with refuelling the three vehicles, helped by Newman, Messelier and Angel. Maria, Carmen and Sofía sat together in the Microbus, and Spenser, after a brief word with Valin, went over and tapped on the glass next to where Maria was sitting. The three women inside all looked at him, and Maria wound down the window.

'I'd like to speak to Carmen, please,' said the American.

Maria turned to her daughter and said: 'Do you want to?'

'Yes,' the girl replied.

'Then do so.'

'I'm sorry for your loss,' Spenser said to Maria.

She nodded. 'Thank you,' she said.

'I'll say a prayer for her.'

'Say a prayer for yourself. You will need it before you leave here. If you are not killed first – you and all your friends.'

'Mother,' said Carmen. 'It was not his fault. We knew what we were getting into.'

The older woman nodded again. 'I'm sorry,' she said to Spenser. 'That was ungracious of me. One life among so many that have been lost is worth little. But she was my eldest daughter. I had such high hopes for her. And look what has happened.'

'I understand,' said Spenser. 'I have lost people too. Friends, family, comrades. Too many. I know what it's like to mourn. I don't blame you for being angry.'

Maria touched Spenser's hand through the open window of the bus, as Carmen climbed out, and she and Spenser went to the edge of the clearing where they were parked.

'The colonel tells me that your family are staying here. Not coming out with us as planned,' he said.

Carmen looked up at him and nodded.

'I want you to come with me to America,' Spenser said. 'On your own if necessary.'

'Why?'

'You know why. You've known since the moment I first laid eyes on you.'

'Yes, I've known. But my parents . . . '

'They would want what is best for you.'

'And you know what that is?'

Spenser smiled. 'No, I can't say that I do. But there is a chance that you might find it with me.'

'*You.* A soldier of fortune. A paid mercenary, who fights for whoever has the biggest purse.'

'Yes, me. I've been alone a long time, Carmen. Years. *Too* long. I don't make a habit of this, believe me. But as soon as I saw you, I wanted you to be with me. That's why I kissed you before. I thought you enjoyed it. I hoped you did.'

'You are an attractive man, Spenser. I can't believe there has been no one for as long as that.'

'Take my word for it. And take my word that I only want the best for you.'

'I do.'

'Then will you come with me?'

'Let me think about it. I will speak with my mother. Perhaps she does not want to lose two daughters in one day.'

'Of course.'

Carmen went up on tiptoe and kissed Spenser briefly on the mouth again. 'Of course I enjoyed it,' she said. 'More than you know.'

'I'm glad.'

'You could always stay here with us,' said Carmen.

'And be on the "most wanted" list of every law-enforcement agency in Colombia? Not to mention the army.'

'There are places we could go where no one would ever find us.'

'You make it sound very tempting.'

'So you'll think about it?'

'I will.'

'I must go back to my mother.'

'Of course.' And he watched as she walked back to the Microbus, looking wistfully over her shoulder once as she went.

Spenser stood alone and considered what Carmen had said. What the hell did he have to go back to in the States? Money. Sure. There was money waiting. Plenty. If they ever made it out, that was. Maybe life wouldn't be too bad in Colombia. Not with a woman like Carmen. But did he want them both to live in fear of a knock on the door at midnight for the rest of their lives? He shook his head wearily. Jesus Christ, what a decision.

Over at the truck that Jesús and Carlos were topping up with diesel from a huge can, Resnick was smoking a cigarette and watched Spenser and Carmen as they talked. He saw their brief kiss and envied their obvious attraction to each other, and looked through the side window of the Microbus at Sofía's lustrous hair.

Jesús saw him looking. 'She is beautiful, is she not?' he said.

'Sofía?'

Jesús nodded.

'She is,' said Resnick.

'If only you could have met under different circumstances . . . ' said the old man.

'I was thinking the very same thing.'

'Your friend: the American with the sad eyes. He also has those thoughts – about Carmen.'

'I think he does.'

Just then, Valin came and joined them. 'About finished, Jesús,' he said.

Jesús and Carlos put the heavy can on the ground, and Carlos screwed on the cap, before returning it to its hiding place under camouflage netting at the side of the clearing, with the rest of the stash of fuel.

'All done, Colonel,' said Jesús, rubbing his hands down the sides of his trousers. 'All the vehicles have full tanks. Certainly enough to get us where we're going.'

'Will you reconsider?' asked Valin. 'About staying, I mean.'

'I think not.'

'OK, I won't argue. But remember what I said about your son and daughters.'

'I will,' promised Jesús. 'We'd better go.'

Everyone climbed back into their vehicles once again, to begin the long haul through the night to the airstrip. By then it was almost four o'clock, and they had only two hours left to make a journey that needed more than three. Valin looked at his watch again as Carlos bumped the truck on to the road, bringing up the rear of the convoy, and in the pit of his stomach he knew they were not going to make it.

21

The miles rolled under the wheels of the three vehicles as they headed towards the airfield, and in the back of the truck Keller broke out rations for himself and Spenser, Angel, Resnick and García.

As Spenser thoughtfully munched on tinned sausage and vegetables, and drank from a canteen of water, he said: 'Sergeant, I may not be coming out.'

'What?' said the German, almost dropping his own can of K-rations.

'I may not be coming out with you,' Spenser repeated. 'I'm thinking about staying.'

'Christ, man. In this God-forsaken hole? After what we've done? Are you mad? Why would you want to stay here?'

'*Cherchez la femme*,' said Resnick.

'What?' said the sergeant again.

'I think our man has lost his heart,' explained the Russian.

Realization dawned on the German's face. 'One of Delgado's girls?' he said.

'That's right. Where have you been, Sarge, that you haven't noticed?' asked Resnick.

'Mostly sitting on top of a hill watching your arses,' said the sergeant. 'But Chris. What are you thinking about? Love 'em, by all means. Fuck 'em if you can. But stay with 'em? Where the hell would the world be if every man did that?'

Spenser and Resnick laughed at Keller's indignation, and even Angel, still deep in gloom from what had happened to Stoner and the McGuire brothers, managed a faint smile.

'I'll have to speak to the boss,' said Spenser.

'I should think you would. What are you doing with your life?' said Keller.

Christ knows, thought Spenser. Christ alone knows.

His mind rewound back to Vietnam. Dust-off at dawn for a strike at a village deep in lush jungle that was so similar to the scenery that was flying past outside. The chopper dropped the patrol close to a village called . . . What the hell did it matter what it was called? It was just another gook village: a dozen hovels, chickens digging in the dirt, and a headman who claimed to love the Yanks. Sure he loved them. Just like all the rest. 'GI, number one,' they called out to soldiers as they went past, then shot them in the back. But hell, who could blame them? It was their country, after all.

They approached the village as a cock crowed, and found cover, then called in for the mortar attack to begin. There were guerrillas in the village, or so intelligence told them. But intelligence had been wrong before, and probably would be again.

Lieutenant Christopher Spenser, aged twenty-one, was in command of a six-man patrol out on a search-and-destroy mission. His radio-man had his headset stuck in his helmet. There was a muffled squawk and he reached for it. 'Go, ten,' he said, then listened. 'Roger that.'

'Guns up on the TOT, Lieutenant,' he said.

'Tell 'em to go for it.'

'Ten, five. Let her eat.'

Then the mortars started to fall on the villages. Huts burst into flames and the occupants, both male and female, ran out screaming. The women carried babies, the children carried cooking pots and bedding and the men carried nothing.

When the last mortar had hit its target, the patrol rose to their feet as one and headed into the village.

Spenser led the way, with to his right a veteran sergeant called Hope. To his left was PFC Beaumont. Behind him, the radio operator, Hopkins, and three more privates, Bennett, Kawolski and Simpson. Beaumont and Simpson were black and Kawolski was a second-generation Pole. Not that it mattered. It just was. It didn't matter either that Beaumont and Simpson were just eighteen.

As they came up to the settlement, something moved in the undergrowth and Kawolski fired off a short burst from his M16 without looking. It was a dog, and died like one: noisily.

As they came to the main street of the village – if you could call a flattened mud path a main street – a black-clad figure appeared from behind a burning hut. Spenser fired on full auto, and the figure vanished into the smoke. 'Check it out, Bennett, Simpson,' he ordered.

'You got it, Ell-Tee,' they chorused, and stealthily went to the corner of the hut and squinted round it.

'It's a woman, Ell-Tee,' said Simpson. 'And she's pregnant. Or at least she was.'

Spenser went to see for himself. The black-clad

figure was indeed a woman, and was indeed pregnant – or had been. His bullets had hit her in the stomach, and she was busy miscarrying and dying at the same time.

'Shit,' said Spenser. 'Medic. Medic.'

Beaumont was the medic, but there was nothing he could do. As the sun rose higher, and the smoke drifted across the paddy-fields, all he did was shoot the woman full of morphine and cradle her head as she and the baby died in the dirt.

The patrol stood around in the morning heat haze and looked at her as she breathed her last. 'Shit, man,' said Simpson. 'What are we doing in this fucking hole? A coupla months ago I was in Philly, and the only thing on my mind was what record to buy on Sat'day. Or what chick to ask to dance. Now look what they done to me. They dumped me out here in a place where we kill pregnant women in the name of the USA.'

'*You* didn't kill her,' said Spenser. '*I* did.'

'Shit, Ell-Tee,' said the young black again. 'We all in this shit together.' He lit a Lucky Strike, and offered Spenser one. The lieutenant accepted and as Simpson gave him a light, he could see that the boy was crying.

Boy, he thought as the truck bounced along the bumpy highway in Colombia. I was nothing but a boy myself. A boy with the blood of a pregnant woman and her unborn baby on my hands. Among others.

There had been no Vietcong in the village. It had been friendly, and the intelligence had been wrong. The patrol dusted off again at nine hundred hours, leaving the destroyed community to fend for itself. The last thing Spenser saw as he looked out of the open door of the Huey was a smudge of smoke against the blue sky, and they were all back at base camp in time for a late breakfast.

The base camp was a little slice of the US transported to South-east Asia. A place where the troops could buy Budweiser and Coca-Cola, Hostess Twinkies and *Playboy* magazine. And listen to Tamla Motown records on the radio: Smokey, Marvin, The Supremes, The Isleys. Tamla Motown: 'The sound of young America.' That was a joke. To Spenser and Simpson, Beaumont, and all the rest, the sound of young America was the rattle of an M16 on full auto.

Spenser's daydream was so real that he imagined he could hear the sound of the Huey as it prepared to land, and he jumped when Keller kicked his foot and screamed, 'Wake up, man. There's a chopper upstairs. Get your fucking gun, for Chrissake.'

Even as Spenser scrambled for the Gatling, the first bullets from the machine-guns mounted in the helicopter began to hit the convoy.

22

The chopper was a Sikorsky HH-S 3C gunship, better known as 'The Jolly Green Giant', because of its size, and had been used to great effect by the American army, notably in Libya in 1986. It had a crew of five, and three 7.62mm mini-guns, similar to the one used by Spenser, poked obscenely from its body, which in this case bore Colombian air force markings.

The first vehicle to bear the brunt of the machine-gun fire from the powerful weapons mounted inside its open doors, and in a gun port underneath its huge belly, was the Microbus in the middle of the convoy. Bullets slammed into it, and Jesús, who was driving, swerved across the road as they punched through the windscreen, killing Maria instantly, stitching a line along the empty seats behind her, next to where Sofía and Carmen were sitting, and pounding into the already dead body of their sister.

Jesús saw the bullets tear through his wife's body, and he let out a roar of pain as the Microbus veered off the road and ploughed into the jungle.

The chopper swept around and came back to strafe the jeep and the truck as Keller and Resnick ripped the canvas cover above them from its metal supports, and Spenser aimed his Gatling at it and began firing. The pilot sheered away as the shells punched through the air, tracers helping Spenser's aim.

O'Rourke, at the wheel of the jeep, skidded to the side of the road, and in the cab of the three-tonner Valin yelled at Carlos in Spanish to stop too, which he did, as Spenser and his companions in the well of the truck kept firing.

The helicopter swept back towards them, its thirty-million-candlepower Night Sun searchlight illuminating the road as if it was day. O'Rourke, Newman and Messelier had left the jeep and taken cover among the trees, and O'Rourke and Newman were firing up at the helicopter with their carry weapons, while the Frenchman reloaded the ARMSCOR with fresh grenades.

Spenser's next burst slammed into the fuselage of the aircraft and one gunner stopped firing as a slug ripped into his leg, which spouted blood.

Messelier fired the grenade-launcher upwards, and by sheer luck, the first projectile went straight through one of the Sikorsky's open doors, hit the roof and bounced back inside the cabin, where it exploded with maximum force. Trailing smoke, the stricken helicopter veered away over the jungle, where it suddenly dropped like a stone and exploded a few hundred yards away.

'Yes,' yelled Messelier, punching the air. 'We killed the fucker.' He did a dance of triumph.

Carlos drove the truck to where the jeep had stopped. 'Status report,' yelled Valin, as he jumped out of the cab. 'O'Rourke, Keller. Any casualties?'

'We've lost the bus,' shouted O'Rourke. 'Angel, Newman, get back and find it.'

The American jumped out of the back of the truck, and he and the ex-para ran back down the road to where the Microbus had pushed into the undergrowth.

There they found Jesús cradling his dead wife, and Sofía and Carmen, white and shaken, holding on to each other for comfort.

'Oh no,' said Angel as he tugged open the door. 'Is she . . . ?'

'Dead,' said Jesús. 'My family is being ripped apart.'

The two mercenaries stood beside the bus in silence. There was nothing they could say, and they knew it.

'I can't go on,' sobbed Jesús. 'This is too much.'

'I'm real sorry, Mr Delgado,' said Angel, and he reached inside the bus to touch the Colombian, who shook off his hand angrily.

'Leave me,' he said. 'Leave us all.'

'We can't do that, sir,' said Newman. 'They know where we are. If there are any jets close by, they'll be looking for us at first light, and we'll really be in trouble. And even if there aren't, the chopper pilot will have radioed through, and some of his buddies might come looking, or send ground troops. We have to move off, and soon.'

'Just leave us. Haven't you done enough? First my daughter, now my wife. I should have listened to your colonel and taken them home this morning when I had a chance.'

'But you didn't, sir,' said Newman. 'And I'm afraid it's too late for you to change your mind. Is the vehicle driveable?'

'I don't know,' said Jesús.

'Here, let me,' said Angel and he slid into the driver's

seat, which Jesús had vacated, and tried the stalled engine. It started first time.

'Do you want me to drive, sir,' asked Angel.

The Colombian nodded, but said nothing.

Angel reversed the Microbus out of the thick vegetation where it had stopped, back on to the road, selected first gear, and with Newman clinging to the outside, drove back to join the others.

When they got back, Newman jumped off the bus and went to report to Valin.

'Oh hell,' said the colonel. 'I told him not to come.'

'He wishes he hadn't, believe me.'

'It's a bit bloody late for that.'

Newman said nothing in reply.

Valin trotted over to the Microbus with Carlos and Spenser close behind, and when the young Colombian saw his mother's body, he wailed and fell to his knees.

Christ, thought Valin. This is all we need. Hysterics from the bloody driver. What next?

Spenser leaned through the window and looked at Carmen. She looked back at him with empty eyes, and said nothing. He didn't speak either, but just walked on to the road and bummed a cigarette off Resnick.

'Tough,' said the Russian.

'And getting tougher,' replied Spenser.

Back at the bus, Valin told Carlos in his native tongue to get in with his family, and said to Angel: 'You drive.'

'Sir,' replied Angel.

Valin then turned to the rest of his men. 'Newman, can you handle the truck?'

'No problem, sir. I've got my HGV.'

'Good, though I don't think anyone will ask to see your licence,' and he looked at his watch as the first faint hint of dawn appeared in the sky towards the east. It was five a.m. – only an hour until take-off.

'Mount up, men,' he said. 'But I think we're right royally screwed.'

23

Angel couldn't believe what was happening to him as he slotted the Microbus with bullet holes in the windscreen into the middle of the convoy. Blood and dead bodies everywhere. And some of them innocent. This was not the way he'd expected it to be when he'd joined Valin's team. Christ, he thought wearily as the Microbus picked up speed. Christ help me.

What he'd wanted to be was a soldier. A regular soldier in the US army. Just like his father had been, and his father before him. Sonny Angelo had fought at Guadalcanal, and Angel's old man, Bobby, had done his time in Vietnam. But by the time Angel had enlisted there were no more wars to fight. Grenada and the Gulf were finished, the Iron Curtain was down, and all there was for him overseas was a short haul in Germany with the drug addicts, unless Clinton got the country involved in some UN shit in Bosnia or Somalia. To be transferred to communications was the last straw. Angel wanted to be out where the fighting was, gun in hand, gum in mouth, wearing shades, just like the photos of his dad in Saigon, *circa* 1970.

So he'd looked for a way to be discharged, and the fight with the MP had been the answer, although he could have done without the time served in the military prison. The fight really wasn't all his fault. He'd fallen in with a bunch of recruits who drank too much, smoked dope, and ingested as many other drugs as they could get their hands on. He had got into a lot of debt, which he could only pay off by acting as chauffeur to one of the dealers who'd heard about his prowess at the wheel.

On Friday and Saturday nights Angel had to drive the guy around a succession of army and civilian bars close to Fort Bragg. The dealer was the proud owner of a restored cherry-red 1959 Plymouth Fury with white leather upholstery, which was not the most discreet vehicle for delivering drugs, but both of them were so zonked it made little difference.

That particular Friday night, Angel had just come off guard duty and was still in uniform. At about ten o'clock he was sitting outside the quaintly-named Stand and Deliver bar, sinking a Bud Lite and smoking a joint, when a jeep with two MPs inside pulled up in front of the Plymouth.

Shit, Angel thought as they got out, settled their equipment belts more comfortably on their hips and walked towards the car.

'Hey, soldier,' said the first MP. 'What's up?'

Angel looked around. 'The sky,' he replied.

'Very funny, man,' said the other MP, a black dude who seemed to be about five feet wide.

'Yeah, man,' said Angel, taking another sip of his beer and a toke on his joint, 'I'm a funny guy.'

'Who says so, your mother?'

'Among others.'

'Gimme your army number and regiment, boy,' said the first MP.

Angel reeled off the information.

'This your car?' asked the black cop.

'No, man,' said Angel. 'Just driving it for a friend, is all.'

'What kinda friend has wheels like this.'

'A rich friend.'

'How did he make his money?'

'Running slaves,' said Angel, looking the black MP straight in the eye.

'Get out the car, motherfucker.'

'You want to make me?'

'Angelo, you're under arrest.'

'In a horse's ass.'

When the big black MP dragged Angel out of the Plymouth, the young recruit lost his temper. He caught hold of the baseball bat he kept under the driver's seat in case of trouble and landed a huge whack just under the rim of the cop's steel helmet, where his neck met his shoulders. The cop went down and Angel began to kick him, as the other MP unholstered his side-arm and dived into the fight.

Angel lashed out at him too, but the MP struck Angel a massive blow on the side of his head with the barrel of his Colt .45, laying him out cold.

Angel got six months in the brig for the escapade, plus a dishonourable discharge. But he got his revenge when he went back to Fort Bragg on his release, and lay in wait for the MPs. He still had a few friends in the town, including the dope dealer, and one night they staged an ambush outside the very same bar. The dealer made a call to the MPs, telling them that a fight was about to break out between the military and a bunch of redneck civilians. Angel had made some enquiries and knew that the white cop, by the name of Jones, was on duty that night. When his jeep turned up, siren wailing, Angel was there waiting. He was dressed in civilian clothes, and the MP hardly gave him a second glance, until Angel walked up to him and smacked him in the face with the brass knucks he was wearing on his right hand, breaking the cop's nose and cheekbone with one blow.

Jones's partner, not the black guy who had been with him on the first occasion, tried to retaliate, but Angel's friends moved in and started to mix it, while Angel made his escape and took the first plane to New York. The episode went down in the legend of the camp.

Soon after, Angel heard about the mercenary scene across the pond, and took a trip to Europe, where he met Valin and O'Rourke and signed up for the mission to Colombia. Now he wasn't so sure it had been the right thing to do, and as the sun peeped over the mountain top, he pulled his sunglasses from his top pocket and put them on, and wondered if any of the mercs would ever get out of the country alive.

24

Valin called O'Rourke on the radio at five forty-five. 'We're never going to make it,' he said tersely. 'Pull over. Out.' O'Rourke did as he was ordered, and Angel in the Microbus, which stank of blood and human tissue brutally exposed to the humid air, did the same, as Newman brought the truck to a halt behind them.

Valin hopped out and ran to the Microbus. 'How much further, Jesús?' he asked.

The Colombian looked at him through eyes still curtained with grief. 'Too far,' he said. 'Another hour at least.'

'Damn it,' said Valin. 'We're never going to catch that plane.'

'He will be back tomorrow.'

'I hope so. Is there anywhere you can think of that we can hole up for the rest of the day?'

'My land is about forty-five minutes away. We can go there, and I will bury my wife and child.'

'Will you come out with us then?'

'Maybe.'

'Your place it is, then. Are there other people about?'

'No, it is quiet and secluded.'

'Angel, you take the lead,' said Valin. 'Will someone show him the route?'

'I will,' said Carmen.

Valin ran to tell O'Rourke what was happening, then headed back to the truck. He was surprised that the party had met no more resistance on the road, and to tell the truth, a little worried. But he mentally shrugged as he took his seat next to Newman and the small convoy set off again.

At six o'clock precisely, as the three vehicles carrying Valin's Raiders were still an hour or so away, the ancient C47 made a pass over the airstrip where it had dropped off Valin's Raiders twenty-four hours earlier, lowered its undercarriage and came in to land. The pilot taxied up to the end of the makeshift runway, feathered his engines and turned the plane round for take-off again. He sat in his patched leather seat and surveyed the clearing. There was nothing to see but the edge of the jungle that surrounded him, and no one emerged to board the Douglas.

The pilot wiped a thin sheen of sweat from his brow, took off his headset and walked back into the body of the plane, where ten men in green fatigues were sitting. They wore no insignia of any kind, and each held an Israeli Galil assault rifle, snouted with a suppressor, as a carry gun, and wore Sig Sauer P228s in holsters on their hips. One of them had been monitoring a powerful radio since the plane had crossed the Colombian border.

The one who had done all the talking so far, and who, the pilot assumed, was their leader, turned from the window that he had been peering through, and said: 'Any sign?' He, like the rest of the men, had an American accent.

'Not a thing,' replied the pilot. He had not been a happy man since the unmarked military transporter had landed at his base and disgorged fourteen anonymous soldiers the previous evening. They had taken command of the C47 and insisted, with the aid of the heavy ordnance they carried, that he take the ten soldiers now sitting in the cabin to meet Colonel Valin and his men, leaving the other four behind to make sure of two things. First, that the pilot returned the next day if by any chance he had to leave them in Colombia; and second, if the worst happened and Valin's men defeated the soldiers, there would be a welcoming party when they got off the plane in Panama.

The leader had paid the pilot handsomely, but even the sight of so many US dollars had not calmed the flier's fears that Valin might object. Physically.

'Well,' said the leader. 'They did the job and got out. At least some of them did. Plus some civilians. A stupid bastard in a chopper dive-bombed them a while back, and copped it. But since then they've been allowed free passage. I've made sure of that.' He gestured towards the radio. 'These dumb Colombians don't know who they've been taking on.'

'The colonel said that they might be delayed,' said the pilot.

The leader smiled. 'That's a nice choice of words,' he said.

'And if they weren't here today, I was to come back tomorrow at the same time.'

'You've told me that already,' the leader said impatiently. 'I wanted this all over and done with by then. Can't you raise them on *your* radio?'

'I don't know what frequencies they're using.'

'You should have asked.'

'*Sí, señor.*'

'We'll wait fifteen minutes, then if they're not here, you get going back across the border and try again tomorrow. We'll stay. Of course, they may have run into something we don't know about yet. A patrol maybe. This is a mess. Why the hell Washington agreed to send them . . . ' He stopped speaking, as if he realized he might be saying too much. 'OK, compadre. Back to your seat and keep a weather eye out. If you see anything – I repeat, anything – sing out.'

'*Sí, señor*,' said the pilot.

When he was safely back on the flight deck with the door closed, the leader, who was referred to by his men only as 'Number One', stood up and addressed them.

'Right,' he said. 'You know why we've been sent down to this hell-hole, and what we have to do now we're here. It's not the most pleasant of jobs, but it has to be done. There are a bunch of half-assed mercenaries running around this apology for a country, creating mayhem in the name of the USA. It was a bad decision made by those fools in the civilian agencies, and we've been sent to clean up their mess the same as we've been doing for the last fifty years. When in doubt, call up the army. You also know that we have no official jurisdiction down here, and if we're caught, no one will admit that we exist. I've been able to use some juice on the military as you heard when I was talking on the radio. But how far it goes, Christ alone knows. These bastards could turn at any moment. And I can tell you they're not crazy about being ordered around by me. The only reason I've got away with it so far is that our orders came down from someone very powerful. Powerful enough to put the fear of God into these Hispanics. What he's got on them I don't know, and I don't think I want to. So I warn you now, as I've warned you before: if this all goes wrong, and any of us – I repeat, any of us – fall into the hands of the Colombians, we'll just disappear. And these guys are expert at the art. So stay close, watch your backs, keep your weapons close, and trust no one except us ten. Understood?'

The nine soldiers all replied in the affirmative.

'Good,' said Number One. 'And God be with you.'

25

Carmen showed Angel the turn-off to her father's land at almost exactly the same time that the C47 was flying back across the border into Panama. The Microbus bumped down a muddy trail that seemed to be leading nowhere, until suddenly it opened out on to flatlands that dipped until they met a small range of foothills, beyond which reared up an imposing cluster of mountains. The jungle had been cleared to provide arable land, and beside a small stream stood a low farmhouse with a large barn behind it. It was an idyllic scene, and for the first time in hours Angel felt himself relax. He drove towards the building and parked in the barn on Carmen's instructions.

The jeep and truck followed the Microbus inside, and everyone disembarked. Immediately Valin sent Messelier to stand guard on the track that they had taken to enter Jesús's land. The Frenchman was under strict orders to maintain radio silence. The rest of the men stood silently as Carlos and Jesús took the bodies of Maria and Carlotta from the VW. Valin offered to help, but he was rebuffed. The two women were carried gently into the farmhouse and Carmen spoke to the colonel. 'We will prepare some food, when we have made my mother and sister comfortable. But until then, please stay out of the house. You are free to go anywhere else on the land but this is a private moment. I'm sure you understand.'

Valin nodded. 'Of course,' he said. 'You know you have all our sympathies. We won't stray far. In case another chopper comes looking for us.'

'There will not be room for you all to sleep inside the house, but you are welcome to bed down in the barn.'

'We're very grateful to you,' said Valin.

After the Delgados had gone, the men began cleaning their weapons, eating and smoking. Angel found a quiet spot and took the bag of cocaine out from his jacket. It was amazing to him that it had survived all he had been through, but it was undamaged. He poked the point of his knife through the plastic wrapper and took a hit. It was good stuff. The best he'd ever tried, and he got an immediate rush which made him feel better.

That was when Newman found him. 'The spoils of war?' he asked.

'Give it a rest, bud,' said Angel.

'I don't give a fuck,' said Newman. 'Every man is free to be the architect of his own downfall. Just as long as you can do your job when we get out of here.'

'I'll do it,' said Angel. 'Don't worry about that.'

'Good.'

'And what about your job?'

'What do you mean?'

'I saw what you did to Gerry McGuire.'

'Me?'

'Who else?'

'One of the Colombian soldiers.'

'Give me a break, man.'

'You didn't say anything to Valin?'

'What would've been the point?'

'He would probably have shot me, there and then,' said Newman.

'But we need you and that Ithaca you're toting.'

'Self-preservation first, huh, Angel?'

'The McGuires were dead. You're alive. I just wanted you to know that I know, and I'm wondering whether I should watch my back when you're around.'

'You're Italian, aren't you?' asked Newman.

'Fourth generation.'

'Then you've got nothing to worry about, son.' And Newman smiled an evil smile. 'They're better off dead, those two. It's their sort that killed mates of mine,' he went on. 'They should never have been allowed to mix with real soldiers. Irish fucking Republican Army. I shit on them.' He smiled again. 'I'm only sorry that the other one was dead before I got to him.'

'Cool,' said Angel. 'You keep quiet about this' – he tapped the bag of cocaine – 'and I'll keep quiet about McGuire.'

'Deal,' said Newman. 'I'm off for a kip. I imagine you won't want one.'

'I'm fine,' said Angel. 'Just fine.'

At the airstrip, the leader had gathered the men round him in the jungle. It was getting hotter, moisture dripped from the trees, and the bugs were using the men in the green fatigues for target practice.

'You know the deal,' said the leader, wiping the perspiration from his brow with a green rag that he then tied around his head as a sweat band. 'We wait here until dawn tomorrow. The pilot's going to make one more trip. That was the arrangement with Valin. If this little band is not here by then, the pilot has no obligation to return. End of story. And as far as anyone will know, they *didn't* make it. These men are the scum of the earth. They will not be missed. But we have to make sure that there are no loose ends. We have to see to it that not one of them, or anyone they've teamed up with, is still alive to talk about what happened last night in Santa Ana.'

'Why didn't someone do something about it before they even got here?' asked one of his men.

'Valin has friends in high places. If they'd never got here, questions *would* have been asked. But they completed their mission more by luck than by judgement, I imagine. So it's just a tough break that they never made it back to be picked up.'

The man who had asked the question nodded.

Back at Jesús's farmhouse, Carmen was staring out of an upstairs window at the barn where Spenser was standing in the shadows smoking a cigarette and looking at the house. I wonder if he will come for me, she thought. I hope he does. Oh please, Chris, just walk up here and take me away. I don't care what happens. Even if we don't live to see another day, it would have been worth it to spend my last few hours with you.

But he didn't. He dropped the cigarette butt and ground it into the earth with the toe of his combat boot, then turned and went back into the barn.

Inside, Valin was talking to O'Rourke and Keller.

Spenser walked over and joined them. 'What's up, Colonel?' he asked.

'To use a phrase from some of those old films, I don't like it; it's too quiet.'

'Can't be quiet enough for me,' said the American.

'Listen, Chris,' said Valin. 'We were spotted on the main road out of Bogotá by that chopper we shot down. Don't tell me he didn't get a message through about our position before he crashed. Since then, nothing. We could have been bottled up half-a-dozen times. Why weren't we? I think something's going on that we don't know about. So we keep a permanent guard on that road coming in here.'

'You can't suspect Jesús. Not after all he's been through.'

'No, of course not. Jesús could've had us all on slabs any time since we arrived. He's one of the few that I don't suspect.'

'Present company excepted, of course,' said O'Rourke.

'This particular part of the company, yes,' said Valin. 'You three I'd trust until hell freezes over. But who knows about the others. They've only been with us for a few weeks, and we didn't exactly seek references.'

Too true, thought Spenser. Maybe now was not the best time to tell him he was thinking about staying.

'Then why put the Frenchman on guard,' said Keller, 'if he's one that you don't trust?'

'But I do,' replied Valin, remembering Messelier's *nom de guerre*, 'The Invisible Man'. 'He's been around the block. Anyway, someone had to be first on. You can have the next turn if you want.'

'I don't mind,' said the German. 'I've always been

happy to take my share of the shit jobs, as you well know, Colonel.'

'I know, Franz,' said Valin. 'Nobody's casting aspersions on you, of all people. Now go and get some sleep, and I'll wake you if you're needed.'

'OK, Colonel,' said Keller. 'That's not a bad idea.'

'So who's screwing us?' said Spenser.

'We'll find out when we get back to the States,' said Valin.

'*If* we do,' Spenser corrected him.

'Pessimism, Chris,' said Valin. 'Isn't that always the way with you?'

'At least I'm never disappointed,' said Spenser.

'I don't know about that,' said O'Rourke. 'Seems like you and a certain lady are both very disappointed right now.'

'Meaning?'

'From the way you've been gazing up at that house, and the way Carmen's been gazing down here, I'd say that if you two don't get together pretty soon there'll be tears before bedtime.'

'Very funny.'

'Not funny from where I'm standing. More like tragic.'

'Mark. Leave it,' said Valin.

'OK, Colonel,' replied the young lieutenant. 'I just figured that life was too short, that's all.'

And with a wink at Spenser he wandered off.

'But he's not wrong, is he?' said Valin, when the lieutenant had gone.

'Colonel, this is hardly the time and place,' protested Spenser.

'You never said that in Saigon.'

'That was a lifetime ago.'

'And how long's a life?'

Spenser looked at his old friend for a long while, then said: 'You don't think we're going to make it out of here, do you?'

'Anything's possible.'

Spenser nodded. 'I get the picture, Colonel. See you later.' And with that he turned on his heel and walked out of the barn, up the track, on to the farmhouse veranda, and knocked on the door firmly.

Carmen opened it. 'I saw you coming,' she said.

'I don't mean to disturb your family,' said Spenser. 'But I wonder if you'd like to take a walk.'

Carmen smiled. 'In the park?' she said.

'I know it sounds stupid, but we don't know who's going to be coming down that road after us today. I'd just like to talk to you for a few minutes. Just in case.'

'In case?'

'In case I don't make it.'

'And if *you* don't, do you think I will?'

'You must. You must take care of yourself.'

'My place is here with my family – what's left of it.'

Spenser nodded. 'Whatever you say. But will you come?'

'A moment,' she said, and went back inside, closing the door gently behind her.

Spenser turned and looked across the clearing to the entrance to the track. 'Come out, come out, wherever you are,' he said quietly to himself.

The door opened again and Carmen emerged. 'Let's go,' she said. 'This way.' She took him around the side of the house and down another set of steps.

They made their way towards a huge old tree that stood alone. 'This was my playhouse when I was a child,' said Carmen, looking up. Pieces of wood had been nailed to the trunk to make a crude ladder. 'Up you go,' she said.

'Will it support me?'

'Baby,' she said with a smile.

Spenser shrugged, and climbed up into the leafy haven, to find a platform of wooden planks jammed into a support made by four thick branches.

'See,' said Carmen as she joined him. 'That wasn't too bad, was it?'

'You speak very good English.'

'I studied hard. Some of us in the family speak it better than others.' She hesitated. 'Or some of them used to.' She began to cry.

Spenser sighed, and awkwardly took Carmen in his arms. She sobbed gently on his shoulder as he stroked her ebony hair.

Eventually she pulled back and looked at him. 'I'm sorry,' she said.

'Sorry? What's there to be sorry about?'

'You were looking for some happiness. I only gave you grief.'

'Grief with you is like happiness with anyone else,' Spenser said.

'Oh, Chris,' she replied. 'No one has ever said anything like that to me before – in Spanish or English.'

He reddened under her gaze. 'I'm glad,' he said. 'I meant it.'

Carmen leant forward and kissed Spenser, and he clasped her to him again.

26

Fifty yards inside the jungle, beside the track that ran down to the Delgados' land, Messelier leant against a tree and considered the situation. It wasn't looking too good, he thought, as he lit a cigarette, and wondered, like some of the others back at the farm, whether or not any of the group would get out of the country alive.

Of course it wasn't the first time the Frenchman had looked death in the face. Not by a long shot. He thought about all the people he had killed while working for his government as an assassin, and latterly as a mercenary, in the pay of anyone who could afford his services.

Death was familiar to Messelier, as familiar as the feel of wood to a carpenter, or the smell of the sea to a fisherman. But one particular death always remained with him. The one that had made him relinquish his comfortable life in France and ultimately brought him to this humid, stinking jungle: the murder of the child, the daughter of a small-time spy and whore. And although he knew that as a merc he'd killed children since – or at least been involved in the deaths of children – he had felt so close to death on that particular day.

It had been a beautiful spring afternoon in Paris,

and the trees along the Seine were in blossom as he parked his Citroën at a meter and set off to kill the woman who had been selling the confessions of her lover to whoever would pay the most. Messelier strolled along the boulevard where she had her apartment and stopped often to gaze into the windows of the high-priced boutiques where he loved to buy his designer clothes. He was in no hurry. It was a lovely day for a stroll, and his information was that she rarely rose before noon, then spent the afternoon pampering herself before meeting her *amour* for supper.

He picked up a bunch of flowers at the florist's on the corner of the avenue. A spring mixture: carnations, daffodils, roses, lilies. An expensive bunch, as befitted a woman of her reputation, and he carried it to her block, with the flowers covering his face in case the concierge was peering out from behind the shutters. The street door was wide open and Messelier took the lift to the fourth floor, then walked along the wide, carpeted hallway to the woman's door and knocked.

'Who is it?' said a female voice after a minute.

'The florist, mademoiselle,' he replied. 'A delivery.'

'One moment.'

He heard the chain go on, then the door opened a fraction. In the gap between it and the jamb he saw a pretty face topped with blonde hair, and he showed her the flowers.

'*Très jolies*,' she said, pushed the door to, unfastened the chain and opened the door all the way. 'Come in, monsieur.'

Messelier did as he was asked and went into the hall of the apartment. The woman was about thirty, very beautiful, wearing a long, black negligée.

'Take them through to the kitchen,' she said. 'My maid will arrange them when she returns.'

She's alone, thought Messelier. Excellent. He went in the direction she indicated, into a large, light, airy kitchen with a view of the Eiffel Tower.

He laid the flowers beside the sink and turned to look at the woman. She *was* beautiful, and it seemed a shame to mar such beauty with death. But he had a job to do.

He smiled at her and said: 'It's a beautiful day, isn't it?'

She agreed, and went to look for a card attached to the bouquet.

Messelier, who was armed with a silenced .38 automatic pistol and a switchblade, looked around the kitchen. On the wall hung a set of carving knives, and it seemed to him appropriate that he should use one of them to dispatch her. He was wearing thin, black-leather gloves and he reached for the longest, most wicked-looking of the utensils as she searched among the foliage of the flowers for the message she expected.

'Your lover?' he asked.

She spun round on one heel. 'What?' she demanded, then saw the knife he was holding, and suddenly looked ten years older.

'They're not from the minister,' he said, 'but perhaps from some of his colleagues. The ones that do not appreciate you selling their most precious secrets.'

'I don't . . . ' she said, and put her hands up to her mouth.

'I am sorry,' said Messelier, and sunk the blade of the knife into her abdomen and twisted it viciously.

The woman let out a stifled scream like a pig being slaughtered, and stepped back, pulling herself off the blade of the knife, which dripped blood on to the immaculate black-and-white tiled floor. She grabbed at her wound, but blood welled between her fingers and she looked down at it and fainted.

Messelier finished the job by lifting up her head and slashing the tempered steel of the blade across her throat. He dropped her body and stepped back to avoid his clothes being stained by her vital fluids.

He washed the knife under the tap and was just about to return it to its place when he heard footsteps in the hall. The maid, he thought. But I didn't hear the front door . . . A little flaxen-haired girl came into the kitchen.

'*Maman* . . . ' she said, then saw the body, stiffened and screamed. Messelier grabbed her and covered her mouth with his gloved hand. There was only one thing for it. She had to be killed too, for he knew, by looking into her wide, terror-filled eyes, that she would remember the man who had been in the room with her dead mother. Messelier lifted her cleanly with one arm and sliced through her windpipe with a single blow of the knife with the other. Then he dropped her next to her mother, where she twitched twice before her heart stopped beating and the blood stopped flowing from the cut.

This time he didn't bother to wash the weapon, but just dropped it next to the two bodies and walked unhurriedly out of the flat.

Once in the fresh air again, he breathed deeply and walked down the avenue to the first café he came to, where he ordered a large brandy.

The assassin was still there an hour later, three empty glasses in front of him, when he heard the scream of ambulance and police sirens, and knew that the maid must have returned to make her grisly find. He watched the public utility vehicles as they skidded to a halt in front of the apartment building where he had done his evil work.

Messelier was so deeply engrossed in his thoughts, and neglectful of his guard duty, that he heard nothing of the faint footsteps on the soft ground, and when the hand on the end of a bare, brown arm grabbed him by the hair from behind, and the other came round his neck and slit his throat from ear to ear with a long-bladed knife that closely resembled the one he had used on the two females so long ago, he almost welcomed it.

When two hours to the minute had passed since they got to the farm, Valin called Newman out from the barn and sent him to relieve Messelier.

The former para jogged off and vanished into the undergrowth. Five minutes later he came through on the radio to Valin. 'Colonel, Newman,' he said. 'Receiving? Over.'

'Newman, Valin. I thought I ordered radio silence. Over.'

'You'd better get up here, Colonel, right now. Over and out.'

'Shit,' said Valin. 'What now?' He picked up his carry weapon and went to find O'Rourke.

Together they headed towards the spot where Newman had vanished, and pushed into the bushes. They heard Newman's whistle as they pushed further into the jungle, then came out to where he was waiting. From a branch of the tree immediately in front of him, Messelier's body dangled on a length of thick wire. The slash in his throat resembled a red-lipped grin, and his uniform had been split open at the crutch and his genitalia cut off and stuffed into his mouth.

27

They left the Frenchman where he was hanging and faded back into the jungle. 'Who the hell got him?' said O'Rourke. 'I thought he was an expert.'

'The only experts in these jungles are the natives,' said Valin. 'I don't think this was soldiers' work.'

'Who then?'

'Bandits,' said Valin. 'Let's get back quick.'

From the direction of the farmhouse they heard the first crackle of gunfire.

'Shit,' said Valin. 'Go, go, go. At the double.'

It was not clear how long the bandits had been watching the farmhouse, or if they had been sent on their mission by some outside agency. Or whether, simply, they were in the wrong place at the wrong time. But what was clear was that there were more than half a dozen of them: small, brown men dressed in rags, all carrying various derivatives of the Kalashnikov AK47, side-arms, swords, knives, bows and arrows, and crossbows, and all determined to kill everyone in their path.

The first volley of bullets slammed into the barn and house, and Keller, who was asleep on two bales of hay, woke with a start, grabbed his G3 and dived towards the door, yelling orders as he went. He didn't know what the hell was going on, but whatever it was, it was trouble.

Spenser, who was still in the tree house with Carmen, came bolt upright as the firing started. They were both naked and he cursed as he struggled into his clothes in the confined and uncomfortable space. 'Christ,' he said. 'What's happening?'

'I don't know,' said Carmen, also pulling on her clothes.

'You stay here,' Spenser ordered, slipping his Star .45 from its holster. 'I'm going to see what's happening.'

'I'll come with you.'

'*No*. You stay right where you are.'

The American dived down the ladder and peered round the side of the tree. What he saw was Keller appearing at the door of the barn, spraying the bandits with shells from his automatic rifle, and the farmhouse door opening, and Carlos appearing in the threshold holding a pistol, only to be cut down by a hail of bullets from among the trees.

For a confused moment the bandits looked like Vietcong to Spenser, and once again he was back in 'Nam, until he pulled himself together, steadied his handgun, and popped off half a magazine in their direction.

One of the bandits threw up his arms and fell face forwards on to the ground, and two more immediately turned their guns in Spenser's direction and bullets ripped up the earth around him and slammed into the tree trunk where he was sheltering.

Shit, he thought. I wish I'd got the Gatling.

Jesús appeared at the doorway of the farmhouse and dragged Carlos back inside, then knelt and fired one of the Heckler and Kochs that Valin had given to the women, and another of the bandits hit the dirt, just as Valin, O'Rourke and Newman came out of the jungle a hundred yards or so to their right and added their fire to that coming from the farm.

The bandits turned their fire on the newcomers, who dived to the ground and rolled behind what cover they could find, still shooting. Another of the bandits was hit and he lay where he had fallen, and Spenser could hear his screams from where he was taking cover.

He hated that. It was always one of the worst memories he had of the war: lying in cover, listening to a fallen comrade or enemy screaming for help. Sometimes the sound went on for hours, or what seemed like hours, until the wounded man lost consciousness or died.

Spenser tried to reckon the distance from where he was to the barn. He reckoned about five hundred yards. He wanted to get hold of his sweet little rock 'n' roller, and as the bandits were occupied with Valin's trio, he kicked away from where he was kneeling and zigzagged towards the barn and his gun. One of the bandits spotted his run and turned his gun in Spenser's direction. The American saw the bullets stitching a line across the ground towards him and threw himself down and felt earth patter across his back. Just as quickly he was up and running again, as the bandit ran out of ammunition and had to change the magazine in his Kalashnikov. Spenser put on a spurt, and saw Keller, Resnick and Angel pumping out covering fire. Then suddenly he was between the corner of the barn and the enemy, and threw himself inside and fell against the wall, panting hard.

'Enjoy the exercise?' said Angel conversationally.

'Fuck you.'

'Nice to see you too, Chris. Where's the little woman?'

'Halfway up a tree if she knows what's good for her,' said Spenser, as, still breathless, he hurried to the back of the three-tonner and retrieved his Gatling.

'This'll do for those fuckers,' he said grimly. 'Who the fuck are they anyhow?'

'Fuck knows,' said Angel. 'They look like a bunch of Crips looking to do some gangbanging, from the state of the threads they're wearing.'

'You wanna feed me?' said Spenser.

'Always a pleasure,' said Angel, and he connected the ammunition belt to the feed of the Gatling.

'Run with me, Angel,' shouted Spenser, and the two of them dashed through the open door and Spenser started to fire towards the bandits' cover. His shells smashed into the trees and undergrowth, cutting a huge swath of destruction through the lush greenery. Branches flew from trees, and others were chopped to the ground completely, as his bullets ripped into the jungle.

Two more of the bandits went down in the onslaught, and Angel screamed above the hammering of the weapon: 'Way to go.'

Keller, Resnick, Jesús, Valin, Newman and O'Rourke added their fire-power to the onslaught and the remaining handful of bandits were mowed down. All except one, who, when his AK47 jammed, threw it to the ground, drew a curved machete from his belt and made a kamikaze charge towards Valin's group. They poured fire at his diminutive form, and saw the shots chopping lumps out of his body. But still he came. The hail of fire they were pumping at him was relentless, but still he wouldn't fall, until finally, with the last of his strength, from ten or fifteen yards in front of their position, he hurled the evil-looking blade he was holding. Its surface caught the sun as it flew through the air, and as it left his hand the bandit himself pitched forward and skidded along the ground face down. The machete struck the side of Newman's neck, and he toppled backwards, dropping his Ithaca and clutching at the obscenity sticking out of him.

28

In the silence that followed the fire-fight, the birds that had risen from the jungle at the sound of gunfire began to settle back into the trees.

Valin dropped his M16, and went to Newman, but it was too late. The ex-para had torn the blade from his neck, but he was drowning in his own blood as the terrible sucking wound took its toll.

Valin clamped his hand over Newman's windpipe, but he knew he was wasting his time, and the man died as he knelt over him.

'Shit,' he said, and wiped his bloody hand on Newman's tunic.

O'Rourke picked up the dead man's shotgun and went over to the fallen body of the bandit who had thrown the machete and fired a round into his head.

'He's dead too. Must be,' said Valin.

'Not dead enough,' said O'Rourke, and fired again and watched the bandit's lifeless body kick as the shot smashed into him.

'Come on, Mark,' said Valin. 'Let's go and see what's happened down there.'

Together they walked back towards the farmhouse.

Carlos was dead from a bullet to the heart. There seemed to be no end to the tragedy that was striking the Delgado family that day. Valin told the rest what had happened to the Frenchman. 'We'd better bury our people,' he said.

'I need a priest,' said Jesús.

'No priest, Jesús. Sorry,' said Valin. 'We bury our dead, leave those bastards out there to the carrion, and get out of here.'

'No,' said Jesús firmly.

'I'm sorry,' said O'Rourke. 'But what Colonel Valin says, goes.'

'Spenser, Resnick, burial detail. Angel, Keller, O'Rourke, let's go and collect Messelier and Newman,' said Valin.

'I will dig my family's graves myself,' said the Colombian.

'As you wish,' said Valin. And with that, they set about their grisly tasks.

It was almost noon before the work was done. Everyone lent a hand with the work, even García. Carmen and Sofía prepared food for the men, as Valin watched the road and the skies for the enemy that he knew could come from anywhere, any time.

The day was hot, and as he watched the men under his command sweating as they toiled, it reminded him of other times when he had seen graves being dug. The graves of Argentinians in the Falklands, where the earth was cold, and the merciless wind blew from Antarctica; graves in the Gulf for the civilian victims of that insane regime; and graves in Britain to bury the soldiers killed in Northern Ireland. He touched the scar on his face. It was a constant reminder of his days in the service of his country before he had been cast aside like an old shoe when the powers that be considered him of no further use.

It was almost as if it were yesterday. Belfast. Christmas, three years earlier. A convoy was heading towards the barracks where Valin's regiment was billeted. In the lead was an armoured Land Rover with bulletproof glass and skirts to prevent hand-grenades being tossed underneath. Then came a dark-blue Rover containing men from the RUC, followed by a ministerial Jaguar carrying Valin and the politician who was bringing seasonal greetings from the people comfortably ensconced on the mainland. Bringing up the rear was another Land Rover, bristling with guns.

As they passed a Republican estate, Valin remembered, the politician turned to him and said: 'It's not as bad as the people back home think it is over here. These houses are really quite respectable.' Just then the first Land Rover hit a land-mine against which even its skirts couldn't protect it, and the vehicle was heaved over on to its side, as the blue Rover swerved to avoid it.

'Get down, sir,' roared Valin, pushing the politician to the floor and drawing his Browning 9mm pistol, as the driver braked hard, and the firing from the ambush began.

The Jaguar was also fitted with bulletproof glass, but nothing could prevent the heavy-calibre bullets that were splintering the car. Valin fired at the muzzle flashes until his face took the force of a ricocheting slug that tore a long groove in his flesh and knocked him unconscious. One man in the lead Land Rover was killed and another two seriously wounded. The RUC officers were unhurt, as were the passengers in the second Land Rover. The minister sustained only minor cuts, as did the chauffeur of the Jaguar. Valin's were the most serious injuries and he was flown back to England. He missed his Christmas dinner, but O'Rourke, who had been on leave, managed to smuggle a bottle of brandy into his hospital room on New Year's Eve. Valin had never been back to Ireland since, and he wasn't sorry.

When the work was complete, Jesús brought a bible from the house and read the burial service in Spanish as the bodies of Maria, Carlotta, Carlos, Messelier and Newman were lowered into the ground.

The mercenaries stood bare-headed in the humid breeze that blew across from the jungle to the mountains, and Valin recited the Lord's Prayer before they began to fill in the graves.

When they were complete, and the rough crosses that Carmen and Sofía had fashioned from odd pieces of wood that they had found in the barn had been set up over the scars in the earth formed by the graves, Valin said: 'I think it's time we moved out.'

'To go where?' said Jesús.

'Anywhere that we can lie low until tonight. It's not far to the landing strip, is it?'

'An hour or so.'

'I don't want to draw attention to it until we have to,' said Valin. 'Any ideas?'

'There is a mountain road,' said Jesús. 'There are caves up there that no one knows about.'

'And you'll come with us?'

'What is there here for me now?' said the Colombian.

'To America?'

'The land of golden opportunity?'

'That's right.'

'And revenge on the man or men who double-crossed us.'

Valin smiled, and the scar on his face stood out. 'But of course.'

'If we make it.'

'We've made it so far.'

'But at what cost?'

'To you more than the rest of us.'

'So the revenge will be all the sweeter.'

Valin touched Jesús on the shoulder. 'Yes, my friend,' he said. 'All the sweeter.'

29

The phone lines in Washington were red-hot.

Bob 'Tank' Tankerton called General Avery in his office near the White House. 'They did it, General,' he said. 'Mission accomplished. I've heard that they razed the factory and most of Santa Ana to the ground.'

'Is this a secure line, Tank?'

'Certainly.'

'Good. Are they out?'

'That's all I know, General,' replied Tank. 'Nothing further. And I've heard nothing from Valin or any of his troops.'

'Any casualties?'

'I heard that the locals dragged some bodies through the town and hanged them from lampposts.'

'How many exactly? Alive or dead?'

'The reports are sketchy on that. But I should imagine they're dead by now.'

'Jesus.'

'Valin always knew that could happen. It goes with the territory.'

'Keep me informed of any further developments.'

'Of course, sir. You'll be the first to know.'

Next, Tankerton spoke to Karl Landers from the FBI, and told the same story.

'That's good news,' said Landers.

'Sure,' replied Tank.

'Worth the money.'

'Yeah.'

'*If* we don't have to pay the balance.'

'Meaning?'

'Meaning that if they don't come out, we're free and clear, and two-thirds of a million pounds better off.'

'Not a nice thought, Karl.'

'But a practical one.'

'I suppose. But then you don't know James Valin like I do. I'd stake my pension on him surviving.'

'I hope you never have to.'

'Nor you.'

'Keep in touch, Tank.'

'Count on it.'

Tankerton's final call was to CIA headquarters at Langley, Virginia, where he was put through to Jack Bernard.

'So they did it,' said Bernard, after listening to Tank. 'Frankly, I'm amazed.'

'I'm not.'

'You always were a fan, Tank.'

'And you never were.'

'Cor-rect.'

'Maybe you'll change your mind now.'

'Maybe. But it goes deeper than that. I always thought that goddam Limey went round with a broom handle stuck up his ass.'

'That's the way they do it in the British army.'

'Sure is.'

'Listen, Jack, I'll keep you up to speed on developments.'

'You do that little thing.'

Tank smiled as he put down the phone, sat back in his seat and remembered how he, Jack Bernard and Valin had met.

It had been in Saigon, in May 1970. Tank had been a captain in the Marines, Jack Bernard had been part of the CIA task force involved in the Air America scheme, flying into Cambodia. And First Lieutenant James Valin, as he was then, was one of the many British SAS personnel who were wearing American uniforms and fighting illegally in South-east Asia.

It wasn't only the British either. German and French soldiers fought side by side with the US troops, mainly on covert missions, while their countrymen sat at home, comforted by the knowledge that their governments were not involved in the costly action in Vietnam.

Like hell. They had all been young men then, pumped up at the promise of action. Who cared that the war was going to hell in a handcart? Who cared that, without the proper back-up of men and equipment, and Nixon doing his usual prevaricating in Congress, and the general public at home becoming even more anti-war with every day, there was no way they could win?

It was a paradise for a professional soldier. Guns to play with. And a bunch of gooks to use as target practice. A free-fire zone for every gung-ho maniac in the land.

It wasn't so much fun for the conscripts, but that was the way the ball bounced. Tough.

The three of them met for the first time at a morning briefing, then went to an off-limits bar that stank of cooked fish and stale sweat, and was packed with girls hawking their wares, drug dealers, currency speculators, souvenir salesmen, and every other kind of low life imaginable. The Rolling Stones were on the jukebox and the beer was cheap. Paradise.

'You're never going to win this war without the full backing of all sections of your government,' said Valin. 'And the opposition is growing. Your president has to put the full weight of his authority behind it, or you'll be sent home with your tail between your legs. The chances are you will anyway. You're fighting a fanatical opposition on their own territory. A territory alien to ninety-nine per cent of your personnel. The North Vietnamese regard it as a privilege to die for one inch of soil. Do your men feel the same?' The question went unanswered. 'Of course they don't,' the Englishman said. 'The same thing is going to happen to the British government in Northern Ireland if the past three years are anything to go by. Look at military history if you don't believe me. The only way to conquer anyone in their own country is complete destruction, or the fear of it, swiftly followed by economic integration. Look at Germany and Japan after the Second World War. The way you're going, you can't win. And it won't be long before you find that out. A matter of a year or two at most.'

'Then we will lose,' said Tank, 'if we're relying on Nixon. The guy's an asshole.'

'Don't talk about the president like that,' said Bernard pompously. Even at twenty-two he'd been a bumptious conservative. 'Especially not in uniform. And you know we shouldn't be in this place. It's dangerous. The VC infiltrate.'

'Just like the base,' said Tank.

Valin grinned, and ordered more beers.

'That's the kind of talk that *will* lose us the war,' Bernard admonished his fellow countryman.

'No. What you're doing in Cambodia will lose the war,' said Valin decisively.

'Not so loud,' said Bernard looking round. 'That's classified.'

'Then how come every hustler in town knows about it?' asked Tank.

'People like you blabbing their mouths off in bars,' said Bernard. 'That's how.'

Tank and Valin looked at each other and pulled faces.

It was one o'clock, and stiflingly hot. Both Tank's and Valin's tropical uniforms were sodden rags, as was Bernard's summer-weight suit, and the fan that turned lazily above their heads did little but move the humid air around the place.

Sgt. Pepper was now on the hi-fi, and Tank hummed along, and ordered more iced beer.

The afternoon wore on, and they continued arguing about the rights and wrongs of the US involvement in the war. Tank knew that Bernard was mentally noting everything that he and Valin said, for future reference, but the more beer he drank, the less he cared. Around two-thirty everyone in the bar heard the buzz of a small motorcycle, and the screech of tyres as it pulled up outside. Suddenly, a fragmentation grenade was lobbed through the hole that acted as a window, hit the back wall, and dropped, to bounce along the stained surface of the bar and come to rest in front of the three of them.

The place began to empty in a second, women screaming and everyone scrambling to get out.

Jack Bernard dived under a table, and Tank and Valin just looked at each other, before Valin calmly picked up the grenade. 'It's amazing how often amateurs forget to take out the pin,' he said in a conversational tone, as he reached over the bar and appropriated a bottle of rice wine. 'I think we deserve this for being so brave,' he said, and removed the cork with his teeth and took a slug, before passing it to Tank, who did the same.

Valin looked around the room for their CIA comrade. 'Hey, Jack,' he called. 'Fancy a snort?'

Bernard had never forgiven Valin for that. Or for being right about the outcome of the war. Or Tank, for that matter.

But the Americans had been forced to work together occasionally since they returned to the USA and Tank had joined the DEA, and they maintained an uneasy truce.

It still made Tank laugh to think of the look on Bernard's face as he crawled out from under the table, and how, when Valin had tossed him the grenade, Bernard had flinched, even though it was safe.

As soon as Tank put down the phone after one of his calls, the person at the other end dialled a number in Leavenworth, Kansas, and was put through to someone who owed him more than one favour.

'Everything copacetic?' he asked.

'As far as we know.'

'Let me know if it isn't.'

'Sure will.'

30

The troops abandoned the bullet-scarred VW Microbus, and took only the ancient jeep and the Ford three-tonner. O'Rourke drove the former, with Keller and Jesús as passengers. The two Delgado daughters, García and the rest of the troops travelled in the truck, Angel driving, Valin riding shotgun, and the rest in the back. All weapons had been checked and Resnick carried his last knapsack full of explosives.

The two vehicles drove up the narrow track through the dense jungle with all personnel ready for trouble, but none was in evidence. They turned in a westerly direction and soon the road started to rise. The jungle receded as the foothills became mountains, and the road narrowed and began to corkscrew. The air thinned, the temperature dropped and the views over the countryside became ever more spectacular the higher they climbed.

They saw little traffic for the first hour, apart from the occasional donkey cart, farm vehicle or pedestrian, until, as they crossed another mountain pass, two black Buick sedans with silver insignia on the doors, blue-and-red panniers mounted on the roofs, and long whip aerials at the back, sped past them in the opposite direction, headlights blazing in the afternoon sunlight.

'Shit,' said Angel as the cars sped past. 'Cops.'

In the jeep in front O'Rourke looked over his shoulder at Jesús.

'State Police,' said the Colombian. 'Bastards.'

The two police cars took the next bend and screeched to a halt with a stink of rubber. There was a brief radio conversation between the cars and then they both made hasty three-point turns on the narrow road before setting off in pursuit of the small convoy of mercenaries.

Angel, in the cab of the truck, and Spenser, who was watching from the back, were the first to see the lead police car coming up behind them. Angel glanced in his mirror and said: 'Trouble, Colonel. The fuzz are behind us.' Spenser shouted at Resnick to tell Valin through the window that divided front and rear of the Ford that trouble was looming.

'Affirmative,' said Valin, who had seen them already.

Angel blasted the horn and flashed his headlights at the jeep in front, and accelerated the cumbersome three-tonner as much as he could on the steep and twisting climb, and O'Rourke responded by putting his foot down in the jeep, to get as much power to the four drive wheels as he could.

But both the jeep and the truck were old, and their engines, although well maintained and tuned, were tired. By contrast, the police Buicks were almost new, both with turbo-charged, five-litre V8 lumps, and were coming up fast.

Spenser and Carmen loaded the Gatling and steadied it on the tailgate of the truck.

'Blow them away,' growled Resnick, and Spenser opened fire. The heavy slugs tore lumps out of the road, stitched a line up to the oncoming bumper of the first

Buick, ripped through the radiator, destroyed the block, imploded the windscreen, and killed both driver and passenger. The heavy sedan swerved, hit the low retaining wall at the side of the road, somersaulted, and flew into space, to tumble down the mountainside and explode in flames. 'Easy,' said Spenser, and winked at Carmen.

The second Buick dropped right back. Valin, squinting in his wing mirror, was in no doubt that frantic radio messages were flying across the airwaves to police headquarters.

'We're in trouble,' he said to Angel. 'We've got to disable that other car. They can follow us for ever, out of range of our guns, and let their pals know exactly where we are.'

'We'll just have to fuck 'em, then,' replied his companion.

'Very succinctly put.'

'Count on me, boss.'

'So how do we do it?'

'Radio through to the jeep. Get them to pull ahead fast. I'll slow down. That guy behind us isn't going to get too close, in case the same thing happens to him as to his buddies. When the jeep comes to a turn-off, it pulls off the highway. Then, when the cops have gone past, it pulls out behind them, and we've got the sons of bitches bottled up. I slow down, the jeep speeds up, I block the way forward, O'Rourke blocks the way back, and we catch them in the crossfire.'

'Good idea, Angel,' said Valin. 'As long as the police don't pick up our call. Or if they do, they don't speak English.'

'Nothing's infallible, Colonel.'

Valin smiled grimly, reached for his radio and called

Keller in the jeep. He explained the plan and the German raised his right arm and leant forward and shouted in O'Rourke's ear. The lieutenant lifted his hand off the wheel and when he did, Angel allowed the three-tonner to slow slightly, and the jeep pulled away.

Angel saw the Buick drop back as the truck's speed decreased, and he made a circle with his thumb and forefinger to Valin. 'Got the suckers, Colonel,' he said. 'The guy who's driving that cop car would last no time in East LA. It's the oldest trick in the book. Bookend the cops and shoot shit out of 'em.'

'Nice friends you've got, Angel.'

'I get around. East Coast, West Coast. You know how it goes.'

'One step in front of the law.'

'That's what shoes are for, boss.' And Angel laughed, keeping one eye on the mirror.

Up at the front, O'Rourke kept the pedal to the metal until Jesús, whom Keller had filled in on the plan, leant forward and shouted: 'Two hundred metres ahead on your right. Mining road.'

O'Rourke put the jeep into a four-wheel skid that sent dust and pebbles flying as he expertly steered the jeep into a narrow lane that was hardly more than a ditch leading to an abandoned mineshaft.

O'Rourke drove the jeep round a slight bend and slammed on the brakes. 'Sergeant, check the progress of the police,' he shouted, and Keller hopped out of the jeep and ran back down the track, taking advantage of all possible cover until he could get a clear sight of the road without being seen himself.

First the three-tonner went past, and then a minute or so later, the Buick with four officers aboard.

Keller sprinted back to the others, gave a thumbs-up and O'Rourke turned the jeep round, and after the German had got into the back, they returned to the main road in pursuit of the police car.

'What a surprise they're going to get,' Keller shouted to O'Rourke.

'Not as big a surprise as we'll get if another carload come up behind us,' O'Rourke shouted into the slip-stream. 'You look out the back.'

And as Keller complied, the lieutenant radioed ahead to inform Valin that the police car was boxed in.

Valin and Angel heard the message and looked at each other in triumph, then the colonel relayed the news through to the well of the lorry, and Spenser prepared to fire again.

'Slow right down, Angel,' said the colonel. 'Let O'Rourke and the rest catch up.'

Angel did as his commander ordered, and gave the labouring engine a respite.

Behind them the Buick slowed too, until O'Rourke saw its red tail lights ahead of him.

'Got 'em, boss,' he said into his radio.

'Stop,' yelled Valin, and Angel slewed the big truck across the road. Spenser, Carmen, Resnick and Sofía dropped down from the tailgate and fanned out, as Valin and Angel joined them, guns at the ready, and García threw himself down behind the first cover he could find.

The police driver saw what was happening, slammed on his brakes and threw the Buick into reverse, just as O'Rourke turned the bend behind him and pulled the jeep into the side of the road and his two passengers tumbled out.

Spenser was crouched behind the retaining wall and opened fire as the Buick's four doors flew open, and the officers inside scrambled for cover. Spenser's burst hit the car broadside and both tyres went down and flames licked from the engine compartment. Then he turned the Gatling on the four policemen, backed up by fire from the rest of his party, and crossfire from the three guns in the jeep. The first of the policemen threw up his arms and fell heavily as the heavy-calibre bullets cut him off at the knees. The second walked into a volley from Keller, O'Rourke and Jesús that left him bleeding his last on to the cracked tarmac. The third and fourth were more fortunate, and reached cover on the hillside, from where they returned fire.

Valin was just about to radio O'Rourke to bring up the jeep, when the Buick exploded, bouncing sideways and sending out a sheet of flame that sealed off the highway.

'I hope to Christ they can get the jeep past,' Valin said to Angel, who was crouching next to him, as bullets zipped past their ears. 'The road's very narrow there. I don't want to stick around here for a moment longer than necessary.'

'They'll have to come in the truck if they can't,' replied Angel. 'Are you going to call them up? We can keep those two pinned down with covering fire while they make it.'

'Yes,' said Valin. 'But thanks, Angel. I might never have come up with that on my own.'

'Sorry, boss,' said Angel. 'It was just a thought.'

'Don't apologize. It was a good one. If we get out of this alive I'm going to make you up to sergeant, if you're interested,' said Valin, keying the radio to reach O'Rourke.

It was decided that the lieutenant would attempt to drive the jeep up to the truck under the cover of fire from Valin's group. And if he couldn't get it past the burning Buick, to abandon it, and leg it up to the truck. Valin was worried about having to rely on only one vehicle. He was well aware that if they came under attack from another helicopter, having just one target made it easier for the opposition to kill and injure the maximum amount of troops in one go. And as for mechanical failure, he dared not think about the consequences. The truck had as many holes in it as a tea-strainer, from their previous engagements, and it was a miracle that nothing vital had been hit so far.

'Right, people,' said Valin. 'Now!' He took aim and fired a short burst at the rocks where he had seen one of the policemen take cover. The rock exploded into chips, and the other members of the squad with weapons opened fire too. García, who refused to fight, hid behind the low wall with his arms over his head, and wished, not for the first time, that the young British lieutenant was still acting as his personal bodyguard.

At the first crackle of gunfire, O'Rourke, who had already fallen back to the jeep, started the engine, slammed it into gear and took off up the hill. He skidded to a halt, to allow Keller and Jesús to dive on board, before he accelerated away with a screech of tyres and made for the Buick, which by then was burning less fiercely. At that point, the level area on the side of the mountain was so narrow that the road on the right-hand side was only separated from thin air and a thousand-foot drop by the retaining wall. Further on, where the truck had stopped, there was a slope behind the wall before the cliff ended, where Valin's people had taken cover.

The jeep's nearside wing rammed into the Buick's back bumper and pushed it slightly out of the way, but the police car was too heavy and the jeep bounced back, its offside front wheel demolishing the crumbling wall, and lifted off the ground as O'Rourke frantically spun the wheel anti-clockwise. The vehicle lurched, and Valin and the rest of the squad held their collective breath as the jeep teetered towards disaster.

Flames licked at one side of it, as the other began to tilt away, until suddenly the front wheel hit rock again and the tyre found purchase. The engine screamed as O'Rourke upped the revs and the jeep leapt forward, only to be caught by a burst from an automatic weapon held by one of the policemen.

Keller took bullets in both legs and his groin, and Valin's soldiers poured fire on to the mountain again, forcing the policeman to duck back into his hidey-hole. O'Rourke pulled up in front of the truck, stopped and helped Jesús attend to the German.

Valin, his men, and the Delgado girls, with Sofía dragging García, made a run back to the truck, Spenser halting in the middle of the road to empty his cartridge belt at the mountainside to give his friends covering fire.

Angel and Valin dived for the cab, and the rest leapt into the back. Angel fired up the engine, and gesticulated to Spenser to get on board, which he did. The young American gave a blast on his horn, and O'Rourke left Keller to the ministrations of Jesús, jammed the jeep into gear and sped off, closely followed by the truck and twin bursts of fire from the two policemen on the mountain.

31

A quarter of a mile down the road, round another bend and well out of range, O'Rourke stopped the jeep for another look at Keller's wounds. He was a mess. It looked like some of the bullets had ricocheted off the metal of the jeep, judging from the jagged holes they had ripped in the flesh on entry, and others at the exit points. All were leaking blood, and the sergeant's face was white with shock and pain.

'This is not good,' Jesús told the lieutenant as he finished tying tourniquets, which he had made from the sleeves of his jacket, around Keller's upper thighs to try to slow the loss of blood. 'I can't do a thing for those,' he said, pointing at the wounds to Keller's groin. 'He needs a doctor.'

Valin jumped down from the truck and ran to the jeep. 'How is he?' he demanded.

'I'm OK,' the German said through clenched teeth.

'No, he's not,' said O'Rourke. 'He needs urgent medical attention.'

'What, here?' said Valin, looking round. 'In the back of beyond? Not to mention that he's one of the most wanted men in the country right now. What do you suggest? That we drop him off at casualty, and leave him to the gentle care of the nearest hospital? This is not the Edgware Road on a Saturday night.'

'No, sir,' said O'Rourke stiffly. 'I suggest that we try and save his life.'

'Sorry, Mark,' said Valin. 'Point taken. You're right, of course. Where *is* the nearest hospital, Jesús?'

'Bogotá. We'd never get within a hundred kilometres of it.'

'A doctor?'

'There is a village about thirty kilometres away. There is a doctor there. But there is a military post too.'

'So we take out the military post, then get the medic to look at Keller.'

'But . . . '

'No buts, Jesús. This is one of my men. I won't have him bleed to death on the side of a mountain in Colombia. We go to the village and get him looked at. Now mount up. Jesús, you show Mark the way. And be careful. We don't know who those police alerted that we were in the area.'

Valin ran back to the truck and O'Rourke, with Jesús directing him, led the way to the village.

About a mile before they reached the outskirts, at an empty crossroads, Jesús asked O'Rourke to stop the jeep. Keller was lying in the back, his face contorted with pain, and blood was dripping from his trouser legs and forming a puddle on the floor. The Colombian got out of the leading vehicle and went back to the truck.

'The military post is on this side of the village,' he explained to Valin and the rest. 'It is nothing much. Just a blockhouse and a small barracks for maybe four or five men.'

'Right,' said Valin. 'Jesús, get back to the jeep and get Mark to pull into the side road and out of sight. We'll follow.'

Jesús went back to the jeep and O'Rourke steered it off the main road and behind a ruined cottage that was the first sign of civilization they had seen for miles. Angel drove the truck after him, and everyone gathered together for a final briefing.

'The jeep and Keller stay here,' said Valin. 'Sofía, if you will, I want you to stay with him. And you, García.'

Jesús explained to the chemist what the colonel had said, and the prisoner nodded.

'The rest of us go into the village and disable the guard post,' Valin continued. 'Then we get the doctor and come back.' He addressed Sofía again: 'If anything goes wrong and we don't return, do what you can for Keller, García and yourself. I know it will be difficult, but whatever you do, don't follow us. Take the jeep as far away as possible and try and help the sergeant. We should be OK, but if it goes all wrong at least there's a chance that the three of you can get away.'

Sofía nodded. 'I understand,' she said. 'I wish you the best of luck.' She kissed her father and sister and embraced them fiercely.

García raised his hand and saluted Carmen and the men. '*Hasta la vista*,' he said. '*Vayan con Dios, compadres*.' Then he and Sofía went to the jeep, where the girl sat in the back next to Keller and held his hand, and García sat behind the steering wheel.

The rest went back to the truck, but before they got on board, Valin asked: 'What's the ammunition situation?'

'Not too good,' said Spenser, and the others grunted in agreement. 'We didn't expect this kind of opposition, did we?'

Valin shook his head. 'So be sparing, people,' he urged them.

'Yeah,' agreed Angel. 'We don't want to come up against any of these guys with just our dicks in our hands.' He nodded at Carmen. 'Begging your pardon, ma'am. Not that you'd have that kind of a problem.'

Carmen smiled back at him. 'I think I get the picture,' she said.

'Saddle up, then,' said Valin. 'Back into the breach. Jesús, you come up front with us, and show us the lie of the land.'

Once in the truck, the Colombian explained that the military post straddled the main road into the village. It was a deterrent to the kind of bandits that they had met at his farm earlier, and who roamed the bleak mountainside, looking for prey.

The truck nosed along the road until the post came into sight. As Jesús had said, it controlled the main thoroughfare of the hamlet, which drowsed lazily in the afternoon sun. Angel pulled up to the barrier that blocked the road and a National Guardsman, uniform jacket mis-buttoned, came out of the hut yawning, and carrying a Thompson sub-machine-gun.

Angel unholstered his side-arm as the guard approached the driver's side and spoke to him in Spanish.

'*No comprendo*,' answered Angel, then poked the pistol over the edge of the window and shot the man in the face, as Valin slipped out of the passenger door, closely followed by Jesús, and the rest of the squad dived out from under the canvas at the back of the truck.

At the sound of the shot, another soldier poked his head out of the hut, only to collect a burst of bullets from Valin's M16. The troops rushed the guardhouse and the barracks beyond, meeting little resistance. Two of the soldiers were enjoying a siesta, and the third raised his hands in surrender as they burst into the guardhouse.

'Ask him if there's any more around,' Valin said to Jesús.

The Colombian did, and the soldier shook his head.

'OK,' said Valin. 'Tie them up, and let's go and find this medic. And listen, see if there's an ammunition store with anything useful.'

32

After the task of securing the soldiers had been completed, and the ammunition store had been plundered for as much ordnance as Valin's team could use, they went in search of the doctor.

His house was behind the main street of the village, if indeed such a title could be bestowed on the tiny, dry and dusty thoroughfare that they found when they pushed on. The shooting from the guard post seemed to have caused little excitement in the small collection of dwellings, and Angel followed Jesús's directions without seeing another human being.

'Some burg,' he said. 'The Las Vegas of Colombia. A one-horse town, and the horse died.'

'Shut up, Angel,' said Valin. 'Just drive.'

''K, Colonel,' said the American. 'Just making a comment.'

'The people will have been frightened by the gunfire,' said Jesús. 'It is not advisable to be too inquisitive in these circumstances. They are probably hiding beneath their beds with their hands over their ears.'

'Let's hope they stay that way,' said Valin.

On Jesús's instructions, Angel stopped the truck outside a tiny brick-built house with a tarnished brass nameplate screwed to the wall, and Jesús and Valin jumped down.

They stepped on to the porch and Valin hammered on the door. After a moment he hammered again, until it was opened by a wizened old woman in a long, black dress and a white apron.

'*Médico,*' he demanded. '*Llame al médico.*'

The frightened woman ran back into the house and within thirty seconds a distinguished-looking elderly man in a black suit, white shirt and black tie came to the door.

Jesús told him in Spanish that a man with bullet wounds in his legs was needing assistance on the edge of town.

The doctor looked at him and shrugged, and then they rattled away at each other in their native tongue.

'He does not want to come, Colonel,' said Jesús.

'You amaze me. Tell him he has no choice.'

'He says that he has retired from medical practice.'

'Tell him he just got back into it.'

Jesús rattled another half-a-dozen sentences.

'He says no, Colonel.'

Valin took the Smith & Wesson auto from its holster on his lap and stuck it into the doctor's midriff. 'Tell him we'll go with him to get the necessary bandages and medication,' he said. 'Or he'll be treating himself.'

When Jesús had spoken again, the doctor shrugged once more, and the three men went into the house, to reappear a few minutes later, the doctor now wearing a dark overcoat and carrying an ancient medical bag.

All three squeezed into the cab, and Angel drove to the next corner, then back to the main street and headed out of town past the disabled military post. Within a few minutes they got back to the jeep.

Keller was delirious, and Sofía was supporting his head on her lap, while García stood by helplessly. 'Thank goodness you've come,' the young woman said to the doctor in Spanish. 'He's getting worse.'

The doctor looked at the state of Keller's wounds, shook his head and opened his bag, but Valin stopped him. 'We're not staying here,' he said. 'It's too risky. You were saying something about some caves, Jesús.'

'Yes. There are a number about fifteen minutes' drive from here in that direction.' He pointed down the road that cut across the highway they had travelled in on.

'Let's go then,' said Valin. 'The doctor can look at him there. Another few minutes won't make much difference.'

Jesús told the doctor what Valin had said, as O'Rourke got back behind the wheel of the jeep and started the engine, and then climbed into the front passenger seat. The doctor got in the back with Keller and Sofía, and gave the German a painkilling injection as they drove.

The mountain reared up again in front of them, and Jesús pointed to a track that led off the road they were following. 'Down there,' he said to O'Rourke. 'Just a few more minutes.'

Before long they came to a towering cliff punctuated at ground level and above by a number of large holes. 'In there,' said Jesús, pointing to one of the openings. 'The cave runs under the mountain like a natural tunnel. We can pass right through, and the airstrip is only a short drive from the other side.

'Sounds good to me,' said O'Rourke, and, flicking on his lights, steered the jeep into the darkness. Angel followed slowly in the three-tonner. The jeep's yellow beams showed a large, domed cave, and O'Rourke stopped the vehicle on the smooth rock floor.

The doctor rattled off something in Spanish to Jesús, who shouted for Angel to bring the truck round so that his headlights would give the doctor some illumination to work in. As soon as he was satisfied, the doctor ripped the unconscious Keller's trousers off and examined the wounds more closely, all the time talking to Jesús.

'He's very bad,' Jesús relayed to the group, while the doctor began to dress the wound. 'Bones have been shattered, and he's lost a lot of blood.'

'Resnick,' said Valin, 'go and keep an eye on the entrance. I want to know if anything's going on out there.'

'Colonel,' said the Russian, and jogged towards the light-filled entrance to the cave.

The doctor finished bandaging Keller's legs and groin and stood back to survey his handiwork.

'That is all I can do,' he said in Spanish. 'Maybe he will live. Maybe not. He is in God's hands. Now may I go home?'

Valin understood what he was saying and shook his head. 'I'm sorry,' he said in the same language. 'But you will stay here until we leave. My man needs care, and you will give it to him.'

The doctor let forth a torrent of words that was too fast for Valin's limited understanding of Spanish, but he got the drift and grinned. 'Tell him to shut up, Jesús, or we'll have to gag him.'

As Jesús gently explained what Valin had said, and the doctor scowled angrily, Valin had a word with

O'Rourke, then went to join the rest of his troops. 'We stay here until tomorrow morning, then set off for the airstrip,' he said. 'Apparently we go straight through this mountain, then head downwards.'

'Sounds OK to me, Colonel,' said Angel. 'I can't wait to get back home.'

'Me neither,' said Spenser.

'Soon,' said Valin. 'Very soon, I promise. And then we can have a gentle word with the person who spoiled what could have been a very clean exercise.'

'And collect our cash,' said Angel.

'That too,' agreed Valin. 'That too.'

Back in the USA, the man who had betrayed Valin's men was making another call to Leavenworth. 'Any news yet?' he asked.

'The plane has returned to Panama, empty. My men have stayed down in Colombia. The pilot will return tomorrow under escort.'

'What *is* happening down there?'

'The remains of the strike force escaped from Santa Ana, then shot down a Colombian air force chopper. A Jolly Green Giant.'

'They have the luck of the devil.'

'Their luck will run out tomorrow, if not before.'

'I hope so.'

'Count on it.'

'No, you. I will be very angry if you fail.'

Then the line went dead.

33

The afternoon dragged into evening, and the party ate a desultory meal of the remains of their rations, leaving only enough for a snack before their departure.

Spenser, sitting next to Carmen in the chilled air of the cave, gave her his jacket to wear. She looked hard and long at him before she spoke. 'Did you mean what you said before?' she asked.

'Of course.'

'Then it seems we have very little choice. I have to come out with you.'

'Collectively? Or me personally?'

'I don't understand.'

'Come out as part of the team, or as a couple.'

'You know very well.'

'Good.'

He leaned over and kissed her, and for the first time in years offered up a prayer. A prayer that it would happen, and nothing else would go wrong.

Sofía continued nursing Keller, who was drenched in sweat and moaning softly. In his delirium he was back in post-war East Berlin, a child of the Nazis and forced to scavenge for food for his mother on the bomb-sites that covered the city like the empty sockets in a toothless mouth.

Franz Keller's father had come back from Russia, a shadow of the proud SS officer who had gone off to destroy Stalin's armies. He sired his only son before dying of tuberculosis in the unheated flat that the small family occupied. Franz Keller had grown up fast. Before he was five he was scrounging supplies from the American servicemen who guarded the Brandenburg gate. He exchanged chewing gum, cigarettes and nylon stockings for black-market food and fuel for the paraffin heater that kept Frau Keller and her son alive during the bitter winters of his childhood.

His mother passed away when he was eleven and he was alone. It was the mid fifties, and while the free world held its collective breath for the economic boom that was to come, young Franz slept in deserted bunkers, discovered the remains that the rats had left of the bodies of his countrymen, fought with other children for the rotting remains of other people's refuse, and learnt to defend himself against the ghouls and monsters who roamed the city in search of human prey.

By the time the wall went up, he was in his teens, and just before the authorities clamped down on travel between the east and west he moved to free Berlin, where he joined a gang of black-marketeers as a runner. He was unusually strong, even after years of poor nutrition, and that, combined with his natural cunning and the ruthlessness he had learnt after years of fending for himself, soon brought him to the attention of his bosses and he moved fast up the ladder. He went all over the country, helping oversee the import of contraband. Especially at the seaports, where one evening in the Star Club in Hamburg, he befriended a young man from Liverpool who was a guitarist in one of the beat groups who played there. They ended up drunk and stoned, swapping a couple of prostitutes all night long, until eventually, hung over and suffering from their debauchery, they breakfasted together in a café down by the docks. Swearing eternal friendship, they parted, never to meet again. The musician was John Lennon, and Keller had never forgotten that night.

By the time he was twenty, Keller was a gun-toting bodyguard to one of the most powerful hoodlums in the gang. He had a flat in one of the smartest parts of the city, a Mercedes, women, clothes and, most important of all to the orphan from the east, more than enough to eat and drink.

As the sixties wound down, and the black market dwindled, a large-scale gang war broke out in West Berlin, as control of the city's burgeoning drug trade came up for grabs.

One night, Keller entered a smart restaurant with his boss, and one of the dozen working girls that the boss squired round the town and then took back to his flat and used for sexual gratification. The kind of sexual gratification that involved abuse and sodomy, where the woman was tied up with leather straps and beaten with a horse whip. Meanwhile Keller would sit in the next room, reading a magazine or watching TV, ignoring the screams from the bedroom.

To Keller it was routine. A night like a hundred others. He would sit at the next table to his boss and his whore, and listen to his boss boast of the week's achievements, and how much money he had made. He would watch him stuff his mouth with goose and potatoes, and run his greasy hands up the whore's legs until he reached her underwear, with no concern about who might be watching. Keller's boss was a pig. But a pig with a big trough. Big enough for Keller to get more than his fair share of the swill.

But that night was different. As they waited in the foyer to be shown to the best table in the place, three gunmen appeared in the doorway behind him. All three carried powerful automatic handguns, and opened fire. The woman took three shots to the abdomen and one to the neck. Keller's boss took eight bullets in all: two to the head, five to the body, and one in his right arm. Miraculously, Keller was left untouched, and he hardly had time to reach under his jacket and unholster the Colt Lightweight Commander .45 auto that he had liberated from an American serviceman late one night, before the gunmen were gone.

Pandemonium broke out in the restaurant. Twenty-one shots had been fired in all. One waiter had been killed by a bullet to the heart. Another had collected a spare slug in his buttock. A female diner was bleeding her last on to the deep-red carpet, which soaked up her blood and hardly showed a stain. One man, who was dining with a woman who wasn't his wife, choked to death on a piece of steak. And at a nearby table, the host at a dinner party for six was killed by a bullet that hit him in the liver before he had settled the bill, much to the disgust of his guests.

Keller's boss was dead before he hit the floor, and the woman died a few minutes later. Keller left before the police arrived. He had checked on the man in his charge, and he knew a dead body when he saw one.

Keller was in big trouble. His other bosses would want to know why he didn't return fire at the gunmen, and would brook no excuses. A couple of bullets in his own body might have mitigated his laxity. But probably not completely. Only his own death while saving his boss's life would have truly exonerated him. But he was unhurt, and he knew that people would soon be asking questions. Embarrassing questions like how much money had he taken to allow his charge to be gunned down. He probably wouldn't be allowed to live long enough to offer an explanation. It would be shoot first and ask questions later, when the news of the assassination got around.

There was only one answer. To get out – fast.

The limousine in which the three of them had arrived at the restaurant had vanished by the time he got outside, but anyway he would have ignored it. He took a taxi to his flat and was packed and gone within twenty minutes. He went straight to the airport, carrying the little money that he had stashed away there, and a passport in a fake name that he had bought months before in case of just such an eventuality as this. Life was cheap in West Berlin in the sixties, and Keller's motto had always been: 'Be Prepared'. He booked a one-way ticket on the first flight to Madrid, ditched his gun just as his flight was called, and no one had come looking for him. He didn't need the hassle of being caught trying to carry a weapon through the departure lounge or through customs at the other end, and he knew he could pick up a new weapon in Spain within a few days. The only problem was cash. He dared not touch his bank account. The gang had key bank employees in their pocket, and Keller knew it would only be a matter of days before his bosses would be after him if he made a withdrawal.

So he arrived in the Spanish capital with just the minimum of luggage and a few thousand marks in his pocket. He stole a car and drove to the coast, where he mingled with the few holiday-makers who were just discovering the Costa del Sol, and he robbed and burgled his way along the strip, until once again he could afford the best hotels and a hired Mercedes.

But luck was not with him. The Germans were also taking their holidays in Spain, and one evening when Keller was enjoying a quiet drink after dinner, he was recognized by one of his old gang. Keller recognized the man too, and left town without even checking out of his hotel. He drove along the coast, dumped his car, bought a one-way passage on a fast PT boat that was smuggling cigarettes, gold, medical supplies and guns both ways between Spain and Africa, and the next day found himself once again penniless, this time in Morocco. He headed south, picking up a car and money on the way, by the same means he had used in Spain, leaving a trail of dead and dying people behind him.

Eventually, when he got to newly independent Burundi, part of the Belgian Congo until 1962, he was captured by a marauding band of tribesmen, and only released when they fought and lost a pitched battle with a group of mercenaries who had been brought in by the president.

Keller was given the option of joining the group or

being summarily shot. Naturally he joined, and fought behind their leader, a former Scots Guards major, for the next five years. The major granted Keller the honorary title of sergeant, and taught him to handle weapons from all over the world.

The major was killed by a stray shot on the South African border in 1974 and Keller caught a boat to the USA, once again using forged papers. His visa stood up to scrutiny in New Orleans and he started a one-man crime wave that took him right across the country to California, where he worked in Hollywood as an armourer and stunt man.

But the German found life on the West Coast boring, and after a few years he drifted across the Midwest, picking up jobs where he could. Finally, he pushed on further, until he got to New York, where, on a whim, he took a boat to Europe, where he ended up one cold winter's night in London. That was how he met Colonel Valin and Mark O'Rourke, and the three had been together ever since.

As Keller lay in the back of the jeep in the dark and frigid air of a cave somewhere in Colombia, it was as if it were only yesterday, not years ago, that he had met the pair of them.

'Another brandy, Colonel?' he shouted, startling Sofía out of her half doze. 'And a pint for you, Lieutenant,' he called, as if across a busy bar.

'Shh,' she said, and stroked his forehead, which was pouring with sweat. 'Shh. Everything's going to be all right.'

Resnick, who had been relieved by Angel at the cave entrance, watched Sofía as she ministered to the sick man. And he watched Spenser and Carmen too.

Resnick was another loner who had not had a steady woman in his life for years. If we both get out of here alive, he thought as he gazed at the young woman, perhaps we could make it a double wedding.

Night fell fast again, and soon after it got dark, Angel found and spoke to Valin.

'There's a lot of noise and light back where we came from,' he said. 'I think there's choppers up with searchlights.'

'They could hardly ignore us killing those police and destroying their cars,' said Valin. 'And then taking out a guard post. If they get close, come and let me know.'

Angel touched the rim of his tin hat, and went back to his post. The sound of helicopter engines rose and fell, but he knew that they were safe unless the spotlights got closer.

Jesús and Valin sat together on a rock shelf, and the Colombian said that the next morning's drive should take no longer than an hour or so, and that they should leave about four-thirty.

'How are we off for fuel?' asked Valin.

'There's enough,' said Jesús. 'Both the truck and the jeep have extra fuel tanks.'

'And if we don't meet anyone on the ride home, we should be back in the USA in three or four days,' said Valin. 'There are three cars waiting in Panama, and three more in Mexico City, complete with our papers.'

'What about us?' asked Jesús. 'My girls, García and me? How are we going to get into the States?'

'I think you'll have to go in illegally. But don't

worry. We know some back roads. Some of the stuff we brought out wouldn't pass muster with the Border Patrol, so we had to cross by covert means.'

'So be it,' said Jesús philosophically.

'And then we get down to business. There's money to be collected, and I know that the rest of the men would agree that you deserve your fair share. You *and* your daughters.'

'Do you think money could replace what we've lost?'

'Of course not. But it will help you all to build a new life. And at least one of them seems ready to do it with one of my men.'

Jesús looked over at Carmen and Spenser, and shook his head. 'It's crazy,' he said. 'Women. What can you make of them?'

34

To the eleven people waiting in the cave, the night seemed to go on for ever. The moon hung in the corner of the sky, hardly moving as the temperature dropped like a stone.

Spenser and Carmen were together under his thin cotton jacket. He had fallen asleep; she could not. Her sense of loss was too great. Angel had been relieved and was snorting coke behind a rock at the back of the cave, while Valin took his turn on watch. Resnick was working on a timing device by the light of a pencil torch close to the jeep where Sofía was still sitting next to Keller, who had dropped off into a fitful sleep. O'Rourke was dozing in the back of the truck on the opposite bench to García, who was asleep. The doctor sat alone, still wearing his coat, and with his battered bag between his legs, while Jesús kept an eye on all of them, a cigarette cupped in one hand and a cocked Heckler and Koch in the other.

Carmen looked at her father's face by the glow of the cigarette each time he took a drag. His features could have been carved out of dark ivory. Poor man, she thought. What he's gone through today. What all of us have gone through. Silent tears began to run down her face as she thought of her mother, sister and brother, laid to rest in cold graves that she would probably never see again. She thought too of the two mercenaries, Newman and Messelier, who lay next to them, and the other four men they had left behind in Santa Ana.

She remembered her mother's work-roughened hands, with which she had gently cared for her as a child, and her brother's strong back as he'd helped with the meagre harvest that was their livelihood, and the way that Carlotta had been a friend as well as a sister, all her life, and her tears flowed harder. She moved closer to Spenser for comfort and warmth in what was turning out to be a cold, hard world.

Outside the cave, Valin looked back across towards the hamlet where they had kidnapped the doctor, and up towards the mountains where they had fought the pitched battle with the police. There was still light and noise from the choppers, but he was convinced they had no idea where his small band was hiding.

A bit of luck at last, he thought. If only it can hold.

As all nights must, eventually this one passed, and at a few minutes to four Jesús and Valin roused the rest of the group.

'Tell the doctor he can go now,' said Valin to Jesús. 'Tell him he'll have to walk. Give him my apologies, but I have no choice in the matter. I don't want him telling the authorities where we spent the night until we are long gone.'

Jesús did as he was told. Naturally, the doctor objected vehemently. But eventually he realized he had no choice, and he picked up his bag and left the cave. Before he went, O'Rourke gave him his torch.

'Don't want the old boy falling down and breaking his neck,' he said.

As he left, the doctor checked Keller, who was awake and in dreadful pain, for the last time, and his prognosis was not good. 'He will never walk again,' he told Valin. 'And there is a chance of gangrene. More than a chance.' He gave the German a final shot, and left pills for him, should the pain get any worse.

As soon as the doctor had walked out of the cave, Valin gave the order for the rest to mount up. Jesús, Sofía and Keller were in the jeep, with O'Rourke driving, and the rest got into the truck, with Valin and Angel in the cab as before. At four-twenty the drivers started their engines and set off through the tunnel. The journey was as easy as Jesús had predicted, and they came out on a mountain road just as their synchronized watches showed four forty-five.

35

The two vehicles began the hairpin descent towards the carpet of jungle below, which was black in the pre-dawn light, their beams cutting a yellow path in front of them.

'Won't be long now,' Valin said to Angel. 'Let's just hope those choppers have gone back to their base, or that they don't get inquisitive if they haven't.'

'Can't be soon enough for me,' said the American. 'Clean sheets and ice in the drinks.'

'Your idea of civilization?'

'Fucking A, Colonel.'

'So what are you doing here?'

'Civilization pales next to this kind of experience.'

'It's like a drug,' said Valin candidly. 'And you know all about that, don't you?'

Angel looked over at the colonel in the dim light from the dashboard. 'What do you mean?'

'You know very well. The little package you've been carrying around in your jacket since we blew up the factory.'

'Well, I'll be damned. You're smarter than I gave you credit for.'

'I just keep my eyes open. Do you intend to sell it when you get back to the States?'

'I know some people who might be interested.'

'I thought you might.'

'There's nothing wrong with making a profit. That's what we're all risking our lives to do here.'

'I could make you dump it,' said Valin.

'And I'd do it, sir. If you ordered me to.'

'What the hell?' said Valin. 'What difference will it make? It's a bad world.'

'Glad that you see it that way, Colonel,' said Angel, and put a cigarette in his mouth.

'But I might need you to do something special for me one day,' Valin went on. 'Are you ready for that?'

'Depends on what it is.'

Valin shook his head. 'No,' he said. 'Whatever it is. You do it without question. That's the only way it can be.'

The cab of the truck was silent except for the roar from the tired old engine.

'I dig, Colonel,' said Angel. 'Just say the word.'

'I will. Count on it,' replied Valin.

Angel slammed down a gear as the incline got steeper, and said nothing more.

The sky began to lighten in the east and with it the spirits of the party. Surely nothing much more can happen, they thought. If, the harder hearts added, the fucking plane turns up.

Meanwhile, back in the jungle beside the airstrip, the soldiers who were waiting had been awake for more than an hour, keeping watch for any sign of movement on the track leading to it.

'What do you say, sir?' one of them said to Number One.

'Who knows?' he replied. 'Maybe something *has* happened on the way here. Maybe they won't turn up at all. There's been a lot of traffic on the police and military radio channels. Our boys seem to be causing mayhem wherever they go. But we've not heard that they've been stopped. Not so far at least.'

'Or maybe they've called in at McDonald's for an Egg McMuffin,' said the soldier.

'Jesus,' said another 'I hope they get a take-out.'

'Me too,' said a third. 'What the hell do they put in these combat rations?'

'Nutrition for our nation's youth,' said Number One. Then he stopped, one hand raised. 'Can you hear anything?' he said.

They could. From across the jungle came the faint sound of heavy-duty vehicles, and from the fading darkness, heading east to where the sun was just about to rise, came the deep roar of twin-prop aero engines.

Then the soldier the leader had posted along the track as a look-out raced from the trees and towards them. He gave a swift salute and said: 'Someone's coming, sir.'

'Time to go time,' said Number One. 'Let's kick butt.'

The journey down the mountain had been uneventful, and as it got lighter, first Angel, then O'Rourke, killed the lights on their vehicles.

They found the entrance to the track with no difficulty, and O'Rourke, closely followed by Angel, turned into it, just as the soldiers at the airstrip heard, first their engines, then those of the Douglas C47 Dakota.

The soldiers spread out to wait for the new arrivals, who happened to turn up more or less simultaneously, the nose of the jeep poking through the jungle, followed by the truck, as the rising sun's rays caught the dull surface of the plane and muddily reflected it across the look-out's eyes.

The soldiers were under strict orders to hold their fire until their leader's signal, and they all sat tight as the plane made its final run and came in to land.

When the truck and jeep came to a halt, everyone disembarked. O'Rourke and Jesús lifted Keller, who was now awake and seemingly slightly better, from the jeep, and laid him gently on the ground. The rest, carrying weapons and equipment, watched as the C47 lost height, and there were relieved smiles all round as their fatigue disappeared at the thought of their imminent departure.

Then one of the soldiers lying in ambush, nervous after his long wait, hot, tired and covered in insect bites, touched the trigger of his machine-gun and loosed a single burst. His bullets tore into the side of the three-tonner, and Valin's team split apart, and dived for cover.

'What now?' said O'Rourke as he found himself next to Valin, behind one of the double rear wheels of the truck. 'What the hell's going on?'

'Don't know,' said Valin calmly, as he let off a burst of shells himself at a green-clad figure he had seen move his position, and fired the last grenade from the ARMSCOR that he had taken from Resnick when the truck was unloaded. It exploded just within the trees, sending the soldiers there diving for cover.

The pilot of the C47, meanwhile, who had not been

too pleased to be forced to return to the airstrip under threat not only from Valin, but also from the leader of the soldiers, was becoming less pleased with every passing moment. If it had not been for the four soldiers Number One had left at the pilot's home base to convince him that an early-morning flight was good for his health, he would have taken a chance and not come back at all. One of them was now sitting in the co-pilot's seat with a Sig Sauer 228 pointed at the pilot's belly, another was peering through one of the windows of the main cabin, and the other two were waiting back there, just in case the unthinkable happened, something went wrong, and Valin's people managed to get out somehow.

'Just for insurance, you understand,' the soldier sitting next to him had explained during the flight, holding up his pistol. 'But I do have a pilot's licence, so don't think I won't use this.'

At the moment of touchdown, the pilot saw the muzzle flashes from the jungle as the soldier opened fire prematurely, watched Valin's group throw themselves into cover, and then jammed on the brakes and slewed the C47 to one side of the runway. Then he turned it as tightly as he could in a full circle, and prayed that he had enough runway to take off again, which he would have been sorely tempted to do if it wasn't for the damned gun that covered him steadily.

Resnick, unaware that the pilot was not alone, and assuming that the fire from the jungle was coming from Colombian soldiers, National Guardsmen or police, saw the plane turn and heard its engines revving, and assumed again that it was about to take off and leave him and his comrades stranded. He was determined to stop it. Grabbing his last pack of HE, he stood up and ran to the jeep, flung himself into the driver's seat, started the engine, jammed it into gear and sent it in the direction of the C47. He skidded to a halt close to the side of the plane, jumped out of the jeep without switching off the engine, grabbed the pack, slung it over his shoulder, and carrying his CZ 75 semi-automatic pistol in his left hand, yanked open the door in the side of the fuselage, and leapt inside as bullets thumped into the skin of the plane beside him.

'Don't shoot at the plane,' yelled Number One to his troops. 'We need the fucker to get out of here.'

The soldier in the cabin of the plane had watched Resnick's dash, and smiled. He stood up as Resnick hauled himself and his knapsack inside. The Russian sensed a presence and looked up into the soldier's eyes and they both pulled the triggers of their guns simultaneously. A burst of 7.62mm bullets from the soldier's Galil hit Resnick in the chest, knocking him down in the aisle, where he lay still, and the soldier took a single shell in his neck and died instantly.

The other soldier kicked open the connecting door between the flight deck and the cabin, and poked the snout of his Sig through the doorway. Through the smoke from both guns he saw his comrade lying dead, and Resnick sprawled on his back, with blood bubbling out from the multiple wounds in his chest. The soldier cursed the mercenary, walked down the aisle, kicked his pistol out of his hand, and was just about to finish the Russian off, when the radio in the cockpit burst into life and he heard Number One's unmistakable voice cut through the static: 'Number One to C47. Come in.'

The soldier left Resnick where he lay and ran back to the flight deck, tore the mike off its hook and said. 'C47 to Number One. Receiving.'

'What's going on in there? Over.'

Outside, Valin's people were by now a little more organized and were returning fire steadily as Spenser readied the Gatling. The only problem was that he was very low on bullets, as the cartridge belts for the weapon were heavy, and only so many could be taken on a mission. And for days he'd been using ammunition like it was going out of fashion.

Carmen was at his side again and they smiled at each other like veterans, which in a way they were.

They had taken refuge in a shallow, dry ditch at one side of the runway, and when the gun was ready they stood up together and swept the soldiers' position with a hail of fire, then dropped down again as their fire was returned.

The soldiers had not fared well in the exchange. Of the ten of them on the ground, three were hit: one dead, one seriously wounded and one with just a flesh wound.

Their leader was furious as he talked on the radio with the soldier on board the plane, the radio man kneeling beside him. Everything would have been fine if some damn fool hadn't fired too soon, he thought to himself as Spenser opened up with the Gatling.

The bullets cut through the thick jungle cover and he heard a man cry out, and for the first time considered the possibility that his mission to exterminate Valin's team might not succeed.

Back on the plane, Resnick opened his eyes to find himself lying on the floor with his chest on fire with pain, and the soldier he had shot lying next to him, his eyes staring sightlessly up at the roof of the cabin. Resnick's blouse was soaked with blood, but his body armour had deflected most of the force of the shells, so that the wounds looked a lot worse than they really were. The other soldier was standing in the doorway to the cockpit with his gun on the pilot, his back to the cabin, talking on the radio handset to whoever was on the ground.

Resnick's side-arm was lying a yard or so from his right hand and he picked it up, pulled himself into a sitting position and then on to his feet, trying not to make any noise, as pain lanced through his chest. Maybe the wounds *were* as bad as they looked, he thought. He was afraid to shoot inside the plane for fear of hitting something vital, so he held his gun by the barrel like a hammer and pulled himself towards the soldier, using the backs of the seats as supports.

He was within a yard of the door when the soldier sensed that all was not right behind him, and began to turn. Using all his strength, Resnick lunged forward and brought the butt of the pistol down on the soldier's neck just below the rim of his steel helmet, and he slumped to the floor.

Resnick holstered his own weapon, picked up the soldier's Sig, steadied himself against the wall of the plane and looked in at the pilot. He was fine. Obviously a pragmatist, he showed little emotion at the way the tables kept being turned.

Using the soldier's belt, Resnick trussed his hands behind his back and went to see the state of play, dragging the pilot with him. The firing was spasmodic by then, and no one was shooting at the C47, much to Resnick's relief.

'We've got to make that plane,' said Valin, firing single rounds into the jungle. 'I'm almost out of ammo.'

'Me too,' said O'Rourke. 'If the bastard thing waits for us.'

Not knowing what had happened inside the cabin of the C47, Valin said confidently: 'Resnick's on board. He'll make sure it does. Come on, let's get Keller and make a run for it.'

They snaked along the ground underneath the body of the truck to where Keller was lying beside the front wheel. He was awake and held his Heckler and Koch across his body.

'We're off,' said Valin. 'Come on, we'll give you a hand.'

Keller shook his head. 'You go, I'll give you cover,' he said.

'Don't be stupid,' said O'Rourke. 'One goes, we all go.'

'I can't walk.'

'We'll carry you.'

'We'll be dead before we get ten yards. Leave me. Give me the ARMSCOR. I've got ammunition and grenades, and I'll give you covering fire. Get the civilians to the plane.'

'I'm not leaving you,' said Valin.

'You've got no choice. I'm not coming. I'm dying. And even if I'm not, my legs are never going to be any use again. I heard what the doctor said. There's no future for me. I'd rather die like I lived, with a gun in my hand. I've got some rounds left. Now go.'

'Keller . . . ' Valin implored.

'Go, Colonel. And thank you for all the good times. We'll never see the likes of them again.' And he pulled himself up on to one elbow and poked his gun around the side of the tyre.

Valin looked at the German and made his decision. In similar circumstances he would do exactly what Keller was doing, and they both knew it. He tossed the ARMSCOR down beside the sergeant and said: 'Goodbye, Keller. It's been a pleasure, my old friend. You're a brave man. Come on, Mark, let's get out of here.' He touched Keller on the shoulder before heading towards the ditch where the rest of the group were sheltering.

O'Rourke tried one more time. 'Keller,' he said, 'that doctor doesn't know what he's talking about.'

'I think he does,' said the sergeant. 'I can feel it. Now go, Mark, and have a drink for me when you get back to London. In that pub in Paddington where we met.'

'I will,' said O'Rourke, and he squeezed Keller's arm and followed Valin.

36

Valin dived for cover as bullets from the soldiers in the jungle whined around him, and he added his fire to that of the rest as O'Rourke left Keller and zigzagged across the open ground towards them. Valin bluntly explained what was happening, and looking at his expression, no one argued. It was that kind of war. Personal. Where friends died, and mourning came later.

Valin saw Keller raise his hand and make a 'Go' gesture, and he shouted: 'Come on. Get to the plane.' On Valin's order, Angel, O'Rourke, Spenser, Carmen, Sofía, Jesús and García scrambled to their feet and, closely followed by Valin himself, made their final run.

Keller opened fire with his Heckler and Koch as they went, and all of them blasted off their remaining ammunition in the direction of the jungle. Keller had loaded the ARMSCOR, and started lobbing fragmentation and smoke grenades. Anything to give his friends the few seconds they needed to get to safety.

Number One, from his position behind the bole of a thick vine close to the edge of the jungle, saw the plan and screamed for his remaining five men to make for the plane. They broke cover and Keller smiled through the pall of smoke that was drifting towards him. 'Come on, you suckers,' he shouted, as he smacked home a fresh magazine, aimed and opened fire, forgetting the pain from his injuries in the excitement of action.

Three of the soldiers went down with the first burst, and the rest dropped into cover and fired back at Keller. Then Resnick got into the act. Using both his pistol and the Sig he had captured, he fired two-handed from the door of the plane while the pilot cowered next to him.

Valin, his men and the civilians sprinted towards the plane, and Keller kept up the hail of covering fire. Luckily for the mercenaries and their companions, the soldiers were trying to avoid hitting the plane in case a stray bullet ignited one of the fuel tanks and they were all stranded in South America. As the group got closer to the C47, Keller hauled himself to his feet, despite his appalling wounds, and pumped round after round at the enemy. He hardly felt the first bullet hit him in the shoulder, his adrenalin was pumping so fast. But a second smashed into his arm; the gun was knocked out of his grasp, and the bullet that ended his life tore through his skull as he scrabbled to retrieve it.

The leader saw him go down and lie still, and he screamed: 'Get after them.' The remaining soldiers scrambled to their feet and set off after Valin's group.

Resnick jumped down from the doorway of the plane. He knew that the bullets from the Galil had done more damage than he had at first thought, and he was beginning to hallucinate. He saw the figures running towards him as the friends he had lost in Afghanistan, and urged them to go faster. They dived through into the cabin one by one, and, seeing the soldiers advancing towards the plane, he knew that he must destroy them.

The pilot ran back to his seat and revved up the engines, keeping one careful eye on the gauges in front of him in case some vital part of the plane had been hit and he might not be able to take off. But everything seemed fine. The oil pressures were up, and the fuel tanks were three-quarters full.

'Go,' shouted Valin, as he dived through the door behind the others. 'Resnick,' he yelled at the Russian. 'Get back in.'

But Resnick was in a world of his own. Deep down he knew that if they tried to take off, the soldiers would destroy the plane out of sheer spite, and as he walked towards them he dropped the guns he was carrying, and put his hands into the knapsack slung around his back and pulled the knotted cord inside that set the detonator to blow.

The three soldiers casually shot him down as they went, but as they passed him by the charge blew, killing Resnick and two of them, and mortally wounding their leader.

As Resnick died, the last impression in his mind was of a night in Afghanistan at another airfield, where he and his comrades had just finished loading the hold of the huge cargo plane known as the 'Black Tulip' because of its paint job. Every evening as dusk descended, it was loaded with the plywood coffins of dead soldiers and flew back to the homeland with it grisly cargo. It was not a job to relish as some of the bodies were days old and decomposition had set in. The smell was horrendous and attracted swarms of black flies that bit at the exposed skin of the men loading the plane. They were issued with masks, but as the heat of the day had hardly diminished, they were more of a hindrance than a help, and most of the loaders dispensed with them. On that particular night, as Resnick was holding one end of a coffin, the soldier at the other end, a corporal of infantry, slipped and fell, the box they were carrying burst open, and the horribly disfigured corpse of a young conscript fell into the dirt. As Resnick and the corporal gingerly loaded the body back into the coffin, one of his arms broke off to expose a heaving mass of maggots that had claimed the body for their own. Resnick had never forgotten the stomach-clenching feeling as they threw the bits of the soldier into the box. As the explosive charge blasted Resnick to eternity, he once again stared death in the face – but this time it was his own.

Valin saw what the Russian had done, and realized that they would never have got away without the sacrifice of him and Keller. He slammed the door and shouted: 'Take it away.' The pilot opened the throttles and started the C47's final take-off from Colombia.

37

Valin watched as the smoke from Resnick's suicide drifted across the airstrip, and the pilot, under the watchful eye of O'Rourke, who had taken the co-pilot's seat, banked the C47 away, and headed for Panama.

The inside of the fuselage shook from the vibrations from the twin engines and boomed from their noise and the slipstream outside, so that talking in normal tones was impossible. 'What about this one, Colonel?' shouted Angel, poking the nameless soldier in the ribs with the barrel of his Uzi.

'I think we'll have a little chat.'

The soldier looked at Valin scornfully. 'You'll be wasting your breath,' he yelled.

Valin shook his head. 'I don't think so.'

'Try then.'

'I assume you were with that lot,' Valin said, gesturing behind him to indicate the dead and wounded soldiers back at the LZ. 'Who sent you?'

'Give me a break.'

'All right. Let's start with a simple question. Name, rank and serial number.'

'Fuck you.'

Valin's hand lashed out and caught him around the

side of his face, and the soldier's head snapped back. 'No profanity, please. There are ladies present.'

'Call them ladies. Fucking spic whores.'

Spenser made as if to get up, but Carmen restrained him. 'Ignore him, Chris,' she said.

'Don't stop him,' said the soldier. 'The odds are just about right. Him armed and me tied up. Spenser, isn't it? Renegade officer. Murderer.'

'And that little welcome back there was a fair fight, was it? A nice little ambush,' hissed Valin.

'Fuck you.'

'And you know who at least one of us is,' said Valin. 'How interesting.'

The soldier shook his head in disgust, then looked away. Valin grabbed him by the chin and turned his head so that their eyes met. 'I'm not playing,' he shouted. 'I want to know who sent you.'

'You never will.'

'Then you'll never live to see your home and family again. You do have a family?'

The soldier was silent. Valin looked at the dead body of the soldier's comrade. Still lying on his back, blank eyes staring upwards, and blood crusted around the wound in his neck. 'Throw that body out,' Valin said to Angel. 'It's making the place look untidy.'

'Sir,' said Angel in reply.

'And him too,' said Valin. 'The live one.'

The young American's eyes widened. '*What*?'

'You heard. Open the door of the plane and throw them both out.'

'We don't have any parachutes,' said Angel.

Valin pulled a 'couldn't care less' face. 'Throw him out anyway, Angel. He's excess baggage.'

'I'll do it if you won't,' said Spenser. 'I was getting kind of fond of Resnick, and Keller's been a friend for a long time. And this dude called Carmen and her sister rude names. I hate that kind of disrespect. Specially from an American. Throw the shit out and let's be done with it.'

'Angel will do it, won't you, Angel. After all, you have to earn your bonus,' said Valin.

Spenser, Jesús, Sofía and Carmen looked puzzled. García was looking around the faces in the cabin trying to figure out what was going on.

Angel shrugged, remembering the bargain he had struck with his commanding officer back in the cab of the truck. 'OK, Colonel,' he said. He poked the soldier again. 'On your feet, pal.'

'You can't do this,' shouted the soldier, for the first time looking worried.

'It's done, babe. You heard the man,' said Angel with a cheery grin.

'Look, I don't know anything. I'm just a grunt.'

'You knew all about Spenser,' said Valin. 'And I'm willing to bet you know exactly who else came into Colombia two days ago with me.'

'Gossip. Scuttlebutt,' stammered the soldier. 'You know the kind of thing. We just got talking.'

'We?'

'Special Services. Out of Leavenworth.'

'You're a long way from home, soldier.'

'Listen, Colonel Valin . . . '

'You know me too?'

'Course I know you. All of you. They gave us a full briefing before we left the base.'

'And they issued you with uniforms without insignia,

and even took your dog tags off you.'

The soldier's hand went instinctively to his neck.

'Nothing there,' said Valin. 'Or did you just lose them?'

The soldier didn't answer.

'Covert activities,' Valin said, and shook his head. 'Naughty, naughty. Now who sent you?'

'Christ, I don't know. We just followed orders.'

'From?'

'Captain Skelton. You left him back there.'

'Shame,' interjected Spenser. 'What exactly was the mission?'

'Terminate with extreme prejudice.'

'All of us?' Valin again.

'Everyone in your party.'

'Civilians too?'

The soldier nodded.

'You came out of Panama with the plane yesterday?'

'I didn't. The ten did. I was left behind with him.' He gestured at the body. 'And two others to make sure the pilot came back. I can fly a plane.'

'So there's a little reception party waiting.'

The soldier didn't reply. He didn't have to.

'Damn it,' said Valin. 'We'll have to land somewhere else.'

'Shit,' said Spenser. 'Is this operation ever going to go right?'

'It will,' said Valin. 'We haven't started yet.'

He looked long and hard at the soldier. 'Sorry,' he said. 'Angel. Do it.'

'Up, motherfucker,' said Angel. 'Spenser, open the door.'

'No,' said the soldier. 'Please. My family.'

'I gotta family too,' said Angel. 'Think how my mom would've missed me if you'd managed to kill all of us. At least *your* mom'll get a letter from your commanding officer telling her that you died in an unavoidable accident. So move your ass, son.'

'My wife. My kids.'

'I'm inconsolable,' said Angel. 'Chris. Door.'

'I'll just warn the pilot,' said Valin, and went to the door to the cockpit and told him that he'd have to trim his craft, as Spenser rose to his feet and pulled the door inwards and the slipstream whipped through the inside of the plane.

'Move it,' said Angel, pushing the soldier with his gun. 'Say a prayer.'

'You bastard,' said the soldier as Angel hustled him towards the open doorway. 'Please. No.'

'Have a nice trip,' said Angel, and shoved the soldier through the opening. The man grabbed the edge, his fingers white with strain, and Angel reversed his gun and slammed the butt down on to his knuckles, making him cry out as the mercenary shoved him through the doorway.

His scream was lost in the roar from outside, and Angel looked down as his figure diminished until he was no longer visible, then he and Spenser picked up the dead soldier's body off the floor and tossed it out too. Angel slammed the door shut and turned toward the colonel and said: 'Done, sir.'

'Good man, Angel. I'm going forward to have a word with our pilot about a change of flight plan.'

He moved to the cockpit door, opened it and went inside, slamming the door behind him.

'Welcome to the real world, Angel,' said Spenser.

'It's been real enough for me these last few days,' he replied.

'How do you feel?'

Angel shrugged and pulled a face. 'Shit happens,' he said, and slumped down into his uncomfortable seat, his Uzi cradled on his lap.

Valin stood between the pilot's and the co-pilot's seat.

'Change of plan,' he said to the pilot in English.

The man looked up at him and said: 'How?'

'We figure we might be met if we go back to your home base. Of course, you know nothing about that, do you?'

The pilot's eyes widened. 'Me, señor?'

'You, señor. Before he took a little walk in the fresh air, our friend told us that there was a little welcoming committee back at your airfield.'

'I know nothing . . . '

'Except how to play both ends against the middle and take a little baksheesh from both sides.'

'It is a hard world.'

'And getting harder all the time. You know what happened to him. How would you like to make the same last journey?'

'Then who would land the aeroplane?'

'We may have lost a lot of men. But there are still some talented people aboard. Talented enough to land this bucket anyway.'

The pilot paled beneath his tan.

'I see you get my drift,' said Valin. 'Now I want you to fly us to Mexico.'

'Mexico. Impossible.'

'Nothing's impossible.'

'Air traffic control.'

Valin laughed mirthlessly. 'You mean you've never done any smuggling in this wreck. Fly under the radar like you did coming in and out of Colombia.'

'Fuel. I'll need more fuel to get us there.'

'What's your range?'

The pilot shrugged. 'Fifteen hundred miles,' he said. 'But I only have enough fuel for a thousand.'

'And how far is Mexico City?'

'Maybe sixteen hundred.'

'One stop then.'

'But we'll need money.'

'I've got American Express,' said Valin.

O'Rourke looked up to the roof. Christ, he thought. Only Valin could hijack a plane and pay for the gas with plastic.

38

'I'll send someone to relieve you soon,' said Valin to O'Rourke. 'But in the meantime keep an eye on our treacherous friend here. I don't trust him any further than I can throw him.'

'You threw the other ones quite a way,' said O'Rourke with a grin. 'About twelve thousand feet if the altimeter in this crate is accurate.'

The pilot paled even more and Valin went back into the passenger section. 'You'll be glad to hear we won't be driving from Panama to Mexico City,' he announced.

'Shame,' said Spenser. 'I was really looking forward to it.'

'I'm sure you were, Chris. No. We've extended our charter, and the brave captain of this low-rent airline is going to fly us all the way there.'

'And we leave the welcoming party twiddling their thumbs in Panama.'

'Exactly. While we fly on over, give them a cheery wave and head towards Mexico.'

'We've got to cross a lot of countries.'

'We'll take the scenic route over the water for some of the way.'

'I hope no one thinks we're muling drugs,' said Angel.

Valin gave the young American an old-fashioned look. 'It's a risk we're going to have to take.'

'If we get spotted by some Latin American air force we could be shot down and all end up being deep-sixed,' said Spenser gloomily.

'Pessimism, Chris. I've told you about that before,' said Valin.

The plane droned on and O'Rourke waited to be relieved so that he could get some rest. He was dog-tired and the noise from the engines was sending him to sleep. It had been fifty-six hours since he had slept properly and he slowly dozed off.

He was in a car being driven down a street in Dublin. In his pocket was a tiny Russian-made .20-calibre PSM. It was very small and slim, with a bullet that could penetrate all known practical body armour. It had been developed for the KGB special ops personnel, especially for 'wet' operations.

And that was precisely what the young lieutenant was embarking on. He and his female driver had crossed the border the previous evening posing as tourists. Now they were looking for the address of a notorious IRA assassin who had fled to the safety of the south, and the hit-and-miss extradition orders that were passed there. He knew that even if he was arrested there, the chances of his being sent north again were slim.

'So be it,' O'Rourke's commander had said. 'You are going down there to fix the bastard. He's been thumbing his nose at us for too long. He's back and forth across that border like a dog at a fair. We're fed up with him. Go and deal with the bugger.'

'That's it,' the driver said, and nodded at a

terraced house with a stone-clad front. She braked the Montego to a halt just around the next corner.

O'Rourke got out of the car, walked back round the corner and up the front path of the house where his target lived, and pressed the doorbell.

A light came on behind the glass quarter-light above the door, and a man's voice said: 'Who's there?'

'Garda,' answered O'Rourke.

There was a rattle of chains and the door opened on a chain. 'Let me see.'

O'Rourke had a forged Garda ID in the name of Hardman. He thought that was amusing. And he held it up to the gap between the door and jamb. The door was pushed to, the chain was removed and the door opened all the way. 'Whaddya want?' said the man who appeared.

O'Rourke identified him from the photos he had seen. 'Pat Davies?' he asked, just to be sure.

'That's me,' said the man. 'What do you want?'

'This,' said O'Rourke, and produced the gun from under his coat and shot Davies three times. At that range he couldn't miss, and the Irishman fell backwards. The reports of the shots had been no louder than hand claps, and O'Rourke pulled the door to before walking to the car without a backward glance.

'Done,' he said when he got into the passenger seat and the driver pulled smoothly away.

On the way back north, she asked: 'How does it feel?'

She was a sergeant. 'Like shit,' said O'Rourke, and lit a cigarette. 'I didn't join up to become an assassin.'

'It had to be done.'

'Oh yeah? In whose name? The great British public. If this ever came out I'd be in jail faster than you can sneeze. And our lords and masters in Whitehall would deny having even heard my name.'

'It's better than patrolling the streets, dodging snipers.'

'Is it? I don't know so much. At least I could get to sleep without feeling like a murderer when I was doing that.'

'Don't worry about it, Mark.'

'I worry that they'll order me to do it again.'

'That's the risk we take doing this sort of duty.'

He shook his head sadly at the truth of her remark. 'I need a drink. Find somewhere decent-looking,' he said.

She did, at an anonymous motel that was part of a large chain. The drink became a late dinner, and O'Rourke suggested that they stay out another night, and when the sergeant agreed, he booked a pair of adjoining single rooms.

O'Rourke woke up at three o'clock with a scream dying in his throat. He had been dreaming about the bloody body of Davies pursuing him through some nightmare landscape.

He lay back down again and wiped the sweat off his body with the sheet.

A minute later there was a tap at the door. He switched on the bedside lamp, got out of bed, pulled on the robe he had packed, then opened the door.

The sergeant was standing outside, her blonde hair down and wearing a robe of her own. 'I thought I heard you cry out,' she explained.

'Bad dream,' he said. 'Come in.'

'Tea?' he said, as she sat down.

'Please.'

He filled the kettle that had been on the sideboard, from the tap in the tiny bathroom, plugged it in, and threw two tea bags into the cups provided.

When the kettle boiled he made the tea and he took her cup to where she was sitting on the only chair, an uncomfortable-looking thing with a straight wooden back. Mark took his own cup and sat on the bed.

'Davies?' she asked when they had both lit cigarettes.

He nodded.

'Bad?'

'Enough.'

'I'm sorry.'

'Me too.'

She put down her cup, stood up, unfastened her robe, pulled if off her shoulders and let it fall to the floor. She was naked underneath. Her body was firm and for the first time he could be sure that she was a natural blonde. 'I'll make you feel better,' she said and walked across the bedroom towards him.

O'Rourke's dream was broken when the Bolivian pilot, who had seen his eyes close, made a grab for the Browning automatic that had almost slipped from his fingers.

The young lieutenant woke with a start and lashed out at the pilot, whose other hand slipped off the joystick. The plane nose-dived. They fought for control of the gun as the plane dipped even more steeply.

Behind, all was chaos as all seven passengers were flung out of their seats.

'Christ,' shouted Angel, 'what the hell's happening?'

Back in the cockpit, the pilot gave up the fight and dived for the controls and managed to pull the C47 out of its dive, just a few hundred feet above the tops of the trees that formed the jungle below.

'You stupid bastard,' said O'Rourke as he regained his seat and Valin came to the cockpit on the run, his Smith & Wesson in his hand, ready to fire.

'What happened?' he demanded.

'Our friend here decided to play the hero,' said O'Rourke.

'The bloody plane nearly crashed,' growled Valin.

'Tell me about it.'

Valin leant over the pilot. 'Are you mad?' he asked.

The pilot shrugged, but his hands were trembling on the controls.

'Go on back, Mark,' said Valin. 'I'll take a turn here.'

39

The unscheduled stop for fuel was in Panama, but at an airfield about two hundred miles from the pilot's home base. He was apparently well known there, and called in on the radio with Valin, gun cocked and pointing at him, and Jesús standing between the seats listening for any hint of treachery in the message. But the pilot seemed to have learnt his lesson, and merely asked for permission to land to refuel. The air traffic controller in the tower casually gave him the OK, and the C47 touched down just after eight o'clock and taxied to where a bowser, manned by two yawning men, was waiting.

They were happy to accept Valin's American Express card in exchange for the fuel, and within thirty minutes the plane was airborne again. Jesús had stayed with the pilot throughout, and nothing more than some macho remarks seemed to have passed between them.

The pilot followed the coastline of Honduras, up towards Mexico, flying low, and the radio was silent.

They landed for the last time at an airstrip just outside Mexico City. The pilot reported to the ATC that he was doing a short-hop charter, and that his compass had broken, and requested an emergency landing.

The request was granted, and everyone offloaded, their weapons broken down and stashed away neatly, and resembling nothing as much as a party of hunters who had been on an excursion and lost their way home.

Valin hired three taxis at the airport, and they drove to where their cars were garaged, taking the pilot with them. No one at the airfield, which drowsed in the afternoon sunshine, seemed too worried at their arrival, and that suited everyone fine. As Angel commented: 'They're too busy having a siesta to worry about little old us.'

At the garage, Valin paid the pilot the remainder of his fee, plus a sizeable bonus, changed cars and headed north towards the USA. They drove through Durango and Chihuahua on main roads, but before they reached the border, they struck off into the desert, the way they had entered the country, and by nightfall of their second day on the road, they had crossed the border on an unpatrolled secondary road.

40

When they got back to the temporary base that Valin had set up in the rented ranch in New Mexico they felt that they could relax for a while. They were all exhausted and went off for some much-needed sleep. But sleep didn't come easy for any of them, and within a couple of hours they were all gathered together in the huge kitchen at the back of the ranch house, where O'Rourke made pot after pot of strong coffee.

'What now, Colonel?' said Angel, lighting a cigarette. 'Where do we go from here?'

'We go to Virginia to collect the money that's owed us for completing our mission. And we find the man who tried to sell us out, and sent those troops to kill us.'

'And?' Angel again.

'And we kill him.'

'More killing?' said Jesús. 'Hasn't there been enough?'

'Yes,' said Valin. 'More than enough. But we left a lot of good people down in Colombia. I can't rest until they have been avenged. I'll understand if any of you don't want to come with me. If necessary, I will go alone. You will still be paid. This was not part of the deal. Everyone here fulfilled their obligations tenfold down there.'

'I'm with you, sir,' said O'Rourke.

'Me too,' said Angel. 'I nearly had my butt shot off half-a-dozen times. Anyway, what else is there to do?'

'Count me in,' said Spenser.

'Where he goes, I go,' said Carmen, putting her arm around Spenser's shoulder.

'And where she goes . . . ' Jesús didn't finish the sentence. 'Besides, I have a little unfinished business of my own.'

'And me,' said Sofía going to her father and embracing him.

'And you, García,' said Valin in Spanish, and explained the situation to the Colombian, who rattled off an answer.

Valin smiled. 'Ramón is up for it. So that means we all are. I'm proud of you. Now what I suggest we do is split up for the journey back north. I won't be happy about our security until we've finished this business once and for all. I'll go with O'Rourke and Ramón. Spenser, will you take Jesús, Carmen and Sofía with you?'

The American nodded.

'And Angel, I imagine you'll want to be off on your own.'

'Yessir,' said Angel.

'Then we'll meet again at a designated time and place and bring this thing to its logical conclusion.'

'I'll go and check the cars,' said Angel.

'Good man,' said Valin, and Angel left through the back door and headed to the barn where they'd left their cars on arrival.

At the start of the mission, Angel had flown into Phoenix, Arizona, and hired a Lexus for the drive to New Mexico. Valin, O'Rourke, Keller and Spenser had come into Albuquerque together and picked up a Chevrolet Caprice station wagon at Hertz, which they had used to ferry the rest of the mercenaries, who had come in on domestic flights, to and from the airport.

Angel checked on the fuel, oil and water on both vehicles, and everything was OK. But they would need another. The three other station wagons that had been rented legitimately for the drive to and from Mexico City were parked under the shade of some stunted trees outside the ranch house, and he figured one of them would do. He went back into the kitchen and said as much.

Valin agreed.

'I'm going to drive to Miami,' Angel said. 'I got me a little business there.'

'How long will that take?' asked O'Rourke.

'Coupla days. Three at the most. Then I'll drop the car off and catch a plane, and meet you in Virginia.'

'Good enough,' said Valin. 'What about you, Spenser?'

'We'll go back to Albuquerque. We'll get a plane to New York, check into a hotel. Maybe do a little sightseeing. Then we'll fly to Virginia too, and catch up with you there.'

'Good. I think we should meet each other there a week today in the bar of the Hilton in Richmond. But don't check in. Just get some transport, and find a motel locally. We'll only be there twenty-four hours.'

Or maybe for ever, thought Spenser, but didn't say so.

41

Once they were all safely away, from the anonymity of a gas station pay phone Valin called Tank Tankerton in Washington.

'Christ, James,' said the American. 'We thought you were all dead.'

'No such luck, Tank.'

'I don't get you.'

'We were stitched up.'

'What do you mean?'

'Sold a pup. Betrayed.'

'By whom?'

'Such perfect grammar. Not by you.'

'Well thanks, James.'

'Don't mention it.'

'Who then?'

'You'll find out.'

'But only you, your men, Jesús Delgado and his family, and the four of us who hired you had any idea . . . '

'Exactly,' interrupted Valin. 'So work it out for yourself. It wasn't my men, or any of the Delgados.'

'What happened to them?'

'The survivors are back here.'

'With you.'

'Not right now.'

'Shit. How do you mean, survivors?'

'Jesús's wife, one of his daughters and his son are buried down in Colombia. And some of my men. Too many. Some of them didn't even get a decent burial.'

'My God. So you're saying . . . '

'I'm saying nothing right now. Got the rest of our money?'

'Sure.'

'The mission was a success, by the way.'

'I know that.'

'No "Congratulations on a job well done"?'

'Sorry, James. I'm just a bit surprised to hear from you like this.'

'I'll take it as read, then. Are you ready to deliver?'

'Of course. When?'

'Soon. I'll be in touch. And make sure everyone's there. We don't want any truants. Same place as last time. Just let them know we'll be in town. I think they'll all want to come to the party.' And with that Valin hung up.

Tank rang Landers, Bernard and General Avery straight away, and told them the news. Within fifteen minutes a telephone rang in Leavenworth.

'What's happening?' asked a voice.

'They're still in Colombia.'

'Like hell. Valin's somewhere in the United States. He's on his way to Virginia.'

'But the plane never came out. A couple of my guys are still waiting in Panama.'

'Bring them home. I think you can draw a line under

the rest. The whole deal's gone to shit. You'd better find out what went wrong.'

'I will.'

The phone went dead.

42

On the day of the rendezvous the cocktail bar of the Hilton in Richmond, Virginia, was dark and air-conditioned cool in comparison with the streets outside, where the heatwave had not abated, and the state capital shimmered in the heat haze.

Valin, O'Rourke and García were the first to arrive at the rendezvous. After leaving the ranch in New Mexico they had driven across country to Los Angeles, where they had booked into the Château Marmont, and spent a week living in room-service luxury, and catching up on their sleep, before flying to Washington DC, then driving down to Richmond overnight, where they were booked into a Howard Johnson. Spenser and the Delgados came into the bar about half an hour later. They had gone to New York as planned, and rented a service apartment in a block overlooking Central Park. Spenser and Carmen had decided to get married in the city when the mission was finally finished. Angel rolled in about twenty minutes after them.

The eight of them looked very different from the last time they had been together. Colonel James Valin was wearing a three-piece suit in cream linen that he had picked up from his tailor in Savile Row the last time he had been in England. O'Rourke was wearing faded blue jeans, cowboy boots, a white shirt and a brown suede waistcoat. Perched on his nose were a pair of sunglasses with purple lenses. García was pure Ivy League in a blue Brooks Brothers suit, pale-blue Oxford button-down shirt and a plain, navy-blue knitted tie. On his feet he wore shiny black loafers. Spenser still wore his baseball cap, and with it, a leather jacket and chinos. Carmen and Sofía were out-and-out *haute couture*, Carmen wearing a pink Versace suit, black nylons and matching pink, low-heeled pumps. Her hair had been put into one thick, dark pigtail and she wore huge sunglasses. Sofía was a vision in yellow: dress by Albertini, accessories by Chanel. Spenser had obviously not stinted with his money. Jesús was wearing a black suit, white shirt and thin black tie in memory of those he had lost. His white hair was cut short and he looked like a Mafia Godfather on his way to church.

Both Carmen and Sofía had wanted to wear mourning too, for their mother, brother and sister, but Spenser didn't want to draw attention as they arrived in town, where they'd made reservations at the local Holiday Inn, and had argued that it was better for the two women to look as though they were simply on holiday. Jesús had reluctantly accepted Spenser's logic, but insisted that he would wear black, and Spenser had concurred.

Angel was wearing a pale-blue Hawaiian shirt, a pink *Miami Vice* suit, white deck shoes with no socks, and his usual reflector shades. He sported a two-day growth of stubble, and his hair was long and unkempt. He had found a Sheraton hotel on the edge of town, and had booked in.

'Watch out,' said O'Rourke as he entered the bar. 'It's Don Johnson.'

Angel sashayed over and joined them, ordered a Bourbon with ice and water for himself from the waitress, took off his shades and winked at her.

He was rich now that he had sold the Colombian coke to a contact in Miami. And he'd be even richer when he collected the remains of his fee for the mission. But not rich enough to forget the friends he had made under fire.

'You're looking well,' said Valin drily.

'Never better, sir,' said Angel. 'But I can't get used to the quiet life.'

'It should get more interesting now,' replied Valin.

'Any chance of another mission?' asked Angel.

'You're a glutton for punishment, aren't you,' said O'Rourke.

'Your next mission is now,' said Valin. 'Maybe later we'll talk about the future.'

'Good enough, Colonel,' said Angel.

'Is the meeting set?' asked Spenser.

'Yes,' replied Valin. 'I had confirmation over the phone this morning.'

'When?'

'Tomorrow afternoon at two.'

'Were they surprised to hear from you?' asked Angel.

'A little.'

'Who did you speak to?' Spenser said.

'Tank Tankerton. Three times. Once on the road soon after we left the ranch. Yesterday afternoon. Then again this morning.'

'My old friend,' Jesús said.

Valin nodded. 'I didn't tell them about García.'

The Colombian perked up at the sound of his name, and Jesús quickly translated.

'No one knows that he came out with us. Or indeed that he even exists,' said Valin.

Jesús carried on whispering quietly to the Colombian as Valin spoke.

'And they'll all be there?' said O'Rourke.

'The same four as last time,' confirmed Valin.

'And they'll have our money?' asked Angel.

'That was the arrangement,' replied Valin. 'One-third up front, the rest on completion.'

'Did he say anything about the welcoming committee that was sent to meet us?' asked Spenser.

'Not a word. But I doubt that Tank even knew about it.'

'One of those bastards is gonna pay,' said Angel.

'Are you armed?' asked Valin.

Angel touched under the arm of his pink jacket. 'I always am these days, Colonel. It's a dangerous world out there.'

'Bring it tomorrow,' said Valin. 'I want everyone but García armed. They searched us thoroughly last time and we went through a metal detector. We're going to have to take that place.'

'Sounds good to me,' said Spenser. 'Pay-back time. I can hardly wait.'

They met for the last time the next afternoon in a diner on a corner close to the building that housed basement 101. They were all casually dressed except for Jesús and García, who wore suits. Sofía and Carmen wore jeans and leather jackets. Everyone but García carried concealed handguns. Between them they had enough fire-power to wage a war, which was exactly what they intended to do if necessary.

They sat together in the diner under the draught of a huge ceiling fan until they were all present, then paid for the Cokes they had drunk and walked together to the building.

The reception area was large, and scrutinized by twin video cameras: one covered the entrance, the other the doors to the lift that connected it with the floors above and below. In front of the lift doors was a walk-through metal detector, similar to those used at airports. There were two men at the desk – both big, in tight, black suits with bulges under the right armpits – and they stood when they buzzed Valin and his companions through the front door.

'Colonel James Valin and party,' said Valin in his most British accent.

'You're expected, sir,' said one of the security men. 'But first we have to search you.'

'Of course. I think this is what you're looking for.' And the colonel took a Glock niner from the shoulder holster he wore under his casual jacket and covered both men. 'Mark,' he said, and O'Rourke took a can of black spray paint from one of his pockets, grabbed a chair from behind the desk and, climbing on it, blanked out the lenses of the cameras. As he was doing so, Angel and Spenser relieved the guards of their weapons, and Carmen summoned the lift.

'We'll all go down together,' said Valin calmly when the lift appeared. When the doors whispered open, six guns were trained on it, but it was empty. They all managed to squeeze in, and Valin touched the button marked 'B101' and they descended to the basement. When the doors opened, the corridor was empty, and the party walked along it, guns at the ready, their footsteps silent on the carpet, with the only noise the hum of the air-conditioning system.

The door to the room that Valin and O'Rourke had visited before was unguarded and Valin gestured for one of the men in dark suits to open it.

The same four representatives of the US government were sitting at the same table as before, fruit and bottled water in front of them, and they all looked up when it opened without a pre-emptive knock. Valin stepped into the room, gun in hand, closely followed by his seven companions and their two prisoners.

'For God's sake, James,' said Tankerton, half rising to his feet. 'What's going on?'

'We've come to settle our accounts,' said Valin quietly.

'But why with guns? What the hell's wrong with you?'

'There's nothing wrong with us. Not that I can say the same for our companions who we left to rot on Colombian soil. But we're fine. A little older, a little wiser, perhaps, that's all. But I'm forgetting my manners. Allow me to introduce you all. You'll forgive me if I'm telling you something you already know. The gentleman who's done all the talking so far is Bob 'Tank' Tankerton, who represents the Drug Enforcement Agency. Next to him is Jack Bernard from the Central Intelligence Agency, based at Langley. Next to him is Karl Landers, Federal Bureau of Investigation, and finally, all the way from the White House itself, is General Ethan Avery.' Then in turn he introduced the survivors of Valin's Raiders and the Delgados, but not Ramón García.

Tankerton looked over at Jesús Delgado. 'Jesús, my old friend,' he said. 'It's been too long. I heard what happened to your family. I'm so sorry.'

'I too am sorry,' said Jesús.

'And your daughters,' Tankerton went on, looking at the young women. 'The last time I saw them they were only babies.'

'I remember, Mr Tankerton,' said Sofía.

'Tank, please. All my friends call me Tank.'

'Tank,' she repeated.

'We didn't know which of you, if any, had made it out until you called,' said Tankerton. 'There were such confusing reports coming out of Colombia.'

'We almost didn't make it,' said Valin. 'Any of us.'

'And who is this?' asked Tankerton, referring to García.

'Someone we linked up with down there. His name is Ramón García. He was a chemist at the factory complex. The Colombian government coerced him into working for them. We brought him out.'

'You did a wonderful job, James,' said Tank. 'Our spies tell us the factory was completely destroyed.'

'They'll rebuild it,' said O'Rourke. 'With help.'

'What kind of help?' For the first time, the man from the CIA spoke.

'The help of this government,' said O'Rourke. 'The kind of help that almost killed us all.'

'I don't know what you're talking about,' Tankerton said.

'*You* probably don't, Tank,' said Valin. 'But at least one of the rest of you does.'

The DEA man looked genuinely puzzled. 'What are you talking about?'

'A traitor. Someone who flew down to Bogotá from the USA, visited the factory and told the authorities down there what was happening. That we were coming, though not the exact place, date and time. Thank Christ only a few people knew that, including you, Tank, which puts you in the clear. Otherwise the plane that took us in would have been shot out of the air, and none of us would be here today. But once in, *everyone* knew where we were, and certain contingency plans were made to stop us coming out again.'

'I still don't understand,' said Tank, looking at the other three men who sat at the table.

'Tank,' said Valin. 'Are you losing your touch? Getting old? When the plane came back to pick us up, along with it came a force of US personnel. No uniform insignia. No dog tags. But US all the same. Special Services out of Leavenworth.'

The man from the FBI interrupted: 'If what you say is true, wouldn't it have been easier just not to pick you up altogether, or to let the Colombian authorities know where you were being collected from, and let them mop you up.'

'No,' said Valin firmly. 'If that had happened it's possible one or more of us might have escaped, to eventually get back here and tell you exactly what I'm telling you now. Unfortunately, the men sent down weren't as good as us. But it was very close.'

His words hung in the air like smoke.

'So who *is* the traitor?' asked Tankerton.

'Like I told you on the phone, Tank, it's one of the three here with you. It has to be.'

'I don't like this,' said the man from the FBI. 'Not one bit. I didn't come here today to listen to this sort of thing.' And he made as if to rise from his seat.

'Stay where you are,' ordered Valin, moving his gun round to cover him.

'Have you got any proof?' asked Tankerton.

'Yes. Do you speak Spanish?'

'A little.'

'Gentlemen?' said Valin to the others. The man from the FBI shook his head. The other two nodded.

'When the traitor went to Santa Ana he was seen by García here,' said Valin. 'And what he told the authorities down there was passed on to the factory personnel. Of course no one down there, or our traitor, ever thought that we'd complete the job, or in doing so bring out the one man who could and would identify him.' He paused for effect, then said: 'Jesús, you know what to do.'

Jesús turned to García, and in Spanish asked: 'Is the man who came down to Santa Ana in this room?'

'*Sí*,' said García.

'What exactly did he do when he came down?'

'He talked to the factory boss, and the military leader from the town.'

'What did he say?'

'He told them that a force of unofficial soldiers was coming to destroy the factory.'

'Did he say when?'

'No. That he did not know. Not exactly. Only that it would be soon.'

'And what happened?'

'We were put on orange alert at the factory, and the military commander drafted in extra troops.'

'And he is definitely here?'

'*Sí*.'

'Would you point him out?'

All the time, between question and answer, Jesús translated for the non-Spanish speakers, and at the last question García dramatically raised his finger and pointed it at General Avery.

'This is nonsense,' Avery spluttered. 'Are you going to believe some Colombian whom no one has ever seen before, over me? A man who has fought for his country in three wars. Who has been decorated for bravery a dozen times.'

'Shit, General,' said Spenser. 'I believe him. I remember you from 'Nam. Always in the DMZ with a freshly pressed uniform and a couple of young WAACs in tow. Hey, man, you enjoyed your wars, as long as there was someone else to fight them for you.'

'Things never change, do they?' said Valin.

'Tank,' Avery pleaded. 'You don't believe this nonsense, do you?'

'Check with Leavenworth, Tank,' said Valin. 'Even our gallant general here couldn't send those men down to Colombia without leaving some record of it. There must be an order in triplicate somewhere. And at least some of them were stranded at an LZ in Panama, waiting in case we did manage to get the plane out. They might be still down there, waiting for further orders.'

Without warning, one of the guards grabbed at Valin's gun and tried to wrestle it from his grasp. Spenser chopped at his neck with his own gun barrel, and the man slumped to the floor with a groan, but before order could be established, Avery stood up from his seat, an automatic pistol in his hand that seemed to have appeared from nowhere, and grabbed Carmen, twisted her gun out of her hand and held her in front of himself as a shield, his arm around the throat, and his gun at her head. 'Put down your weapons,' he ordered. Everyone did as Avery said, weapons thumping to the carpet, and as the general looked at Valin, his mouth curled in contempt. 'You think you're very clever, don't you?' he spat.

'Not at all, General,' replied Valin. 'Anything but. But we did what we were sent to do, despite your efforts to the contrary.'

'Damn you,' said Avery, and tightened his grip on Carmen's throat. 'I should shoot you where you stand, like a dog.' He shook his head. 'Another time, Colonel. I'm sure we'll meet again.'

'It will be my pleasure,' said Valin.

'I'll be leaving now,' said Avery. 'If anyone follows, she's dead.'

'You'll never get out of here alive,' said Tankerton.

'I think I will,' replied Avery. 'But if I don't, nor will this bitch.'

'You bastard,' said Spenser, and made a lunge for Avery, who shot him in the shoulder. As the shot rang out, and while Avery's attention was elsewhere, Jesús bent down and picked up the gun he had dropped earlier and fired once without seeming to aim. The bullet hit Avery in the head, blowing out the back of his skull, and splashing bone splinters, brain and blood across the wall behind him in a red crescent. He fell to the floor, blood gushing from the gaping wound, letting go of Carmen. The girl ran to Spenser, who was leaning against the wall, his hand staunching the blood from his wounded arm.

'That was for my family,' said Jesús.

'Good shot,' said Valin coolly. 'Do you believe me now, Tank?'

Tankerton looked down at the general's body and shook his head. 'Christ, James,' he said. 'I would never have believed it if I hadn't heard it from his own lips.'

'I'm glad you did,' said Valin. 'Are you going to be all right, Chris?'

'Thanks for the thought, Colonel,' said Spenser wryly, as Carmen tore the tail off her shirt to make a rough bandage. 'It's not the first time I've been shot, but I think a doctor might be in order.'

'I'm sure we can get you one, just as soon as Tank completes his side of our bargain.'

'What?' said Tankerton, furrowing his brow.

'Our fee,' said Valin. 'Not only did we destroy the cocaine factory, as per instructions, but we've just saved your government the cost of twenty years for General Avery in a safe little prison somewhere with cable TV piped in and *nouvelle cuisine* three times a day. Not to mention the scandal of a trial. So come on, Tank, cough up. There's a good chap.'

Tankerton took a suitcase from under the chair he had been sitting in, and slid it across the table.'

'There you are, James,' he said. 'Spend it in good health.'

22 Books offers an exciting list of titles in these series. All the books are available from:

Little, Brown and Company (UK) Limited,
PO Box 11,
Falmouth,
Cornwall TR10 9EN.

Alternatively you may fax your order to the above address.
Fax number: 0326 376423.

Payments can be made by cheque or postal order (payable to Little, Brown and Company) or by credit card (Visa/Access). Do not send cash or currency. UK customers and BFPO please allow £1.00 for postage and packing for the first book, plus 50p for the second book, plus 30p for each additional book up to a maximum charge of £3.00 (seven books or more). Overseas customers, including customers in Ireland, please allow £2.00 for the first book, plus £1.00 for the second book, plus 50p for each additional book.

NAME (BLOCK LETTERS PLEASE) ....

....

ADDRESS ....

....

....

☐ I enclose my remittance for £_____

☐ I wish to pay by Access/Visa

Card number

Card expiry date
